The Ever

I. Allan Sealy is the author of two novels, *The Trotter-nama* and *Hero*, and a travel book, *From Yukon to Yucatán*. He divides his time between his homes in the foothills of the Himalayas and in New Zealand.

THE EVEREST HOTEL
A Calendar

I. Allan Sealy

TRANSWORLD PUBLISHERS LTD
61–63 Uxbridge Road, London W5 5SA

TRANSWORLD PUBLISHERS, C/O RANDOM HOUSE AUSTRALIA PTY LTD
20 Alfred Street, Milsons Point, NSW 2061, Australia

TRANSWORLD PUBLISHERS, C/O RANDOM HOUSE NEW ZEALAND
18 Poland Road, Glenfield, Auckland, New Zealand

Published by Anchor – a division of Transworld Publishers Ltd

First published in Great Britain by Doubleday, 1998

This paperback edition published 1999 by Anchor

A catalogue record for this book is available from the British Library

ISBN 1862 30043 7

Typeset in 11/14pt Adobe Caslon by Falcon Oast Graphic Art
Printed and bound in Great Britain by Cox & Wyman Ltd, Reading, Berks.

For Deepa Rose

Contents

Every morning at sunrise the women come out of the forest and set out on the path to the city. They file down the track balancing headloads of firewood on pads wound from cloth that will be sodden with sweat before they reach the market. They have been lopping since first light. Always they stop under this pipal tree hung with the fibrous flasks of weaver birds' nests, and they rest. Dust coats their feet; silver ropes their ankles, their whole fortune. They talk of the ferment in the hills, so many women held in the valley, so many men gone to the plains.

Sometimes they talk about the hairy man: how once he strayed across their path in a stand of flowering teak and stood very still looking straight ahead, like a child imagining himself invisible. And how they scattered and fled, dropping their loads of wood.

Sometimes they talk about husbands and children and the price of things nowadays, sometimes they salt their wounds.

'My children's children won't forget what those wretches did to me,' their leader repeats. The others nod in silence. No-one will forget the night the loggers came.

A breeze stirs, lifts the sweat from their foreheads. As they sit under the whispering canopy of the big tree, a weaver bird's nest falls at their feet. A dungeon with a balcony. The youngest picks it up and looks into its funnel for eggs. It is empty, but she tucks its long topknot into the waistband of her sari to carry the nest home. Baya nests keep ghosts from your door.

When they have rested they heft the loads once more, pausing to get the balance back. Necks braced against the weight, torsos rigid from the strain; their hips wiggle above quickly stepping feet. They go their way without looking back.

At the edge of the forest they have left behind, the trees have a lank emaciated look from repeated lopping. Fresh leaves, new May growth, will cloak the mutilated stumps. But, deeper in, trees are being cut down and trucked away. Bare patches appear on the hillsides, like mange; in time, a whole bare hill. The springs and waterholes are drying up, the animals have to travel further to *drink. Fires light up the night sky; the mountains are burning. The villagers blame the loggers, the loggers blame the villagers. The green of the water courses vanishes with the passing of the rains and the trees grow further apart. Thorny lantana has come from somewhere else to fill in the barren spaces; parakeets expel its seed in new glades and shriek like demons as they swoop on the next thicket. The highway through the forest has been widened. Monkeys come down to the roadside in clans to scrounge and steal; they have learnt to open the new foil packets of potato chips. From behind a tree, through the blind of his eyelashes, Ramapithecus watches.*

Summer

J ETH, *May–June, is the first gusting of hot winds, the singing of an empty tap, a carpet of hailstones on a withered lawn.*

FROM HER WINDOW SEAT RITU WATCHES THE BRIGHT RAIL of the down line glide.

The train jolts and sways, grappled to the earth, but the other track floats serenely, drawn steel rubbed into a beam of light. A branch line appears and glides beside it, making three, then vanishes, dispatched to the other side. The carriage wheels stutter over the crossing then settle back into their rhythm.

The land beyond the track is flat and white with caked dust. Clay pits surround a brick kiln whose furnace will shortly make a hot day hotter. The scrubby acacias that over-hang the ditch are too few to warrant cutting down and carrying to the furnace. Presently ploughed fields return, and farmers twigging bullocks as they ride their wooden harrows. A lake with water hyacinth fills the window, its surface dotted with points of purple light. Then a pond where men wade among dark crimped leaves collecting water chestnuts.

The gradient steepens, the train slows, and as the track curves around a wooded knoll the sun comes up. A stream appears, its bed clogged with boulders, and now the track song turns guttural with trestle bridges and culverts. Without warning the train enters a tunnel; when it bursts from the darkness it has left the plains behind.

Here the holdings beyond the track-side fallows slope into forest, the upright sal that clothes the foothills. For twenty minutes the train skirts a range of what look like anthills covered in jungle, more brown than green. The proper moun-tains, Ritu knows from books, will be clad in oak and rhododendrons and conifers, but these smaller hills crouch under familiar trees: sal, teak and silk-cotton, the trees of her own hills a whole day's journey to the south. Eventually the train leaves the low hills behind and crosses a valley of orchards and rice paddies. On the far side of the valley, bandsaw blue on the horizon, are the true Himalayas.

Sister Ritu's destination, the railhead of Drummondganj, commands the valley between the two ranges; the town is neither of the plains nor of the hills.

The branch line returns, then arcs away along an embank-ment. Other tracks rumble under the train, signalling the approach of something more than a way station. The first houses of Drummondganj appear among shacks and poor shops. At the outer signal the train slows to a halt by barbers' and cigarette vendors' stalls of rough unpainted packing-case wood. A butcher's flyscreen door has been painted black and white; the paint clogs the mesh in a pattern like a crossword puzzle. When a customer goes in Ritu glimpses the butcher's holy pictures, a vision of arms and knives. Next door a barber rubs the day's first chin with a large crystal of alum.

The train starts up again. A new track appears, slides under a donkey engine and splits into a dozen sidings: this will be it. Ritu stirs herself. The traffic drawn up at the last level crossing was city traffic; she watched a citified Sikh leaning his scooter under the barrier to get ahead.

Level crossings touch a chord in Ritu. Her father kept one in the forest. There the gate didn't come down, but swung shut. White, its two red half-discs met when it shut to form a warning sun. The ratchet bell going as you pushed. Their two-room quarter adjoined, with a bed of marigolds at the door and a garden of cockscombs and lady's fingers. A fenced-off grove of mahua trees. The only house with a handpump. Whitewashed not in October, for Diwali, but in December. Christians.

Ritu waits till the train comes to a full halt, suffers the elastic tug at the end, which always brings on nausea, then sketches a minute cross under her chin. A small chin, hardly there, the flaw in a profile that once let her mother entertain notions of a good match. Misreading the girl.

Tea is her present need, and there outside the carriage door is a zinc-faced trolley with cups and a steaming kettle. The kettle whinges, the bloom lifting and settling on its aluminium. Ritu hears the bubble in its throat but steps around the trolley, lugging her suitcase, and slips into the stream of passengers. Her tread suggests someone unaccustomed to level ground, but she has come from the big city. Loose paving stones, not tree roots, are the hazards her feet have learnt to memorize. She wears sandals, the strap on one mended outside Old Delhi station by a cobbler of great dignity.

At the gate she sees the colours of her order, dove-grey and white. Sister Neha is there, a young nun of her tribe from the village up the line in the forest, and an older sterner face that says, without meaning to, Superior.

'We're so glad Mother sent you,' this face says, softening. 'It was getting very difficult.'

Neha fusses with the air around her friend.

'Sister Neha will take your luggage.'

'No, no!' Ritu reaches for her suitcase, but finds the handle already taken.

'Sister Neha will take your luggage.' Pitched as before.

'EVEREST HOTEL', reads an old sign high up in the foyer, the blue letters so faded a traveller's doubting soul turns gratefully to newer, gaudier promises: 'A/C, Fax, TV in every room'.

Ritu takes in her surroundings with frank curiosity: the billboards, the beggars, the soldiers, the weighing machine with its flashing lights. Custody of the eyes, notes Sister Cecelia.

Cecelia herself has just registered a detail that escaped her on the way in. There is no scramble of scooter rickshaw drivers. There are in fact no scooter rickshaws parked outside, no cars. The paved yard beyond the portico wears a deserted look. As the nuns step outside a man presents himself. Baingan coolie, with a long sardonic face and large bloodshot eyes, specializes in women travellers. He can find them a ride, a room, the town's famous rice, ready-bagged, at a better price.

'Wait here,' he intones, and they obey. 'There's no point going that way,' he adds today, rolling slow eyes towards the main road. 'They aren't letting any traffic through.'

'Oh, the *strike*!'

In the midst of her troubles Cecelia had forgotten. She took a back lane coming, and all seemed normal there. Now she stands in the arch, a head taller than the young nuns on either side, and frets. Time is a more perishable commodity to her than to most.

At length Baingan returns, suspense slowing his progress. 'In the lane beyond that tree,' he says, and refrains hammily from pointing, 'is a scooter driver who will take you home for fifty rupees.'

'The fare is fifteen.'

Baingan's lantern jaw shifts to accommodate a smile. 'Not today, Sister.' The sisters are known; it is also known that unlike the blue-and-white sisters they have no jeep. 'But let me talk to the man.'

And again Baingan sets out across the empty forecourt, looking about him with elaborate nonchalance.

'Forty-five,' he says, returning.

'Twenty-five,' replies Cecelia, on God's account, and they close at thirty.

Baingan can supply a chandelier or a racehorse or an emergency safety pin. At home he has a partridge that tells fortunes. His sons may be scooter drivers.

There is some looting going on on the main road. The strike leaders have lost control. A tyre shop has had its shutters forced and three men are rolling tractor tyres in a zigzag race, like dwarfs at a circus. Other men come running when they see the scooter rickshaw.

'Where to in such a hurry?'

Baingan's son is all charm. 'Just taking these sisters—'

'My friend, there's a strike on. Where have you been living?'

'We're only going to the next corner,' says Sister Cecelia, pointing. 'We have a suitcase.'

'Madam, this scooter can't take you anywhere. There's no traffic allowed in the city today.'

Cecelia sits back and folds her arms. Baingan's son gets out and leans on his machine, then takes a cloth and begins to polish it. Neha and Ritu have their hands in their laps, the suitcase pressing on their knees where the waxed twine has begun to bite.

'What's this, what's this?'

More men have come up, swaggering.

Baingan's son grows anxious. 'Just taking these holy sisters.' Now he sees his way to a smashed windscreen and leans into the rickshaw to whisper urgently.

'You'd better get out.'

'Out they'll have to get,' says a man with a stick, tapping the back of the rickshaw where a slogan reads, 'THE BRIDE HERSELF IS THE DOWRY', and underneath, 'Hypothecated to Punjab National Bank'.

Sister Cecelia, nearest the door, stays where she is. Neha bows her head. Ritu grips the handle of her suitcase, feels the leather thong wound around where her father mended a split seam.

A young man leans into the scooter and whips out a pocket comb. He runs his thumb along the teeth with a pinking sound. Then he studies himself in the rear-view mirror and, with great deliberation, does his hair while passing his eyes over the passengers behind him. His friends snigger, then grow serious. One of them says to no-one in particular, '*Out.*'

'Out,' everyone agrees and it becomes a chant.

'Out! Out!'

Sister Cecelia closes her eyes and tilts her head back. Glancing at her, Ritu recognizes that look from certain paintings.

The man with the stick can read defiance, too. He comes to the front, leans his whole weight against the scooter and feels it budge: three wheels will tilt. From the other side comes an answering push. The scooter is surrounded by men happy to push and pull. A rocking is set up. Baingan's son is now pleading with his passengers, but Cecelia's eyes are shut fast. The procession of martyrs passing there does silent battle with prudence. But how to climb down? On the other side, Ritu blinks. This is not the crisis on which her life must hinge, surely. Neha, in the middle, is simply afraid. Hell must be like this, with grinning demons.

Unaccountably the rocking stops. A man is standing by the entrance, stooping a little in order to look into the rickshaw, but also because that is how he holds himself under the mass of his shoulders. He wears lawyer glasses with tumbler-bottom lenses that distort his eyes. His T-shirt and pimply skin make him look younger than his thirty years. He has cut himself shaving, at his prominent Adam's apple, and forgotten to comb his hair, but his clothes and bulk command respect. One of the organizers, from the way the crowd parted to let him through.

'Sister,' he addresses Cecelia.

'You!'

His eyes swim. 'Sister, you must go home immediately.'

'That is what we're trying to do.'

'No, I mean, not in this scooter. Today there's no traffic in the city. But please go home, now. Already there's been trouble. When the police arrive there'll be more. Let me get you a coolie.'

He slides the suitcase out, the plates of his shoulders shifting, and puts it on the road beside the rickshaw. The crowd, now many heads deep, murmurs satisfaction, but waits to see the action through, as if to say, A crowd has face, too.

Cecelia steps haughtily from the rickshaw, her prayer for an honourable release answered. Neha and Ritu follow.

'You want your own state, Brij,' Cecelia says, in possession of herself again. 'Call it the state of Anarchy!'

'It can't be worse than what we have.' Brij half smiles. 'I'll get you a coolie.'

But even as he turns a siren sounds. A short wail, then a silence more trying than the siren. And then an extraordinary sight.

Down the road comes a jeep, regulation grey, with officers and constables including policewomen in khaki, but stencilled in red under the windshield are the defiant words, 'AKASHKHAND GOVERNMENT'. Uniformed separatists! Even Brij is amazed. The movement is more organized than he, an erratic cadre, supposed. Behind, in sedate pursuit, rolls another jeep with the state's proper name and its salaried police. The demonstrators howl and cheer the front jeep on, then taunt the state police. But behind the police jeep is a blue truck that brakes sharply. Chains rattle and the tailgate crashes down, riot police jump out. The crowd doesn't wait. Men are disappearing down lanes off the main road.

'Come with me,' Brij calls.

But Ritu has made a discovery.

'My suitcase!' she whispers, her blood turning to sand.

The suitcase is not there and Baingan's son darts around his rickshaw to make sure.

'It's gone!'

'Wait here,' Brij shouts, racing after the last of the crowd. He stops and calls, 'No, don't wait. Go on home. I'll come there.'

A handful of demonstrators, courting arrest, have not dispersed but stand in a jittery group till the police charge them swinging lathis. The next sound splinters, bamboo on bone. Then they too break up and run.

'What is this?' an officer shouts at the onlookers from the station. 'A circus? Go home!'

The nuns turn away. Ritu is numb, the rope of sand twisting in her veins.

Bougainvillea blazes at the gate.

Red as the sun on a level-crossing gate, as a lineman's flag, as a planet signalling. Ritu pauses to admire, in spite of her loss. Clusters of red bracts, transparencies. She picks one, rubs the membrane between finger and thumb.

Custody of the hands, Cecelia notes.

In the sullage drain by the boundary wall a stray dog lies on its side. Dark water ebbs along its ginger coat, soothing mange. It lifts its head to greet the nuns, turns humid eyes on Ritu. She returns an absent smile.

'Everest' says the plaque set in a moss-stained gatepost. A fine flowing script worked in marble, black set in moon white. Ritu admires the workmanship. Nowadays all marble scripts are crude square-cut capitals.

She turns again to the dog, whose head is twisted back and up; its black eyes meet hers in mute entreaty. You're lucky, she thinks, you have nothing to lose.

'It was mostly books.'

Ritu steadies the cup, feels the tea surge like sweet poison. Her mind is rummaging in the missing suitcase. The exalting dispersion of loss has begun to crystallize in glimpses of lost particulars: the cherished book of ferns, six paintings of specimens on cartridge paper, the reed sewing box.

A pressed ebony leaf in her Augustine.

She has seen her room, big, high-ceilinged, with skylights. A ceiling fan with an inverted cup at the top of a long rod. A bedside table, a cupboard with bare shelves. That will now remain bare, newspaper-lined, bitter with neem leaves.

She simply unslings the cloth shoulder bag and lays it on the bed. Unpacked! Then sits on the bed and cups her chin in her hands and stares at the floor. Red polished cement, pitting. Her bones rehearsing the vibration of the train.

Cool green soap, a new cake, on her palm. An old enamel dish, white with a dark-blue rim, in three parts, the middle part with holes. Beeswax light tunnelling in through the bathroom sluice.

'Towel,' Cecelia says, coming up behind her with one and going out.

Water, tepid at ten, but running. Ritu runs it over her, keeping her hair dry, then buries her face in the towel and stands in limbo, the whole rickshaw rocking. Bathed, she puts her travel habit back on and steps into the hall. A gloomy octagon, lit from the high windows at the landing of a staircase at the back. Light also filtering through the vestibule, shimmering on the wine-dark floor. She narrows her eyes: did that shimmer part to admit a mongoose? Reek of phenyl twined with incense and candlewax and Brasso, a convent bower. Then a newer, cheerful smell. She traces the sounds of tea-making to the refectory, where Neha is setting out a plate of coconut biscuits.

'I'll make you some scrambled eggs.' Spoken, except for the word *scrambled*, in their Gond tongue.

'Tea – just tea!'

Sinking into the nearest chair.

'That's—' *Cecelia's*, Neha was going to say, when Cecelia came in and took another chair.

'Neha will make you some breakfast.'

'I think I'll wait till lunch.'

'Then try one of these.' Cecelia passes the biscuits.

'Everest' on the plate in the same flowing script. The crest a buckle fastening the plate's broad band of royal blue. In the round of the crest a white mountain outlined against a sky worked in fine blue hatching. Near the base the hatching dissolves into dots. Then a single swung line, cloud or hill, dividing the mountain from the name, rock riding on word. *Everest*.

Heavy china, smooth under the thumb, from the building's hotel days. Discouraging kitchen hands and souvenir hunters. The nuns have learned to negotiate a cavernous hotel kitchen. The refectory is the old pantry. The big old dining room, reduced to four tables, is for the lay inmates. 'You can have a fresh habit when Perpetua gets back. She keeps the keys.'

Ritu nods, absorbed in the table, reading its grain. Teak from the forests of her hills; old hills, far older than these fold mountains. Gondwanaland. That forest now under her fingertips, silent, dark, mutating. Wood in covenant with rock, unlocking its mineral body, quenching its fire, changing its course. Cells blundering towards order and clarity, instinct with the eye's jelly. Her nail finds a groove in rock older than measured time.

So the Sister Superior feels it right to rouse the girl.

'What was in the suitcase?'

'Books mostly.'

'Prayer books?' Kindly, but steering.

'Botany books.'

'Botany!' Dropped like a coin on the table, spinning there.

'And some paintings, of plants. I do botanical paintings.'

'Nature studies?' Cecelia once did some herself. 'I thought they used cameras nowadays.'

'Yes, or line drawings. It's a hobby. I started painting at Loreto.'

So, a college nun.

'Anything else? Valuables?'

'No, just books. And photographs. Oh, a shawl.' Looking across at Neha. The shawls of their tribe are striped maroon and cream. 'My mother made it on the loom at home.'

'Your shawl!' Neha, crossing to the old fridge, stops in her tracks. Her mother, in the next village, wove her one too; everyone's mother did. 'How *wicked*!'

'We will pray that it is found. In the mean time you can have clothes and linen from the storeroom. Neha is your size. Perpetua will give you any toiletries you need.'

The oldest nun at Everest is out calling with the youngest, Sister Tsering.

'And you can get . . . suitcases . . . here.' Cecelia bridles at the word, once inert now faintly obscene, like death itself. 'Like the one you had. For that matter, Mr Jed has a whole roomful of trunks.'

'Mr Jed?'

'The landlord. He lives upstairs. He's an old man, but' – Cecelia makes fists in the air – 'big. He says he's ninety.' Ritu sees affection, as for a child, in the smile. 'Last week he decided to stop eating. Hasn't touched a thing since Friday. Tsering takes up his tray, but he won't touch it.' The smile twisting down.

'How is he now?'

'Since yesterday he's refused to see anyone. He's bolted the door and lies up there singing.' Cecelia straightens her back. 'Vulgar songs.'

'Is he . . . ?' Ritu doesn't quite touch her temple.

'He can be perfectly sane when he wants; other days he'll talk nonsense from beginning to end. Up till last month he was writing a book; now it's just marks on the page. The Devil's dictation, he says. I could take his advice on Everest matters before. We have other inmates, you know, who need looking after. Tsering is our nurse, but lately she's had her hands full just looking after him. Which is why I wrote to Mother. She tells me you've worked with older people.'

'We had four in the house.'

Overhead the fan blades slacken, like a loss of will. At the same time the fridge shudders and goes quiet.

'Eleven o'clock,' Cecelia says, looking up.

'Power cuts,' Neha glosses for her friend from the capital and goes to shut the windows. Heat glares through the grilles. At every window Neha shakes the curtains as she draws them. On the verandah she lets down the purple chicks and fastens the stays. The polished floors take on the colour of congealed blood. In the chief rooms the floors are bordered with tiles that now appear to enclose pools of uncertain depth. Neha pads from room to room, wading silently through stone like a ghost accustomed to some earlier level.

'Doesn't he have any relatives?' Ritu asks.

'The relative is the problem. He has a nephew or grand nephew, a young man who thinks he owns the place already.'

'He lives here?'

'He comes and goes. He was here last week, threatening to move in. He lives in Delhi but leaves some of his things in the annexe. Mr Jed is always upset for a couple of days after his visits.'

From the hall come the jangling chimes of a grandfather clock.

'It runs half an hour late,' says Cecelia, when the mutiny of springs and hammers has subsided. 'Let me show you the rest of the place.'

But crosses first to the dresser and opens a drawer.

'Here is your napkin.' She rolls the white linen on the sideboard and passes it through a silver ring. 'This is your napkin ring. And this will be your place, next to Tsering.'

'The winter rose,' says Ritu, stopping at the chapel threshold.

She has never seen one except in books, and now under ash glaze on the border tiles.

Cecelia bows, accepting the gift. She likes knowledge in nuggets, but will guard against abstraction. Especially, she suspects, in this young nun.

'It's in all the rooms,' she says genuflecting. 'The next prayers are at noon, but you can have a few minutes now and then I'll show you Everest.'

She leaves Ritu alone.

The room is a rectangle, painted pale blue, with windows beyond the altar at the far end. A brick wall out there at some distance. Trees. Dark inside. By the brass cross a vase with plastic lilies. Ritu closes her eyes till she hears Cecelia's footfall on the threshold. They step out into the octagonal hall together.

'The chapel used to be the library. We moved the books next door into the parlour. On this side here is Perpetua's room. That,' Cecelia points across the hall, 'is the office, and that next to it is the Superior's room.' *My* being bad form.

Ritu grows conscious of another presence, materializing from above.

'It's not lunchtime, Miss Sampson,' Cecelia says, turning towards the staircase.

'No?' Miss Sampson stops on the last step but one. She is frailty in yellow marble, the veins picked out in indigo. 'I was quite sure it was the bell.'

'It must have been the Latvian.'

'Of *course*.' Miss Sampson rolls milky eyes. 'It would be.' The Latvian flirts with Buddhism and bells. 'Anyway, it's so hot upstairs. Power cuts! Never a power cut under Nehru!'

'This is Sister Ritu.'

'From the capital? We've been expecting you.' She takes Ritu's hand and holds onto it. 'Well,' she looks enquiringly at Cecelia, 'if it isn't lunchtime let me show her my domain.'

The tug is upwards; for a new face Miss Sampson will mount the stairs all over again.

'You remind me of someone,' she says, stopping to look at the young woman. Then takes her arm and begins the ascent. 'Let me lean on you, dear. Usually I have the devil's arm,' she says, tapping the end of the banister which has been elaborately carved into downturned claws. 'Everest gets hotter the higher you climb. That's the local joke. On the roof, where *he* is,' she jabs a nicotined finger, 'is *hell*.'

From the landing the octagonal hall at the heart of Everest makes a keyhole shape, taken with the narrow vestibule. A large black table, once a dining table, stands outside the office door with a telephone on it, its varnished top reflecting the cupola above. The landing windows, crudely papered over, leach a murky light that thickens into sediment at the bottom of the stairwell. Ritu is looking down into a pond, the winter roses blue lotuses. Cecelia a carp suspended in the middle, now flicking her way across the hall, the slow grey fins of her

29

habit furling and unfurling. Picketed at the foot of the stair, the grandfather clock begins another bitter jangling.

The alarm clock! Ritu remembers. Her mother's gift was in the suitcase, too. It falls away from her into the muddy pool. Let it go.

From the kitchen comes a faint crepitation: mustard seed popping under a lid, pinpricks of sound like distant gunfire. The two women climb into another sound, a low melodious ululation that grows louder with every step.

'That's the twins,' Miss Sampson explains. 'They have pride of place.'

Prem and Pravin, nine, have the first room at the top of the stairs. They are sprawled across the one bed, side by side, fallen back as if from sitting, a welter of paddling hands and oscillating heads. Above them, immobilized, hangs a new ceiling fan. A gluey bubbling, *mbo*, *mbo*, *mbo*, issues from their lips, their private language. It binds them, though they do not touch one another, cannot bear to be touched.

'Dressing them is Sister Tsering's treat,' notes Miss Sampson, who must live down the hall from them. 'An uncle left them here for just a couple of days – six months ago.'

She shepherds Ritu back out into the corridor.

'The stair goes on up to the roof, but Jed's had the door bricked in. So Tsering has to go all the way round the building and up the fire escape.'

Hot up here, Ritu thinks. What must it be like for him? She looks up the last flight of stairs at the blocked-off door and thinks she hears someone pacing there. Imagines a figure, all hair and horror, but pleading eyes, turn and shamble away.

'This end of the corridor is for the men,' Miss Sampson is saying. 'Major Bakshi has the first room. He's away at the moment. Drinks like a fish behind Cecelia's back. Next door is the seaman.'

They pass the door with the padlock and come to a room that looks like a stage set. All the furniture has been drawn into one corner, as if the occupant found so much space oppressive after a lifetime in a cabin. Or wished to avoid leaks in the roof.

'He was a sailor, or something,' Miss Sampson whispers. Out loud she calls, 'Any news from Lithuania?'

Only when he stirs do they see the hammock, tied across the balcony. And the birdcage, silhouetted against the window.

'*Latvia,*' the mynah calls, and adds, for the record, 'No.'

But Miss Sampson has already drawn Ritu away to the ladies' end. 'Tsering's here, next to the twins. Opposite her is a goongi.' She mimes a deaf mute. 'Nobody knows her name. She just turned up one day. She won't be in.' Miss Sampson whips open and swiftly shuts the goongi's door, sealing off the squalor she will sometimes peep at. 'Then there's Miss Chatterjee, who doesn't leave her room. Pregnant, if you please, at sixty-nine. And then there's me.'

Balsam and nicotine hang on the green air in Miss Sampson's room. And calamine, to stretch the skin. Money plant festoons the mantelshelf, swamping the green runner. A green chenille counterpane casts its duckweed fringe over the slippers crowding under the bed. The fur-lined pair in olive plaid are home to her pet mongoose, though in summer he sleeps under the commode. By the window a long-legged lampstand balances a goglet with a narrow neck, the mouth covered with a crochet doily, its beads green.

'Oh dear!' Miss Sampson rushes to the tallboy to slip a knitted cosy over her valve radio. 'Getting careless.'

She turns, dejected now. Dust is the enemy, and it's winning; every mote a spy. 'Drummondganj wasn't always like this,' she complains. 'We hardly needed fans, you know. No dust. Loo was unheard of.' She sees Ritu inspecting her row of certificates framed on the wall.

'I lost everything except those. The Army gave us ten minutes to pack before the rioters came. When we left the house was already burning. I was a nutritionist before the war. I treated Nehru before he became prime minister.'

Ritu remains in profile, her head lifted and revealed.

'*That's* who you remind me of,' Miss Sampson whispers, half to herself.

Ritu turns, looks directly at her.

'*His* wife.' Pointing up at the roof.

Green eyes, Ritu sees. Dusty green, like roadside milkweed.

In the chapel are Perpetua and Tsering. Waiting, their backs say.

The Superior has spoken generally of lateness at midday prayer, a homily that could only apply to those who go calling before lunch. Today they have been to old Brother Memen, carrying papayas from the Everest trees, and have come back early. While Cecelia waited in the office for Ritu.

Cecelia begins at once, but the nuns lean out and smile across her at the newcomer. Ritu is further distracted by a trace of black mustard seed on the air. Kitchen smells at Everest migrate to the farthest room.

Lunch is chicken, in honour of the new arrival, made with vinegar the night before and allowed to steep. The mustard seed has alchemized plain cabbage, bought at great cost from a cart at the gate, but Neha's skills are overshadowed by the events of the morning.

'Poor thing!' says Perpetua, laying down the serving spoon. She and Tsering listen aghast to Cecelia's account of the missing suitcase. 'These people!' Perpetua is from Kerala, she cannot forget. 'Complete ruffians,' she adds, clarifying.

'We heard the firing,' Tsering says, 'from across the maidan.'

'They fire into the sky,' Cecelia points out.

'They should call out the Army,' Perpetua says, returning to the chicken. 'One army truck and they run. Now they'll have a flag march, when the damage is done.' She helps herself and passes the dish to Ritu. 'You don't worry,' she says, 'we have everything you need here.' She gives her keys a quartermasterly jingle. Then her jaws go to work, one heavy foot beating time on the floor. Her toes are carved ebony.

Overhead the fan remains motionless. Everyone is sweating. In the silence the pantry tap suddenly begins to sing. Cecelia frowns; taps should be properly turned off. Neha absorbs the reprimand with a bowed head. More air than water passes along the pipes nowadays, the tap a telephone whose gossip exhausts all the dry bends of the city mains back to the depleted waterworks.

'What a summer! Power cuts. Water rationing. Two hours a day. And they've built a big dam in the hills; you must have heard.'

'We have an underground tank,' Cecelia says, 'but it's running down.'

'So, just two baths a day,' Perpetua complains.

'And we make sure all taps are turned off.' Cecelia's extra twist has worn out several washers. She knows it, but can't stop her hand.

'The neighbour has a booster pump,' Perpetua says, splaying the bones of a chicken wing.

'We can't be *sure*.' Cecelia lifts a hand.

'*I'm* sure.' Perpetua wages a daily battle with the neighbour, Mrs Puri, whose roof tanks are just visible through the refectory window. 'When I have proof I'm going to make a report.'

In the water war Perpetua's whole armour is a monkey wrench and a keen ear. She has learnt the language of piped water, mastered its weird diphthongs and glottal stops. She patrols the entire length of the Everest pipes looking for leaks. For the rest of the summer Ritu will look out of a window and see her in the midday sun, frozen at the outdoor tap, her head cocked, listening for the telltale water hammer. Or moving along an invisible line across the burnt grass towards Mrs Puri's boundary, holding the wrench before her like a diviner.

'And then, God help her!' Perpetua puts down the wing, the bones picked clean.

'Sister!'

Perpetua beams at Neha. '*Good* chicken!'

Neha is in the parlour with a Catholic magazine, flipping the pages.

Around the walls of the fan-shaped room are the bookcases she dusts daily, a small padlock on each.

'Why the locks?'

Ritu has just come in. Drawn to the nearest bookcase, she tilts her head, reading off in the dark: Arnold Bennett, Maud Diver, Marie Stopes. No particular system that she can see. Neha drops the magazine and says, 'Sister Cecelia found one of the inmates selling off books to a kabariwallah.'

'Not Major Bakshi?'

'How did you know?' Neha is surprised into their Gond

tongue, but returns quickly to English. Vernaculars encourage factions, particular friendships.

'Miss Sampson showed me round upstairs.'

'Yes, it was the major. He drinks.'

Ritu goes to another bookcase. *The Perfumed Garden. A Rose among Thorns. Miss Lily.* Gardening she's keen on.

'Cecelia has the key?'

'No, no. Mr Jed.'

Of course. His books. 'What's he like?'

'Mad. You'll see. He has rooms full of things downstairs, but he lives on the roof.'

Neha suddenly remembers the suitcase. She can feel it still, jammed against her knees. Her frown line returns.

'Anything you need, just ask.'

'I lost my nail clippers. *Our* nail clippers, sorry!'

'You can borrow mine – sorry, *ours*!'

They laugh together, softly. The heat works like a drug on their eyelids. At home they napped in the afternoon.

'You know the Nakta road?' Ritu has been back. 'It's been metalled. There are tempos running from the checkpost.'

'The mahua will be in bloom,' Neha murmurs. White fleshy petals, sweet in the mouth, in the nose. The musk hangs rotting even at noon, not perfume but the corpse of perfume.

They carry the forest in their heads.

A quarter-past three.

Ritu rests on the pallet that will be her bed. On her back, looking up at the fan. Her feet to the open door. Closes her eyes, uncrosses her feet. Custody of the limbs.

A scuffle at the skylight. She opens her eyes. Two lizards

are fighting a territorial battle high up near the ceiling. She waits for the sickening fall, but one lizard gives in and darts away, expressionless in defeat.

At half-past the fan comes on, grinding hidden teeth. The first air from it is hot ceiling air. She shuts her eyes against it. A photograph slips under her lids: a young man in uniform, her brother. In his grave, hardly grown. She thinks of summer afternoon baths with him at the handpump, the water flying, their screams. Afterwards wet feet on the burning track.

Here the heat is dry. It doesn't stop at the skin. Moist heat clings, defines. This runs through you, makes a ghost of you.

Her eyes stretch suddenly wide open. The photograph was in the suitcase. A knock at the door. Perpetua standing there, respecting the rule. Only the Superior may enter unaccompanied.

'Come and get some clothes from the press,' she calls. 'Then we'll have tea and I'll show you the compound.'

'This is the annexe.'

Perpetua says *anexi*, like everybody else. 'Jed's nephew stays here when he's in town. He's not here now, thank God.'

The annexe is in fact separated from the main building by a drive that leads to the garage, whose iron doors stand open showing an old Packard, canary yellow.

'Jed's baby.' Perpetua runs a finger along the mudguard to check for dust. Ritu, who has never seen a vintage car, admires the elaborate chrome of the mounted headlights.

'The goongi keeps it shining. Great polisher. She should have been a nun. Back here is Thapa's room. He's our nightwatchman and gardener. Used to be Major Bakshi's batman.'

They step past the garage, making for the backyard. The smell of buffalo dung, rich as cigar smoke, hangs over Thapa's quarters; from the shed behind his lean-to comes a breathy sniffing and the clink of a chain as an animal lifts its head. Thapa's door stands open. The afternoon sun is streaming in through a small square window. The man's possessions are stored in a trunk under his string cot. A brass pot and clogs keep the trunk company. Dung has been used to harden the clay of the floor, leaving a vegetable glaze. Thapa's table and clothes horse is a single upright chair.

'Here,' Perpetua beckons mischievously, and draws Ritu into the doorway.

On a shelf set in the opposite wall are Thapa's shaving things: mirror, brush and stick, a cut-throat razor, and a plastic soapdish with a lump of brown soap. The sunlight has turned a bottle of red hair oil into a smoking jewel. In the middle of the shelf are framed pictures of Thapa's goddesses. One who smiles as she rides a tiger, a smile so radiant that there are moments when Thapa, standing before her, grows dizzy. And the other who dances with blood on her tongue, brandishing a curved sword and wearing a necklace of human heads.

But Perpetua is not pointing to the mantelshelf. Higher up, her glance says.

More gods up there, calendar gods, but hanging on a nail beneath them is the object Perpetua means. Thapa's kukri. Sheathed and suspended among the constellated gods like a dark crescent moon.

'You can count the notches in the hilt,' Perpetua says with a conspiratorial bulge of the eyes. Then puckers her lips and draws a finger across her throat where the dewlap trembles.

They stop at the byre to greet Thapa's buffalo, a black hulk with great glistening eyes and patches of pink around its nostrils.

'Our milk supply,' Perpetua says, patting the spots. Ritu winces at the nosering, but the holding chain is around the creature's neck. Stacked in a corner are the dung cakes Thapa cooks on.

They go around the back of the house to the other side, the city side of Everest.

'That's the fire escape,' Perpetua points as they turn the corner. 'The only way up to Jed.'

In spite of its functional intent, the fire escape is a spiral stair of some elegance. It has the lines of a museum skeleton, and it is a kind of dinosaur. Built in an age when iron could be an adornment, before joinery became a matter of spot welding, it wears a disdainful air, standing aloof from the building it serves, a structure in its own right. It is made up of jointed steps, each step a fish-plate cast with its vertebral disc. The discs laid one upon the other form the column at the centre. The balusters that lock the steps in place are heavy grade iron, and so is the rail that links them, yet both have a refinement which shames the flimsy rods and rails of modern stairs. It's hard to say which force predominates: the downward thrust of the central shaft or the upward spiralling of the banister. The whole stair soars and is anchored.

Beyond the stair, squatting by the outside tap, is the goongi. She is scrubbing pots with a pad of crab-grass that she dips from time to time into a mound of ash. With every stroke the slack flesh of her arm jiggles, but she is strong, even muscular. She rams a pot against the ground to get a better grip on it, and scours with little skipping turns. Then rinses off the scum under a thread of water from the tap, and watches the aluminium bloom again.

The sun is low, glittering in the thread. An oakleaf

butterfly has settled on her head. She feels something there, but her hands are covered in scum.

'Oh ho! Who's all dressed up for a wedding?' says Perpetua creeping up on her. 'An ornament in the hair – and what a fine sari!'

The goongi shrieks with laughter. Such a one, Perpetua.

'Not your wedding by any chance?'

The goongi is doubled up, giggling, but turns serious when she sees the new sister.

'This is Ritu.'

'Hrooon!'

The goongi rinses off and stands up clucking. She has cropped white hair, albino eyes and skin, and toenails blue as fish scales on both big toes.

'*Arré*, you've left the tap running!' Perpetua addresses her with *tu*. God, a lover, a dog, merit such familiarity.

The goongi squawks. How to explain that for the last several days the tap won't turn off? She squirms, gloom descending. Let the black wing touch her and she can sulk for days.

'New washer needed, no?' Perpetua mimes a wrench. 'Or a new washer upper!'

The wing has lifted. Miraculously the butterfly has not moved through the whole exchange. Or it might be a leaf, with arching nerves.

The leaf splits in two and flits away. Perpetua exclaims, claps her hands. Hands twisted with arthritis, Ritu notices. The goongi watches the butterfly go.

Cecelia comes out to join them.

The rose garden is hers. By the old OUT gate is Thapa,

bent over a short-handle broom, sweeping up leaves. Several leaf piles show he has been working all evening. He ducks his moon face in a swift greeting, bending still further.

The bamboos are shedding, but there are new leaves like pennants at the top. In the east the sky is olive green; storm clouds are gathering above the dark lychee grove. The lychees are clusters of pink ornaments, a persistence of colour in the fading light. The heat is a rock, immovable.

'What is that smell, Thapa?' Cecelia would like to know.

'Don't know, Sister. It wasn't there this afternoon. Must be something dead.'

The smell gets stronger as they near the IN gate. Lantana has sealed off the other gate and spread along the front wall, but its evil-smelling little posies are not to blame.

'The drain needs cleaning,' Cecelia says, reaching the gate first. 'I've called the municipality three times now.' To Ritu she says, 'It's hard to manage such a big compound with just one man. And Thapa's a good worker. Gardener by day and chowkidar by night. I don't know when he gets to sleep. When do you sleep, Thapa?'

'I sleep.'

'It's the dog,' Ritu says, staring at a dark shape in the drain. 'The one we saw this morning.' So it wasn't play, that look, it was mortification, the look of a creature forced to die in public.

'Thapa. Tomorrow you must go get the sweepers.' Who alone will touch the thing.

Embers of bougainvillea on the wall.

Everest a dark mass, lights coming on.

With the first stirrings of dust come snatches of wild singing from the roof. Jed.

Now this old ram of Tollygunge
He knew a famous trick.

'Don't listen to his nonsense,' Cecelia warns, unusually loud, as they hurry up the drive. Custody of the ears.

The storm takes care of that. Windows are crashing, palm fronds rattle overhead. Neha and Tsering will be rushing about indoors fastening bolts, Miss Sampson pacing in her room, the goongi cowering in hers.

On the roof Jed's mouth takes dust. Grit gets in his eye, his fine hair lifts like thatch. Sand whips the soles of his feet, stings his earlobes, but he's laughing.

He loves a storm. Always has, from earliest childhood. While his little sister buried her face in the pillow Jed would creep out onto the verandah to look. Once even into the garden, where the wind built a tower of dust and rose petals around him.

He somersaulted in the air . . .

The lights go out. The local substation taking no chances with overhead wires. Now an unearthly paleness filters from behind the churning cloud mass in the east. It lights the lychees on the trees from below, shows up a mole on Cecelia's chin. The bamboo clump has begun to clack and groan.

And landed on his – if you don't believe me, sir
You think I'm telling a lie . . .

Jed is shouting into the wind, a schoolboy again. He

clambers out of his bathtub, comes to the parapet overlooking the garage and pisses onto the row of periwinkle pots below. The wind frays the twisting yellow rope, the same jaundiced colour as the sky, and slaps it against the limewashed wall. The storm begins to lash Everest, straining at the latches, battering the forward row of rooms upstairs. A pantry window blows in and dust coats the Everest plates in the rack, the hanging blue-rimmed cups.

Thunder to wake the dead. Rain in sheets, flying spray.

Morning. Cool blue air, wet black earth.
The garden washed clean, wrung out, devastated. Branches down. Leaves strewn everywhere, new green among the brown. All Thapa's leaf heaps levelled. A red carpet of fallen lychees; armies of ants moving that way.

Ritu, drawn towards the gate by some puzzling absence, realizes halfway down the drive that the bougainvillea is missing. She unlatches the gate. There it is, blown off the wall and into the drain. Dead grass and shredded polythene bags are caught in its hair at the level the storm water would have reached. The drain is washed clean. The dog has vanished. From across the road comes the roar of water in an old canal.

After breakfast, a visitor.
A regular visitor to the roof, by the iron stair, but today at the front door, ringing the bell. With a suitcase in his hand.

Brij holds up the other hand by way of warning as Cecelia appears.

'It's empty.'

Cecelia is disappointed for Ritu, who has come up behind her. 'It's empty,' she repeats quickly, to spare her the torment of hope.

'Just one or two books,' Brij adds, handing it over. 'I found it lying open in a back lane.'

For Ritu it's riches. Precisely which books can wait in this lottery. She thanks him and returns to her room.

Cecelia invites Brij into the parlour; she has something more to say. He sits blinking at the bookcases while she goes to order tea, which presently Neha brings on a tray, with coconut biscuits.

'I haven't seen you call on Mr Jed lately,' Cecelia begins.

'I was there last month, but ever since this trouble . . .' His voice drops.

'Akashkhand.' Cecelia irons the word flat. 'What do you hope to gain?'

'Control of our lives,' Brij answers, but flushes because his own life is so directionless. 'At present all the decisions are made by people hundreds of miles away.'

'Plains people,' Cecelia puts in, smiling, an outsider herself.

Brij nods. 'They don't know anything about the hills. How can they make laws for us?'

'There are representatives from here.'

'They don't count. The state's too big. They don't even know we're here. We need a hill state.'

'The great mountaineer would agree!' Cecelia points up at the roof. 'Except he's on strike, too!'

Brij looks up from his clasped hands. 'Is he not well?'

'No. He's stopped eating. Hasn't eaten since Friday.' She counts off the days on her fingers. 'That's three days. He won't see anybody, won't even answer.'

She pours tea. Brij takes a cup, frowning, but will not touch a biscuit now.

'If he won't answer . . .'

'Oh, he's alive, all right. We hear him moving around up there. He kicked Tsering's tray downstairs when she left it outside his door. Last night, when the storm came up, he was singing.'

Brij smiles, a fellow storm-fancier. Connoisseurs of lightning, he and Jed have often sat up on the roof judging a display at the horizon. Judging God.

'Tell me,' Cecelia says, reading the smile, 'what attracted you to him?'

Brij is unprepared for so direct an assault. He buries his nose in the cup, but must come up for air.

'Same thing as everybody. He's famous. You can address a letter, "Mr Jed, Drummondganj," and he'll get it. So I came to see him.' He shrugs. 'We're neighbours.'

'I know.' Brij lives across the high wall from the convent. 'But you kept coming.'

'We get on well.'

'Looks like it.'

'We talk.' He puts his cup down, full stop.

'Maybe he'll talk to you now.'

Brij rises at once. 'Yes.'

'I'll get Sister Ritu. She hasn't met him.'

The book of ferns.

The book of mushrooms.

A botanical pharmacopoeia.

The shawl is gone, of course, but Ritu runs her hand along the silk lining of the suitcase: Navin's photo, her parents'.

And, under the bottom flap, her paintings.

God is merciful. Cecelia finds her on her knees.

'**M**r Jed!'
No answer.

Jed is navigating his bathtub, his stick the tiller.

Nightjars by a well. Sleep. Go on, drift back ninety years. This tub is that cot, enamel white sheets. Slippery enamel edge of sleep. Remember lying there, two years old. By day the flour mill, *chuck-chuck*, by night the nightjars, *chuck-chuck*. Ninety years unravelling.

There.

Truth in this moment. *That* moment recovered. The two are one. Ecstasy. Pure sound, unclouded light.

Chuck-chuck. Music won't do it. Nor will meditation. You must sleepwalk back. Slip out through the bars at the edge of sleep. The outer gate is always open. Slip away.

'Mr Jed!'

Jed stirs wrathfully, feels nightjars and flour mill retreat.

'Breakfast!' Cecelia has brought a tray.

'Go away!' Urgently. But the cot is a bathtub again.

'Porridge and toast. Hot!'

Gone, bugger it! Truth turned into porridge. Not that he hears words any more, not plainly. He hears cadences, knows the measure of 'breakfast', the pitch of 'Jed', the subterfuge of 'porridge and toast'. As he knows the Bach *Requiem* by its profile. He hears the ghosts of sounds. Watches words settle and vanish like breath on his shaving mirror. He rubs three days' growth.

'Go away,' he is moved to repeat, and then, as to hens, '*Hoosh!*'

'You call him, then,' Cecelia whispers.

Brij swallows, the Adam's apple bobbing. It comes out as a bellow.

'*Jed Saab!*'

Jed stirs again in the empty tub. That voice he knows. He shifts the game leg, rests the bad foot on the rim of the tub. One of a row of old porcelain tubs with lion paws taken long ago from the bathrooms of Everest and abandoned on the roof. His roof. No sleep in them either, he's tried them all.

Bends his good knee for support. Two orange stains show where the water once ran in, making, with the knee, three peaks. The old chrome faucets have gone to humbler pipes, to the kabariwallahs, carrying with them their absurd titles, HOT and COLD, like decayed nobility. Nowadays we're grateful just for running water.

Four water tanks bulk on the roof like ship's boilers, bristling with rivets gone orange. Only one is serviceable and it's never more than half full. A maze of pipes designed to torment an old man – his shins bear witness – delivers water, hot in summer, cold in winter, to the house below.

Now he's past water, a rock.

'*Yama Raja!*'

Jed frowns but can't suppress a rush of pleasure. So, he's back. *The godson I should have had instead of that twerp. Too late, of course, like everything else.*

Already he's cranking himself up, on arms once athletic. Sculler's arms, climber's legs. A big frame still. His stick making a gong of the bathtub.

They hear and fall silent. He knows they hear, grows furtive, takes his time.

'I *said* don't bother me,' he barks, reaching the door. But his hand is reaching for the bolt, which drops with a clatter.

Emissaries standing there, not two but three. And he in his pyjamas with the sun behind him.

'I've told you not to use the bolt,' Cecelia chides. Her voice glosses over the past three days. 'What if something happened to you?'

Jed is not fooled. 'The day something happens to me, Sister, you and I will celebrate.' He stretches out the last sibilant lecherously and jigs his shoulders, then turns to the young man, smiling. Not *young*, but not ninety. Not thirty, likely, but he's never asked.

'So.'

'Yama Raja.'

Cecelia goes to step over the threshold with her tray. Jed's arm shoots out to bar her way. The arm with the stick, his Moses rod.

'Please behave, Mr Jed.' Cecelia bustles, entering into the drama of it. 'We have a new sister here.'

Jed's arm remains outstretched. His head turns to the new-comer before his gaze has left the godson. When his eyes do find her he widens them roguishly, old habits dying hard.

'Sister Ritu, Mr Jed.'

Ritu dips her head. Jed's eyes go on widening.

Fay.

She sees a demented prophet, the morning sun pouring through him. Ears flaring red. Behind him a graveyard of old bathtubs and bedsteads. A couple of coal cooking ranges parked like small-gauge locomotives, the furnace doors marked 'Birmingham'. And pages, strewn about.

'You can't come in,' Jed snaps. But crooks his elbow to admit the young man. 'Nachiketa,' he jerks his chin.

Brij steps in, abashed. The staff tilts sharply back to bar the way behind him.

'Another day,' Jed intones for the nuns, stern to pantomime. He loves an audience, this king from bark or papyrus.

'You've dropped something.' Ritu reaches down to pick up a page of hieroglyphs.

He snatches it from her. 'That was the storm.' He hands the page solemnly to Brij. '*The Book.*'

'*Of the Dead,*' Brij offers the nuns, and is at once sorry.

Jed frowns. 'A photocopy,' he demurs, 'of a photograph, of a corrupt edition.'

Brij does Jed's legwork, photocopying, hunting up, mailing, sorting. And lends an arm or shoulder. But today is not quick enough. A moan from Cecelia reaches him before he can turn.

Jed has crumpled where he stood, and Brij can only break the fall.

Pain.

In the ghost toes, he realizes, before passing out.

The Egyptian Book of the Dead.
     The Kath Upanishad Dialogue of Yama, King of the Dead, and Prince Nachiketa.
     The Tibetan Book of the Dead.
     The Drummondganj Book of the Dead.

Atlases without maps. Jed is writing the fourth in a series. He is equipped to, is honorary secretary of and nearest neighbour to the Drummondganj cemetery. Everest and the cemetery share a boundary wall. If Jed should go, as he no longer does, down the iron stair and out the Everest gate, turn right and walk fifty paces, he would come to another gate, the outer gate of the cemetery. Another forty paces across open ground, where men stack piles of newspaper and papier-mâché egg trays and boys burn old cycle tyres, would bring him to a lych-gate whose steep shingled roof recalls English graveyards. A tablet set in the gate declares the ground sacred.

The cemetery is a haven for gamblers.

Above the gothic arch of the lych-gate is inscribed the word, 'EVE-R-EST', with the R at the point of the arch, making two words of one. If Jed were to pass through the gate and turn right he would come to the wall, now breached in places by men and animals, he shares with the dead. Everest the mansion marches with Ever-rest the cemetery.

Sacred to the memory of
ISOLA AMY RATTRAY
beloved daughter of
JAMES and HILDA RATTRAY
who departed this life at Drummondganj
on 2nd May 1851
aged eleven years and two months
leaving her parents desolate
Thy will be done

The Knave of Hearts rides Isola Rattray's grave. Till the King of Spades slaps seigneury. There are hoots from the circle of watchers. The players remain unmoved, then one of them lays out his hand on the tablet in disgust. Spitting delicately the frayed remains of a cigarette.

An avenue of cypresses divides Everest the cemetery into old and new. The gamblers prefer the newer, lower tombstones. Pillared mausoleums brood in the oldest quarter. Everywhere the tombs decay in drifts of grass, railings torn up, obelisks askew. Marigolds and pumpkin vines hide uneven ground. Snakeholes. A ribbed pumpkin has fattened beside a fallen urn. Pinned to the rind, a gauze dragonfly.

Trees are constantly springing up out of crumbling stucco. Pipal, mango, yellow oleander. Assorted palms. Only the cypresses were ever planted. And a bay hedge that has grown into trees.

The chowkidar and his family have the gatehouse but live under the trees. Major General Hubert Eldridge Foley's Doric pile keeps their firewood dry. Six string cots stake out a yard of clay. A man squats by the handpump, covered in lather; nearby a girl washes clothes on a gravestone.

Sacred to the memory of
JOSIAH STEPHEN BILPIN
Additional Magistrate of this City
Murdered in his bed by dacoits
5th December 1911
Beloved of all who knew him.

The charnel house of the family Parsons is stacked with dung cakes. A hand dipped in reddle has left its print on the truncated cross to appease cobras.

But no-one will touch the long black coffin truckle parked at the lych-gate, its arms sticking up into the sky. And beside the gate, on the modest eminence of Captain Frank Wilkin's tomb, is another untouchable, the chowkidar's pet and cemetery mascot. A great black he-goat, sphinx-like but majestically horned, incurious, regarding all creation with sovereign and equal contempt.

Meredith Carling, *of cholera*. Sophia Hope Ware, *of brain fever*. Lieutenant Arthur Eldred Leacock, *in action against the Gurkhas*. Jeremy Rowland, *stung to death by wasps*.

Jed knows them all. Can give chapter and verse, script and missing letters, the lead prised out and sold by weight.

He has dwelt on each, transcribed all.

But one especially. 1942. A plain railing about the plinth. At the headstone a frangipani fans its leaves, pours shade, lets fall a creamy flower. In the branches a dove, calling softly . . . *fay, fay.*

T hey carry him to his proper bed.

But he's fouled the sheets, so they lay him on the floor with a pillow under his head while Cecelia goes downstairs to fetch clean linen.

Ritu turns the mattress which he has not let Tsering touch. Silverfish, crickets dart from underneath, feelers going. Their fine black litter is spread like poppy seed on the plywood base. Brij picks up the bed easily and carries it out onto the roof, where he knocks it repeatedly against the parapet. A scorpion falls out and begins to walk away with its tail lifted. He crushes it, then canes the mattress. Remains there while Ritu sponges down the patient.

Jed is lifted back onto the bed, on fresh sheets. His eyes are closed, but he's breathing.

The porridge is cold.

R itu lets her eyes roam over the room.

Sitting beside the bed, on double duty. She takes in the desk, papers, a collection of glass paperweights. Bubbles expanding in purple glass. Galaxies.

No bubbles in the glucose drip, Jed's new navel cord. Brij fetched it, helped her rig it up. She runs her eye along the tube again to check. His veins ropy, knotted; old vaccination marks like craters on the smooth triceps. The flaccid remains of developed musculature: age always sadder in athletes, she thinks. Beyond the bed, his wardrobe, padlocked. Through the bathroom door she can see a clothes-horse with a worn towel on it, stiff and grey. Yellowing underwear on clothes-hooks with china knobs.

No pictures on the walls, not even a calendar. But in the corner an old gramophone, open, a record on the turntable. She goes to it, bends to read the blue label. Looks back at the man.

Jed's great stone head on the pillow, his white rick of hair. Long fleshy nose, carved lips.

She returns to his poky bathroom to wash her hands again. Wash the thing away, gross slug. Expensive soaps he uses, or used, now cracked and flaking. Then she escapes onto the roof where the sun is already hot, the roof steaming a little from last night's rain. Not the true rains yet.

Everest stretches below her. The gate with its bougain-villea, put back up by Thapa, the gravel drive, the portico. Bamboo creaking in the corner by the other gate as the sun clears the topmost leaves. She follows the parapet along the side of the house, looking down on a row of periwinkle pots directly below, the flowers a vulgar pink with mauve centres. There's the lychee grove, the odd mango, a row of Chinese orange trees. At the boundary mature silver oaks, jacaranda, rosewood. A majestic silk-cotton with upstart eucalypts crowding it. Beyond the wall, bamboo all along the Canal Road, then orchards, a riverbed, fields. Then forest. Climbing to the jagged peaks of that same anthill-like range she skirted on the train. Near enough for the outline of individual trees to be visible against the sky.

The parapet ends, becomes a low balustrade; she has come to the back of the house. A chair is pulled up against the balustrade. His, from the dentures left there. Also a glass of water half full, with a film of leaves and dust. She shakes the brown bottle beside it. No sound: the capsules have gone rubbery, stuck to the sides. It's the fifth day since his fast began. She sits, to see what he sees. Against the boundary is a walled garden in decay. There is an arched entrance at the end of a half-buried path from the house, a pergola inside along three walls. A kind of garden house at one corner.

Beyond the boundary, at right angles to it, extends a stone wall. To one side is the cemetery, to the other are automotive workshops. From up above the effect is of two panels hinged at the wall. Green, with glimpses of white marble to the left; to the right, black oil-soaked earth with glints of machinery. The wall has been breached in places, chassis parts hung on it, stones carried away. Paths disappear from it into the graveyard brush. Outdoor toilet and gambling den.

Everest's own wall with the cemetery is not perfect. Every year one course of bricks falls away. Cracks, as from a quake, have appeared where it abuts the garden house, and a whole raft of brickwork has fallen in. A pipal tree straddles the wall, its roots too involved to tackle any more.

Ritu gets up and follows the balustrade to the fourth side, the city side of Everest. Above the city sprawl rise the mountains, today a hazy wall of blue. On this side of the roof are the water tanks at one end and Jed's room at the other. Down below is the kitchen, with kitchen smells rising, the pumphouse, and the outdoor tap by the water meter. There are few trees on this side, perhaps to preserve the view of the mountains, but Ritu finds this range less appealing than the lower hills on the other side. She steps over the many pipes, past the row of empty bathtubs and abandoned cooking ranges, and comes back to the iron stair. Iron she loves, from a childhood by the track. She leans over to count the steps: forty-seven. Every fish-plate solidly cast and bolted, yet the whole stair vibrates when climbed. Low or high, it answers every foot.

The neighbours on this side of Everest have built on the boundary wall, the last of a series of extensions to the main house. A single flight of concrete steps serves the flat facing Everest, where a wash line hung with a woman's undergarments stretches across the narrow terrace. On the terrace parapet is a pot of basil. Ritu is turning back to Jed's room when she hears a cry come from this upstairs flat, the wailing of a woman pushed beyond endurance. At the same time she sees Perpetua down below, marching towards the boundary, wrench in hand, treading an invisible line that appears to join the Everest mains tap and the pot of basil.

The pulse is gone.

The civil surgeon hooks his stethoscope back around his neck and turns to Cecelia, shaking his head. Jed is finished.

No moan from Cecelia, but the blood drains from her head as she crosses herself. Ritu undoes the drip while the civil surgeon writes out the death certificate. Cecelia, with nothing to do, goes to the light switch and turns it on. Stands at the door looking out at the sky.

Twilight outside, the crows fussing in the silk-cotton. A sickle moon low in the sky, bright edge on a dark stone. A mask, Cecelia is already thinking, and thinks back to the one mother made of Dadda in Poona.

Make one. Wax, was it, or plaster? She has both, Perpetua will have. She accompanies the doctor down, summons all the nuns to prayer.

No plaster, so that night they melt chapel candle stubs on the kitchen stove.

Burning.

Snow that long night when the tent was down at base camp and Dorji went missing.

Settling on the forehead, furring the eyebrows. He'd like to brush it off but his hands are warm in the bag. Let it fall, blanket you. A wind could start up any minute, then you'll be glad of the cover. Down on down, this first snow. Seedfall the porters call it. Sleep, sleep.

But now it begins to bite.

Brush it off for Godsake. His whole being in revolt, but chained.

Burning at his nose now, the nostrils closing up. Shake it off.

He stirs. The stone head masked in wax.

The Coming Forth By Night, he calls it afterwards, laughing with Brij. And Brij, who wasn't there, can share the joke. But Ritu, who was, can't forget.

Nor will Cecelia, who first felt a movement under her fingers, under the hot wax. Drew back her hands from the shock of it, wax clinging to her fingertips, hardening on her palms. Fright on top of snowburn. Immediately lifted the mask, which broke in half at the nose.

Breath of life from the nostrils. Scalding.

The whole head shifted, wax crumbling. Perpetua screamed. Ritu's bird-bright eyes stared, her heart banging.

Days later, as she sweeps the room, a wax bead on the floor will give her a turn.

'Omelette.'

A command. There is a hotplate now in Jed's room, an old Baby Belling. At breakfast there's still electricity.

'And toast. No butter.'

Ritu cracks two eggs over a soup plate and beats them with a fork while the oil heats in the pan. She had planned scrambled eggs; the onions and green chillies are chopped and waiting.

The head shifts again. 'Soft boiled.'

Ritu's hand stops in mid air. 'You said an omelette.'

'Soft boiled.'

'All right.' She can eat the scrambled egg herself. 'Are you sure, now?' She looks hard at Jed, whose eyelids are fluttering as in dream sleep. The chin appears to dip. She puts down the soup plate and takes the frying pan off the stove. Half fills a saucepan with water and puts it on instead, then goes out onto the roof because she can never watch a pot. Custody of the nerves.

Perpetua is down there with her wrench. She sees Ritu and brandishes the wrench by way of greeting. Ritu smiles and waves. Remembers something else that was in the suitcase, her father's gift of a fountain pen, and feels a pang. Looks up at the vultures wheeling, specks in a bleached sky. Grace in so clumsy a creature. Suddenly the same cry she heard yesterday: a drawn-out crowing that today sounds like a cock. On the wash line above the pot of basil the woman's knickers flutter like prayer flags. From the cemetery lane comes a steady clinking; across the other wall the panel beaters have started up.

The pot! She hurries back to Jed's room where the water's bubbling madly.

'Scrambled.'

She looks up sharply. Something in the tone says, Testing.

Her own head says, Soft boiled you said, soft boiled you get, but then she remembers the onions and chillies and sweeps them into the frying pan with the back of the knife. He needs the C, the old devil. Eating again, anyway.

The next day she sets a menu: Tuesday is omelette day. He's passed out of Tsering's care.

'*Soft* boiled!'

She cracks the eggs into a bowl, watching him. The eyelids wobble, show a glint. He's quick to kill it, but not quick enough. She catches the sudden contraction, the abrupt frown that accompanies it, childlike in its mistiming. Now she recognizes that reflex: there have been other times. Late last night she took it for a twitch. He's been watching her.

'Don't you ever sleep?' Helping him up.

He takes the plate, eats greedily, with concentration. Cutting the omelette up into strips. When he's finished he licks the knife lasciviously and looks at her.

'I haven't slept for fifty years.' He measures out the words like an actor. 'There are documented cases. I've corresponded with a man in Tangier who hasn't slept for sixty years.' He lets his eyes close. After a pause, opens them on her. 'We rest.'

'You don't dream?'

The gaze sharpens, frankly appraising. Nobody has asked him that before.

'I would give,' he lifts and drops an ineffectual hand, 'anything, for that.'

She tries to imagine fifty waking years. Her life twice over. But can't. Easier to imagine fifty million, fin drawn into feather, a rib drifting through flesh, dropping away.

'Don't try,' he smiles. The first smile she's wrung from him in five days. 'It's like being dead, except people won't go away.'

She washes the plate in a basin, lets the pan soak, hands

him his tea. Toast crumbs underfoot, and coins of wax she missed.

'Turn that on,' he says gently, setting down his empty cup and nodding at the gramophone.

She confronts the machine with its weird chrome mushroom. 'What do you do?'

'Crank it up.' He winds a handle in the air.

The turntable begins to spin.

'Blow the dust off. Hold that yellow cloth on the record. Lightly. Now the needle.'

It falls heavily, skidding on the shellac. He winces. Bach *in medias res*. It's an old record, even compared to the others. Skipping, scratching, more pain than music. Casals turned to dust. Well, fair enough. The frown relaxes, he lowers himself onto the pillow, shuts his eyes.

She doesn't understand the music, doesn't care for the constant onion-skin crackle. Pads from the room and goes down the iron stair.

The sheets are harder to take, at first.

Once, sometimes twice a week, he will wet the bed. He hates himself on such mornings, torments her. She puts a plastic sheet between him and the mattress, suns the old mattress. Devises a washing system with the row of old tubs. Bleach, soak, four rinses, but the stink remains. Once a day she helps him to the bathroom.

The mask is up on the wall, looking down at him. Cecelia thinks it's ghoulish now, but he insisted and she backed down. Her wax, but his face, or half of it. Brij had it cast in plaster and she was astonished at the detail. Every eyelash caught, frozen shut. The fine sweep of them together, the lids down, asleep at last. Jed laughs at the mockery of it; the mask laughs back, a cross between death's head and Commedia. His dentures, the second set, are back in a tumbler. The first set he wears, even in bed. Other touches of vanity she discovers in this once handsome man: a pocket comb on the bedside table, uncorrected short sight. And something else.

One day she finds him conducting the music from his bed. Eyes closed, forearms up, resting on the elbows, the hands sketching figures in the air. She crosses to the gramophone, lifts the needle.

He goes on conducting.

'He's not mad at all,' she says to Cecelia at dinner. 'Just deaf.'

Cecelia, who was not taken in either, says, 'There are other days.'

In the morning Ritu is washing bedsheets, moving from tub to tub. His favoured tub she leaves alone. When she returns to the room the bed is empty. She checks the bathroom, goes back out onto the roof to look there. He's gone.

A tapping on the stair, wood on iron. He's on his way down, naked.

She goes after him. He hasn't got far. His stick caught in the balusters. He comes quietly, is meekly led back to bed.

But the next day he's waiting at the top of the stair when she comes up. The stick a staff again, sceptre and spear. Naked again.

'Shoo!' he jabs at her.

'Mr Jed . . .'

She looks him in the eye, will stare him into submission.

But he lunges again, and this time she feels the point in her ribs.

'Hah!' He felt it, too. She retreats. Success arouses him. He advances on her, all eyes and rod. Flailing, clattering. She backs down the stair and into Brij.

'Yama Raja!'

Brij has never seen Jed like this. But the words work their magic. Jed's rod goes down, he stands exposed, sees himself. What's he doing here? But must gather up his dignity.

'What brings you here?' he asks, offended at neglect.

'I came to see how you are.'

'I'm as you see me.' Miffed.

'I had to go to my village.'

Jed tilts his head, considering, then relents, nods once.

'The water level is rising. It's reached the lowest houses.'

Brij is conscious of talking across Ritu. He steps around her, giving her the outside, and takes Jed's arm. Jed leans on him, is carried back up the spiral stair.

Jeth, *June is a blowtorch. Air and fire fused, wind spurting flame. By mid-morning the loo has begun to stir, feathering the dust, riffling the verandah chicks. The clump of bamboo creaks. Bright corridors open up in the air and are instantly filled with moving sand. The body tingles, takes on more heat, grows light. Now the lychees are ready for picking; the same heat that torments Miss Sampson clarifies their glaucous flesh.*

At eleven the fan stops.

A table fan because the ceiling has no hook. Like the gramophone it's old, with a simple wire guard that evokes the entwined serpents of medicine.

Ritu sits by the bed, fanning Jed with a bamboo-plaited fan in such a way that she shares the breeze. In half an hour the room is an oven.

'A bloody baker, not an architect,' murmurs Jed.

Ritu sees him rising like dough and smiles. *Softer! Whiter! Lighter!* the local bread boasts. Jed is unsliced brown. Crusty enough, she thinks. She stops fanning. A wasp come in out of the sun is making desultory stabs at the whitewashed wall, like a sunblind climber. A lizard darts from behind the mask to investigate and stops short, eyes glittering. Ritu sees light through the chink in its neck.

'Listen,' she says to Jed, forgetting that he hears by rote. It's the cock crowing again, but this time she's sure it's a woman. Describes the racked cry to Jed.

He chuckles. 'Home is the sailor!' And returns to his thoughts.

She quits the oven for the roof. The sky is scratched enamel; the empty bathtubs are lozenges of blinding light. The roof a bagatelle board for air currents that lift her habit, flap the veil. Waves of heat ebb through the skin, as body and air merge. She pauses by a broken washbasin whose tap says, cruelly, COLD. Grit on the porcelain. The water pipes are burning hot. Down below she sees Perpetua, wrench in hand, cross the brown expanse of grass, casting no shadow. Twelve o'clock, then.

Under the shared pipal tree, on the other side of the broken wall, a head-shaving is in progress. A young brahmin scalp emerges, yellow under hair. The black locks drop sullenly among stillborn pipal leaves, tender green scrolls that will never open. A car roof hung on the broken wall wrinkles the air above it. A pair of feet stick out from under an old taxi, the toes straining towards some cool stream.

'A mug of water.'

Ritu returns to the oven. 'What?'

'A mug of water.'

She fetches it from a bucket in the bathroom. Standing water, last night's. He dips first one hand then the other in it and sighs.

'Now, pour it over me. Go on.'

She does, limb by limb, ending at the neck. It pools in the cup below the Adam's apple, a tarn. She feels the change herself as his closed eyes roll.

'We used to break off icicles and stand them in the saucepan for tea water. The last to melt won first cup.' Looking at her like a Boy Scout.

She asks slowly, so he can watch her lips, 'What was there to collect up there?'

'I was a climber before I collected. But no, there was nothing to collect above the snowline.' He looks out through the door. 'Except some footprints, once.'

Her eyebrows go up. He smiles.

'I photographed them. For the world.' She hasn't heard, hasn't read. He's spared the ridicule then, but feels a pang all the same. He has become history, not just dubious history. 'A row of them, right by our camp, each foot the size of two regular feet. Three of yours. Not boots: you could see the toes. They said it was snowmelt, the sun acting on old prints, widening them. But the edges were crisp enough.'

'So what was it?'

He opens his eyes and stares at her. Then drops his gaze and shrugs.

She jerks her head back. The cry again. But, no, this one's

coming from the other side of Everest. She goes to investigate.

'Hroo!'

It's the goongi, calling up to the roof. When Ritu appears she performs a ballet of hands and points repeatedly to the clump of trees in the backyard. Standing among the tree trunks there is an old anthill. She's pointing to that.

Ritu repeats the gesture for Jed. A hand parachuting down, fingers dangling, wriggling. Then the other hand lowered the same way, again and again.

'The ants are still climbing down,' Jed translates. 'No rain.'

'What's this Yama Raja business?'

Brij is on his hands and knees working a stiff brush along a crack in the roof when Ritu's sandalled feet come up, the toes slender as a bird's. The habit a cool grey wall that ends above her ankles.

Brij straightens up and drops back onto his calves in one fluid movement, brush in hand. 'He was writing the local book of the dead,' he says, and shrugs.

'Yes?'

'So I called him Yama Raja. The God of Death. He didn't know the story of Nachiketa.'

'What is the story?'

Brij puts the brush down. 'Nachiketa was a prince who went to meet the God of Death.' He picks the brush up again and begins to flick at the dust where he left off. The crack forks, then forks again, a dry riverbed that he follows compulsively to its source. 'The god was away, so for three nights Nachiketa waited, fasting. When Yama returned he was impressed, so he granted Nachiketa three boons. First

Nachiketa asked for forgiveness, then for the way to heaven, and Yama granted both boons. The third boon was the secret of death. What comes after life? Yama said, "Ask for immortality instead. Ask for jewels, for heavenly women." But Nachiketa was determined. So Yama told him the secret.'

'Which was?' Because Brij appears to have finished his story.

'There is no death. The soul doesn't die.' It doesn't sound convincing, so he soldiers on. 'If you free yourself of all attachments on earth you put an end to the cycle of re-incarnation and gain eternal life.'

'Oh.' She feels let down, too. Always this sense of disappointment. You're led to the brink of special insight and then – words.

Brij works for a while in silence. Then her silence oppresses him into speech. 'Sister said the main leak is in the sailor's room, which must be somewhere here.'

Ritu looks at the roof, imagining where the staircase would be. 'Or *here*,' she says.

Brij looks again, measures invisible metres, and agrees. He begins to brush where she indicated. He is easily swayed, and knows it, and the knowledge makes him uncomfortable. He's happy doing other people's odd jobs. Cecelia just happened to mention the leaking roof and he found himself offering to tackle it. He worries that someone might think him a stooge.

His father does. 'Look at your brother,' he points through the mesh of their sitting-room door. Raju is already at work in the oil-black front yard, priming the hydraulic pump. Presently he will water-blast the undercarriage of the day's first car. He has on his grease-stained work clothes; so has his father. Brij examines his clean fingernails. He was just thinking of stepping out to do some photocopying for Jed, to chat with the photocopy man by the law courts. There's a lawyer friend, too, who always has time for a cup of tea.

'Take a good look,' his father repeats. He gets up, fishing in his pockets for the starter brushes for the Ambassador on the hoist. 'Give Jed Saab my salaams,' he says and lets the swing door slam.

Brij looks vacantly about the room. It's tiny and ill lit, with mismatched chairs and a grimed look. A film of mineral grease covers everything, especially the dark-blue walls, though no single object has an actual stain. Against the grubby upholstery his trousers look excessively fresh, the crease indecent. He sits there till the compressor motor goes on, then slips out.

'What will you use to fill the cracks?'

The young nun talking. He hasn't dared to ask her about the suitcase.

'There's a new epoxy resin we use in the workshop,' he says, finding a guilty sort of pleasure in the *we*, 'but it's expensive. I'll probably just use cement.'

From the terrace with the pot of basil comes the now familiar cry.

'What is that sound?' Ritu asks.

Brij hangs his head to cover his confusion, but she's seen his embarrassment, so leaves him and goes back to Jed.

Lying there, eyelids fluttering. Unsleeping King of the Dead.

From *The Drummondganj Book of the Dead:*

*T*he seat of the soul is in the viscera at no great remove from its supposed keep, the spinal cord, between the sweetbread *and the liver. The soul appears as a blister, no bigger than a seed pearl, that fades within seconds of exposure to light. It is a bubble of ether, colourless, odourless and tasteless, but not without sound, for in escaping it emits a distinct sigh or susurrus, lasting up to two seconds, by which time the bubble is emptied and life may be said to have departed. Nor is it impalpable, for as it passes from the body in question it may be proved upon the living skin, flowing over the enquirer's hand or other part most pleasurably (as when a velvet kerchief is drawn between the toes).*

The soul does not pass directly to Yama's kingdom. It passes first to the nearest mask, or, if there are none available, into either a gramophone or the table where a gramophone has sat, and resides there a space, revolving. The soul then passes to the city of Canberra. After a millennium it enters the statue of a sparrow, whence it migrates to Neptune's moon, Triton, and may spend many aeons there. Chilblains blight its passage thence to the Café Rose in Muzaffarnagar, where it disports among flies on a calendar. Hell is its next sojourn — for who shall 'scape whipping? — and there it sits supping with a long spoon, listening to the best tunes. Only then does it return to harrow the grave, releasing all secrets taken there; the sound of these escaping is like an express train on a bridge. Some time it must then spend in the cooling tower of an aerated water plant in Upper Volta, whereupon it passes to the rain shadow of an electron chain in the supercollider under the former Mexican state of Texas. Simultaneously it may be found on the leeward side of an electron chain at the opposite end of the universe. Yama, great leveller, imposes this itinerary on all who would enter into his kingdom.

These are, of course, preliminaries.

'He *is* mad!' Cecelia says.

Frowning at the page Ritu has brought to the office at her request.

'There are other days,' Ritu replies, with a smile. The handwriting is her own. Jed has been dictating.

A frog croaks loudly from the cesspit outside the kitchen, a single parched syllable, like a request for clean water. Rain is on every mind at Everest.

At bedtime Ritu examines a sore spot on her ribcage. It's where he lunged at her with his stick. The skin is not broken, but a mark like an ink blot has appeared under the left breast. She turns off the light and lies there with her hands folded under her head, staring at the firefly sparks the old fan throws on the ceiling around the rose. She was sent here for humbling, she knows, and that means not answering back. But she felt obliged to take his part. Why?

Suddenly she remembers last night's dream and flushes at the details. Has he penetrated her cloudland already? Her blood begins to murmur, a steady pounding, as of an ocean she's never seen. He stands over her, a black crag. Moisture in the crevice shames her. She turns sharply onto her side. Yet part of her is clinically amused at the exorbitance of it. She falls asleep to the wittering of the fan.

Next morning she stands on the roof looking down into the walled garden and sees for the first time the outline of a buried pool. She goes down the spiral stair to investigate. Instinctively she leaves the gravel to walk on grass, even dry crab grass, then enters by the arch and finds herself in a derelict arcade. Brick-on-edge underfoot, set in chevrons, a three-sided gallery flanged with yellow stone. On the fourth side a fountain set in the wall, an ape's head that once spouted water into a projecting half-moon basin. The overflow would have run into a wider half-moon pool, whose contours she glimpsed from up above.

A little work would uncover it.

A sunken garden, she realizes as she leaves, and steps out into Perpetua's path. Today the wrench is missing, but the old nun manages to look busy. She listens with half an ear to Ritu's proposal.

'A fountain!' She laughs her rollicking laugh. 'We're lucky to get half a tankful of water during the night. Wait another week, there'll be plenty of water,' she adds, looking up at the sky.

'Who needs a fountain during the monsoon?'

'Correct! In Kerala we don't need fountains.'

Ritu turns her gaze on the mountains, whose blue filters through a screen of dust. 'What is this dam they're building?' she asks.

'Very big one, with foreign aid. That boy Brij comes from that side. He can tell you all about it.'

Heat. With it a stillness that approaches the heart of time.

From the bamboo clump comes the cry of the brainfever bird, mounting, *moré pihu! moré pihu!* to a pitch scarcely bearable. Then the plaint breaks off abruptly and the silence is taut with rebuke. Ritu stands in the doorway looking out onto the roof. On market day the village girls sang the pihu's song at the height of summer, mimicking the bird.

> *Why does he not come?*
> *My love! My love!*
> *Who can there be in the city*
> *To detain him?*

She steps out into the sun to see if she can spot the bird, but can't. There are labourers at work, repairing the canal – migrants, from the vivid saris of the women carrying the rocks. The water level in the canal is low. Beyond the canal is the town jail, its high back wall stepped to match the lay of the land. The canal is stepped, too, with waterfalls at intervals along its course.

'The high gate is the morgue.'

She turns sharply to find Jed behind her. Out of bed for the first time since his fall. He looks past her and points down the Canal Road.

'Death Row,' he says. 'That's the old native Christian cemetery. Beyond it is the Muslim graveyard, and beyond that the Parsees have a graveyard, too. Though there are a couple of Parsee graves at Ever-rest.' He breaks the word in two when speaking of Everest the cemetery. 'And right down there, where the river is, is the Hindu burning ghat. They say the sweetest lychees grow down there.'

The river shows a stony stretch, more bed than stream. A braid of shallow water runs along either bank, narrow enough to step over. Beyond the farther, steeper bank there are clearings in the forest under cultivation. Ritu's eyes pick out the gold of laburnum, purple jacaranda. Then the clearings dwindle and the true forest begins, sloping gently to the crest of the jagged range. The sharp fall is on the other side, down to the plains.

The bird starts up again, *Thirsty! Thirsty!* Staring at the dry forest Ritu picks up another more monotonous call, the coppersmith. No songs about him in her tribe, yet he filled her childhood afternoons like a clock. *Tunk, Tunk, Tunk,* hours without end.

In the afternoon the sky turns black.

Clouds sail overhead, hiding the sun, but come apart without any fall of rain. Before they disperse they cool the day down, helped by breezes from the east where the thunderheads are milling. The thunder is still an abstract growl at the horizon, a tin sheet rumbling in the wings. The hills, Ritu's hills, have shrunk to cardboard cut-outs propped against black velvet. Lightning forks down among the peaks.

Jed's ear, deaf to high bird calls, picks up a familiar vibration on the iron stair. Only one visitor bounds all the way up, two steps at a time, without a pause: Brij.

He knows why he's there. Lightning buffs, the two men have spent hours on the roof gazing out across the proscenium of the low hills where the display usually occurs at this time of year. They applaud with restraint, do not automatically prefer fork lightning. There are subtleties to sheet lightning, of colour, tone and value, that the older man has explained.

Today they are joined by a third watcher. Ritu appears beside them, then takes Brij's seat because he will not sit while she stands. Brij leans on the parapet steadily looking out. More clouds have come up, diffusing the late sunlight, bathing Everest in glassy light. Where the cloud bank ends sunlight streams across the valley, touching isolated flame trees in the forest, stoking crystals of limestone. Above the horizon the sky is wrung cheesecloth, flapping with unexpected lights.

'Master! Master!' Jed applauds a blush out of the cave of a seashell.

Ritu tires first, dropping her gaze to the garden. At the foot of a lemon tree she sees a clump of lilies newly opened.

'They weren't out yesterday,' she says.

'Thunder lilies,' Jed says, following her gaze.

'Is that what you call them?' she laughs, delighted.

'Yes. Vulgar things.' It's the vermilion he despises. 'Now *spider* lilies. There's a lily for you.'

'Or moon lilies.'

'Moon lilies!' he snaps. His tone says, What would you know about them?

And gets up muttering, the show over. Stalks off without a by your leave, so Brij and Ritu exchange a glance.

'What are moon lilies?' asks Brij the next morning. Today he applies a tar-based sealant; Cecelia didn't think cement would hold. But he's lost a week. It could rain any day now.

'I'll show you,' Ritu says on an impulse, and goes down to fetch out a painting from the suitcase.

Brij watches her go, strangely elated. He sits on his haunches, the pourer poised, staring at a crack in the surface that looks like frozen lightning.

Jed, who didn't notice her go, recognizes Ritu's footfall on the stair coming up. When she enters the room his eyelids flutter, the old blue lizard tongue shifting drily.

'Tea,' he decides, out loud.

Ritu walks past him with the painting. Brij has jumped up and come across to her. He holds his tarred hands up by way of warning, then clasps them behind his back. Ritu must hold the painting up for him.

'Tea!' An edge to Jed's request now.

She ignores him, looks critically at the painting, seeing where she lost the balance in what is, after all, art not nature. Another turn of the vase would have brought the leaf around to fill this white space and left a speaking blankness on the other side where it was needed. The petals wrong, too.

71

White on white is always hard.

Brij can only look with the eye of passion. She could show him a botched first wash and he would praise.

'Tea, tea, tea, tea, tea, tea, *tea*!'

She is prepared to go on ignoring Jed, but Brij, finding himself compromised, ushers her in without actually moving.

'Show him,' he suggests.

So she does, still smarting from last evening. But now it's Jed's turn to sulk, his eyes shut fast, eyebrows pushed up virtuously. Where has she seen that look? The mask, she realizes. It's on the wall, looking down without looking. But his eyes open at last, sneakily, looking for sympathy but finding the lily. He stares.

'*Lilium lunaris*,' he says at length, tea forgotten. Classifying, not reading. 'Very good. For me?'

A child's question, so her *yes* is tentative, as if unsure whether this is spoiling. But already he's looking for a place where it might hang. There, under the mask. No, the light's wrong. On that wall, then. So he sees it first thing as he gets out of bed.

'I could have it framed,' Brij offers.

'Good,' Jed agrees. 'A black frame. Matte backing, grey. Take it to Ajanta Studio, ask for Zero, skinny chap.' He turns to Ritu. 'Hold it up there. Yes, fine, fine. Good.' A civil pause. 'Now, can we have some tea?'

She makes three mugs.

'Sister Perpetua tells me you know all about the big dam,' she says, handing Brij his mug.

He stiffens and says, finally, 'I know about the reservoir.' Looks across at Jed for help, but Jed's eyes are roaming the ceiling, his lips moving silently. He has not heard the question. Jed, to whom all things come: people, houses, paintings. Untouched by the waters lapping behind the dam. Jed, back from the dead with no news. It sounded curt, so Brij adds, 'Our village is going to be submerged by the lake. The water has reached our house. The lowest houses are submerged already.'

She stands there picturing it. While Brij, easily distracted, looks at her, other waters roaring in his ears.

'Are there villages already underwater?'

'Fifteen,' he answers mechanically.

'How many more will be affected?'

'More than a hundred. And one town. They've built a new town higher up.'

'Do people live there?'

'Some. The water hasn't reached the old town yet.'

'And the villagers?'

'They were given land. Some have come to the city.'

'Your family came here?'

'We came before the dam. But our relatives are still there. Were there: they were evicted last week. My grandfather, cousins.'

'Sister Perpetua says our water supply will improve once the dam is functioning.'

Brij draws his lips down. 'The pipes lead to the plains,' he says.

The fan goes off as they speak. 'Maybe the power supply will improve,' Ritu laughs.

Brij would like to say that the power lines go down to the plains, too, along the canals, that the people of the catchment area should be paid for their water and their electricity. But he's afraid of sounding like a pamphlet. Ritu finds his reticence pleasing: Jed would pontificate. Brij sits there hunched forward, shoulders like hassocks, his fingers knotted about the mug.

Jed's tea is cold. He sits up in bed and gulps it down like water. He's not untroubled, as Brij supposes. He's haunted.

And now twice over, by forgetfulness. He has begun to forget the great sorrow of his life. It can make him whimper in the night. Sorrow, sudden piercing sorrow, without an object. So it's everywhere, despair smeared over everything. It taints the farthest star.

Brij goes back to work unaware that he's tarred the mug.

There is a handcart in the portico with a large crate on it.

The carters are undoing the rope around the crate while Bunny explains his errand to Sister Cecelia.

'It's a present for Uncle. A satellite dish.'

'But we don't have a TV,' Cecelia points out.

'That's coming,' Bunny says. 'First I wanted to set up the infrastructure.' He's a tense balding man with a rapid flow of words. 'Or rather superstructure.' He corrects himself and turns to chivvy the men. 'Careful, *careful*!'

'Have you talked to Mr Jed?'

'I wanted it to be a surprise. He needs something to occupy him now that he's confined to bed.'

'He isn't confined to bed. And he's still writing his book.'

'Good. It'll give him ideas. He needs stimulation.'

'He needs rest.'

'Exactly. I'll get a remote control.'

'Maybe you should go up and ask him. Before you unload it.'

'Correct. But I have to pay off these men.' He helps the men unload the crate and hustles them off. Then he runs up the fire escape to the roof.

His tread is so light that only the humming of the whole stair alerts Jed. The hum means trouble, if he remembers, and today his faculties are intact.

'Not Tinkerbell, is it?'

'Uncle! It's me, Bunny.'

'Well, fancy.'

'What's all this I hear about you going on a hunger strike? Thapa said you died.'

'Well, I'm back.'

'Good. You look on top of the world.'

'I'm here.'

'That's the main thing. You just rest. Build up your reserves. How's the book going?'

'What book?'

'Cecelia told me. I thought you were keeping the cemetery records. I never knew we had a writer in the family. Listen, I know an agent.'

Jed has closed his eyes. 'What do you want?'

Bunny is not dismayed. He raises his voice. 'You need company,' he says, looking around at the painting, the mask. He picks up a record from the rack, blows the dust off it and puts it down. 'This place needs cleaning. I suppose they've dumped you up here. Sisters of whatisit? Whatever. I know their tactics. Sweet talk, then sit back and wait.'

'For what?'

'You know.'

'What would you do?'

'Me? I would get you a TV. In fact, I've already got the dish.'

'The what?' Jed's eyes flick open.

'A satellite dish. That way you don't have to rent a cable. Do you know in America they have seventy-two channels?'

'They have electricity, too.'

'Well, once the summer's over the power cuts aren't so bad. You can get a generator. Diesel is cheap. The Olympics are coming up. You mark my words, you won't regret it. You'll wonder what you did before. Anyway, that's all theory; the dish is here.'

During the night a cloud comes up from the west, covering the stars and turning the moon red.

Six drops of rain fall like soft fruit on the zinc roof. Jed dreams of a high valley where a hairy creature slips out of a cave at sunset and makes its way to a stream. It stretches out on the bank and drinks, dipping its chin into the water, a beard forming there. Then it crawls along the bank till it comes to a mat-like shrub with tiny blue fruit. *Gaultheria trichophylla*. It picks the berries swiftly, with both hands, cramming them into its mouth and looking over its shoulder as it eats. When it has eaten it rolls over and drags its back along the bristly leaves, moaning. The moaning grows louder. It's in Jed's throat, a deep dry lament because the creature's hair has dropped away.

Jed is floating on his back, calling. Awake, but not in. Watching himself from the wall. A young woman comes in, changes his sheet, his pyjamas.

'Blue! Blue!' He's calling. 'Scratch there, *there*!'

Jed, who, when this trouble started, instituted a regime of exercises, mental exercises, to rejuvenate the brain: that's his way. But this is past will, this is chemistry, failing cells. The cells are the will. You failed chemistry – he recalls an exam from the remote past – now chemistry fails you. This on a good day, and there are still some. He's learnt to cherish them.

On a bad day he can order nothing. Can't even piss straight, he wakes up thinking, but can wallow in it. Later the words will pour out, still connected, sentences still, but breaking up now. Lines are easier, and songs, and antics. And the bad days are getting more frequent.

Outside, the cloud cover is still there, but it's a dust cloud, fine desert sand churned up and carried 500 miles. For two days it hangs over the valley. By day the sun is hidden; by night there are no stars. On the third day the goongi signals from below: a parachute falling upwards. The ants are climbing back up. Brij, inspecting his tar seal, relays the message, but Jed is still unreachable.

Ritu unpegs the dry sheets on the line, and looks askance at the new addition to Everest's roof. It sits beyond her wash-tubs, gleaming whitely through the murk, the last in a series of bowls. Set in a stanchion just where Jed's chair is, it looks up and out. The dentures and vitamin capsules are back on the balustrade, shaded now from the sun, but Jed has lost something of his unimpeded view to the oval bulk of the satellite dish.

The Rains

A SADH, *June–July. The first drop of the monsoon. Always the same fat sound, warm with shipwrecks, fastings, ululations, granaries. Exhaling Arabian salts, breath of a stranded oyster, a rock orchid opening in Bhutan, mist off a cardamom hill. Tasting of sweat, the sweat of the finger that carries it to the tongue. Children hold out their tongues, and old men, but always it strikes the chest bone, one sharp rap, then the warm flat trickle, discharged so quickly of freight and obligation. Good heavy drops, half the rice crop's virtue, ecstasy in the lapwing's gullet, fear in the anthill.*

THE GOONGI WILL BE GROVELLING BEFORE HER PHALLUS.

I've watched her strew petals on the anthill, looking over her shoulder in case Cecelia is watching. Worshipping with a force I can only salute. A force I would trade Everest for.

You're hiding your face. Where are you? In me, says Succour Superior. Well, what's this stone in my chest, then? *And* yours, or why have you abandoned me? Curdled me as cheese. In this desert of porcelain and rusty tanks and dish stuff. What is it? Silicon? A dish for collecting signals with no tube to decipher them. Bathtubs catching rainwater and letting it go. Why do we waste the monsoon? I must build a harvest tank. Get Brij.

Give him Everest.

Or the nuns?

Or that thieving cousin?

Or keep it for myself, seeing as I am immortal.

Go on, strike me dead. One small thunderbolt. Go on, you old sod.

Where's your little vessel, by the way? With my tea? Still heat in this old ram, but he needs coddling. How she hates handling it! Must feel *some*thing. She's human. Yes, sir. Little beauty: Miss before Sister.

All misses at Everest. Near misses, maybe, but misses all the same. Misters included. Look at the neighbours. Fertile ground all round. Mistress Puri, six, God help us, and more to come. Dixit's niece, is it, down the lane has *eight*. Breeding, pullulating on every side. No misses there.

But *here*!

Miss Sampson. *Miss* Chatterjee. The goongi. *All* the sisters. Major Whatsisface. His batman. The veggie twins. Even Brij, across the wall. He's past thirty, must be. *And* that balding git of a cousin.

And Immanuel Jed. Yama Raja. Sometime surveyor, flower-hunter, mountaineer.

Absolute miss.

Jed is weeping.

The rain comes down harder now. He watches it fall on him, sees a pool begin to form around the plughole where his heel is lodged. The toes splayed like gear teeth on the good foot. Feet that were once handsome. At the American hospital the nurses came to look, to lament the surgery.

Fallen arches on Ritu's feet. On the iron stair now, then on the threshold, now hurrying across the roof to him, sandals slapping wetly.

She takes his arm, dispraise in that stiffness, though she says nothing. Helps him up, claps the stick into his free hand. Together they cross to his room, where he stands like a child being towelled dry. Lifting his arms. Looking down at his thing. As a child he always ran out into the first shower of the rains. Sees himself at five catching raindrops on his tongue.

The rain is loud on the tin roof.

'Has the TV arrived?' he shouts above it.

'He's gone,' Ritu answers, 'your nephew.'

'*Cousin*. Not far enough removed. Gone where?'

'Sister Cecelia threw him out for drinking. He and the major got drunk last night and pulled up all Thapa's corn, so Sister had Thapa lock him up in the garage. This morning she sent him off.'

'And he just went?'

'He said he had to go anyway, on business.'

'His father's business, the rogue. Do you know, his father sold all the brass bolts from St Xavier's church when he was twelve?'

She lets him dress himself in the striped blue pyjamas he

now wears night and day. Jed, who wore starched cotton suits in summer and bones in his collar. Who wore a raw silk Indian jacket every day the British ruled, and switched to British suits the day they left.

The rain has spread a sheet of spray on the pukka roof. How is the sealant holding up? Ritu wonders, looking out across the wet expanse, so different from yesterday. The row of empty bathtubs glows through the spray. All along Canal Road the bamboo clumps are bending, lashed by the rain. The farthest clumps are pale ghosts whose silver wash absorbs the grey-green of the distant forest.

Jed is back in bed, eyes shut. Lying in the tub before she came, looking straight up into the falling rain, he trained his eye to follow a single racing drop. Falling into it.

Fay appeared then, rain riddling her clear body. Laying out her water garden with seeds he posted from remote valleys. In wax paper packets tied with sewing thread, then wrapped in felt and then in squares cut from old raincoats and, lastly, hessian. His duplicates.

And then the teeming locust rain turned white and began to sting. Hail! A little white drift forming at the plughole. Half an hour of that and he could have frozen there. On the roof in the heart of June, packed in ice.

'Whose garden was that,' Ritu asks, 'at the back?'

He looks hard at her, at the low straight eyebrows, the lobeless elfin ears, wondering again if this is Fay come back in the flesh to torment him.

'Yours,' he says to test the ghost, but her puzzlement is plain, so he adds, 'now.' And puts a question of his own. 'Is the wistaria still there?'

'There is a creeper, but nothing else. Did you plant it?'

'The lady of the house did. The summers have got so hot I keep expecting it to die. You can smell it up here sometimes, like cinnamon. In China it's the flower of waiting.'

'And the fountain?'

'That was hers, too. It died more or less right away. The hotel people got it going again, but it didn't last. She decided she didn't want the apehead spouting water. I've never seen it go myself.'

The rain clears at midnight, leaving a marbled sky.

Jed goes out onto the terrace to greet the freshness, his stick tapping tentatively as he crosses the still wet roof. Alive, still. Life, this intoxicating night, intolerably alluring, even dredged with corns and chilblains and an ingrown toenail on the phantom foot. A full moon dusts its white light from directly overhead. Innumerable fragments of white cloud falling away on every side: ice-floes on a polar map, their outer edges bronzed. Stars pulsing in the spaces. Heavy shadows under the trees, but the ashen light of open ground filters into the dark.

He frowns.

In the shadows of the lychee grove is a figure. The figure is dancing.

Jed stares. He cocks his better ear, but all the leaves are dripping. The figure moves deliberately back the way it came, like a jumper marking out his steps. Four steps picked out, then unpicked. At the end of each unpicking the figure pauses, readying itself, then dashes forward with one arm raised up and brings the arm sharply down. The lunge is so violent it wrings a grunt from the figure. A human voice, just. Then a space in which the man hums a mournful hill song, muffled by the wet air and the spongy darkness. When the melody runs out the man returns to his measured dance.

At the edge of the grove is an old frangipani, its fat half-human fingers tipped with creamy flowers. Little by little the figure has been approaching this tree in its dance. Now it marks out its steps, retreats, pauses. Darts forward and springs. As it clears the grove the moonlight freezes it in mid-air, and the dancer's sword arm flashes.

At once Jed knows the man. Thapa the Gurkha, dancing with his kukri.

A branch falls to the ground, lopped cleanly.

Next day there's more rain.

The monsoon has broken. Now that the ground is soft for digging Ritu asks Thapa to relay the walk from the house to the walled garden. She pegs out a length of string to guide his pick, but when she returns after mid-morning prayers she finds his line has strayed.

'Along this line, Thapa,' she says, plucking the taut string.

He looks up from his digging, considers the string, then goes back to his curving line. 'That line is crooked,' he says, talking to the ground.

Every day over the next week she waits till Thapa has finished laying the bricks he carries over from the ruined kiln at the city corner of Everest. When he has gone she straightens his crooked line. The next day he unstraightens it. Cecelia, who favours the straight line herself, watches the contest with some interest, but cannot despair when Thapa wins.

SAWAN, *July–August. Worm-casts ziggurat the lawn where the grass is returning to green. Grass springs up, too, on the open ground to the city side of Everest, where the only trees are a thorny pomegranate by the old handpump and a twisted custard apple that overhangs what remains of the kiln. A hundred years ago the winter rose tiles were baked on the spot with clay from the jail pits. The ground is clayey roundabouts and the water-table changeable; it's only since the rains that the handpump draws water, though now the pressure in the mains reaches up to the roof tanks. Nearer the gate the land is low and rainwater pools easily. The frogs are loudest there; they go quiet only when someone walks up the drive. Mosquitoes breed among the mosses, growing fat and slow with cold frog blood.*

In the driving rain the farthest bamboo clumps on Canal Road return to ectoplasm. Bent double in the wind their profile develops like an old albumen print. Another gust and they fade from view.

Up on the roof Jed is daft, unapproachable. One floor down, Miss Sampson worries about her pet mongoose. There are snakes about, and Jowar is a wanderer. The monsoon is an unsteady ally: it has put an end to the dust but it has penetrated her hip and both knees. Also, she frets about her odour. Sweat plagues the Latvian too; he swabs half his florid face and shifts the toothpick to the other side of his mouth, cultivating patience. In the other wing the twins roll their heads like a counterweighted clock. Sweat beads their eyebrows, eczema attacks their webbed toes; their tongues loll and thresh by turns, shaping a sound that could for all that be satisfaction. On her bed Miss Chatterjee is a beached porpoise a thousand miles from her native sea. Her eyes are tightly shut to let her focus on the growth in her womb that may yet prove to be a child.

And gliding in and out of every upstairs doorway is Tsering, moving serenely among her charges, balancing a succession of trays.

Downstairs, old Perpetua malingers in the linen press. Now that the taps are gushing she has abandoned her boggy beat, put away the wrench. In the pantry the coconut biscuits have gone limp. Neha, dreaming of her wet forest, lets slip an old china platter. The rebuke takes five minutes of the Superior's time; Cecelia was in her office answering letters with curious stamps and worrying about what the rain might do to the washable ink of letters just addressed.

Ritu, fetching her towel off the line in the back verandah, finds a cluster of mysterious eggs stuck fast at the selvedge. On the front verandah the goongi sits out this season of witchery rattling four tamarind seeds in the cup of her horny pink hands. A wrong throw will call up churails with tusks for teeth and feet turned back to front. A good throw could summon a husband.

In the garage Major Bakshi sits on the running board of Jed's Packard, drinking rum and water with Jed's cousin, who has come back with a crate of bottles but no TV. And in his room behind the garage, gardener and chowkidar, batman and factotum, Havildar Man Singh Thapa, retd, steps up to the mantelshelf and, standing on tiptoe under the gaze of his particular goddess, returns to its cradle of two nails in the wall the short sword of his life.

'There's a book,' Jed begins, well again. 'If you don't mind, some time, not right away.'

Ritu looks up from mopping the floor where last night he had an accident. Concentration, but also the smell, worse during the rains, has brought a frown to her forehead that's still there when she looks at him.

Fay. That same small frown. How silently she would slip into bed after one of their quarrels! Tense, indrawn, hardly breathing, hardly there at all. Lying down in one swift motion: all grievance summed up in that economical movement. Frozen in reproach.

Perfectly still now, these forty years, coming apart down there under the cypresses. That whole generation made still. Jed alone moving, among strangers, waiting. If it were not for Brij he would feel nothing for the young. At one time they came to worship, to gaze; now even that is done with.

This young woman, for instance. Would she, out of succour, say, take his dry tongue in her mouth, join his old speech with hers? But she's waiting.

'It's a law book, family law. In the last bookcase on your

right as you come in from the hall. It has a leather binding, fat, with gold letters. *Family Law*, on the top shelf. But *don't*,' he twists her a smile, 'look at the book next to it, whatever you do. The one with the green spine.'

She doesn't return the smile. Can he be testing her? She who liked exams, did well.

'I'll get it for you now,' she decides. Puts down the mop and goes at once. It's the challenge, she knows, but also it's access to the library at last; ordinarily she would finish what she was doing.

'It's locked,' he calls after her. 'The keys are here, in the fish.' The fish is a shallow dish with tarnished sockets, once a mould for aspic. 'The small brass female key.' Grinning suggestively as he draws out the *female*.

She takes up the ring and goes out without a word. It's raining, so she returns for an umbrella. Downstairs, the library smells of fenugreek, lunch in the making. She always looks forward to Fridays, potatoes with green fenugreek, and always mortifies her palate, taking less than she would like.

The lock opens easily. She stands back, swings open the glass doors. There is *Family Law* on the top shelf. And the green spine beside it. She reaches up, glancing instinctively over her shoulder as she does.

Her hand falls on the green book. Absurd. That it should happen? Or that she should fear a book? Absurd. She takes the book down, composed, secure, with the same assurance that made her put down the mop and come straight here. What is there to fear?

Opens it.

And shuts it with a clap. But the picture has sped into her brain. She feels the image lodge in the eye, feels its atoms seethe and harden behind the lid like grit: Japanese, eyes, skin. A man and woman, a parted kimono, his nakedness, coupling. And the focus narrowing still further, on a central zone of simple, almost vegetal forms that burn when they should simply be.

She replaces the book, her lips moving in unbidden prayer. 'Hail Mary full of grace, the Lord is with thee,' and again the same line, over and over, as if the rest of the litany were blotted out. Her feet have carried her to the Superior's office. And Cecelia is there, licking an envelope. But what is she to say? How to explain the confusion of books? The straying of a hand?

'He wants a book,' she hears herself saying, 'from the library.'

'Didn't you find it?'

Cecelia would have heard her go in. Now what? 'I looked at the book beside it. It was . . . it was not . . . decent.'

Cecelia nods. 'He has some objectionable books. They will be destroyed, when they are ours to destroy. What was the book he wanted?'

'*Family Law.*'

'Give it to him. I'm surprised he can still read. He may ask *you* to.'

Ritu returns to the library, fetches down the book and carries it upstairs, conscious of having failed, still trembling from the upheaval in her head since the moment, impossibly remote, when she put down the mop.

He looks hard at her as she comes in, allowing himself a little smile.

'Didn't take a little peep, did we?'

'We did.'

His eyebrows go up. 'And?'

'There was nothing special.'

'Nothing at all? Remarkable.' He takes the volume from her. 'The youth of today!' he sighs, turning the pages perfunctorily. Then snaps the book shut. 'Well, nothing special here either, really. You can put it back.'

She would like to toss the book out the window, but puts it down on the table.

'Tea?' she asks.

'Lovely.'

She makes herself some, hands him an empty cup. Jed is not amused. Always better at dishing it out. But mimes satisfaction now.

'Delicious!'

'More?'

'Please.' He holds his cup out, then, as she relents and begins to pour, he lets it fall. 'Oh, *sorry!*' he grins.

The shattering frees something in him, lets a devil swing out of bed to elaborate. The tumbler, for example, is break-able. 'Sorry!' The bedside table can be knocked over. 'Oh dear!' A pile of shellac records will cascade to the floor. 'Now who left those there?'

It could go on, she's standing there unmoving, but Brij has come in. The sight of that young man is always calming. Only now Jed is breaking up himself. Tears, old tears unshed, are working their way out of him, old sobs tearing him apart. The shame of it, the shame. All he wanted was a kiss.

At ninety he'll accept charity, pocket the smallest change.

The apehead fountain continues dry.

But its lower basin is a stagnant pool, and the ground about it is rank with gloryweed. Ritu knows about snakes, steps with care down there. When she was a girl in the jungle she fell asleep once under a tree and woke to find a cobra curled up in her lap. She will never forget the half-hour she sat unmoving, waiting for Navin to come looking for her. How he took a stick and thrashed the bushes roundabout to wake the creature. How it stirred and simply slid away, how she sat there dazed, then ran home screaming. To this day a bag or parcel in her lap can shock her; once the weight of her own folded hands as she dozed made her sick with fear. Now she carries a stick and strikes the ground ahead of her as she walks.

Mosquitoes cloud her path, fasten on her wrists and ankles. At the lighter skin, where her watchband lay, a bite is coming up. She returns to the arcade, stepping gladly onto brick. At the end of the passage she comes to an old door. Her hands are damp as she undoes the lintel chain; between her fingers the heat has blistered into minute pearls.

A workroom, from the shelves and hooks in the wall, but the tools are gone except for a heap of rusted metal in one corner. There's a rough table up against one of two shut windows, but the remains of an elegant planter's chair and a couple of peg-tables suggest something more than a garden shed. She forces the window above the table, letting in air and light. Outside, near enough to touch, is a eucalyptus trunk, wet and grey and plastered with leaves from a hanging branch. The leaves recall a remedy of her mother's.

By the end of the month she has made a workplace of the room. Here she brings leaves and pods and sometimes whole plants for study in the free hour after lunch. Her paints and brushes are here, and also a row of glass bottles – Jed's vitamin empties. In the last bottle is an inch of eucalyptus oil.

Everest Eucalyptus Oil.
A hand-painted label on the familiar brown bottle. Jed

has first rights. He smears a little on the inside of his wrist, making a prissy face, and holds the wrist up to his nose. Inhales and jerks his head back as if stung.

'Clears the sinuses, too!'

Cecelia, up on an inspection tour, stretches her wide mouth in a smile. 'You'd be better off with a mosquito net,' she says. 'Shall I get Thapa to cut you some bamboo poles?'

Jed shakes his head. 'Mosquito nets are for virgins. I've ordered three bottles of this stuff. Brij tells me you can't get it in the market.'

'Sister Ritu has enough to do without going into business.'

'She tells me Thapa does the actual work.'

'So *that's* why he was up the eucalyptus tree!'

'He does the stripping and pressing.' Jed's eyes bulge wickedly as he strokes the words. Language at least he can caress.

'I'm thinking of switching Sister Ritu's duties with Sister Tsering's.'

Jed looks up sharply.

'I want *six* bottles,' he says carefully, a veiled threat in every syllable. 'And Sister *Ritu* looks after me.'

The apehead enters her dreams.

She is tending a row of moon lilies in planters. It's a roof garden where a brass band, a wedding band, has abandoned its instruments and disappeared to take a break. Their folding chairs are in disarray, the sinuous instruments balanced on them, waiting. For ever, something in their abandonment says. It is dusk and a light breeze flows from the evening star. She is making her way with a watering can from pot to pot on the parapet when she looks down into the compound and sees him. An apeman moving through the trees by the anthill. He is the colour of the anthill, of a guava tree trunk. She is so startled she knocks over a planter. It falls to the ground with the sound of a large gourd cracking open. The creature stops in his tracks and shuts his eyes to make himself invisible. After a safe interval he turns his head slowly towards the sound and sees her on the roof. They stare at one another until he can no longer hold her gaze. It's a look of straining to understand, ending in bafflement. He walks on, sustaining an enormous erection. She sits down slowly on one of the folding chairs, taking the horn into her lap. It's not a dream she can confess to, she knows, even in the dream.

Brij stands on the roof looking out at the low forested hills.

This is Ritu's favourite spot; it's where they sat to watch the summer lightning. The hills sweat a film of monsoon vapour into clear sky. Every tree on the slopes is distinct. The air is washed clean. Scraps of cloud snag on the peaks and unravel, vanishing into the wet blue. Brij is dizzy following them; the clouds are still, the hills toppling. He has come to see how the sealant is holding up.

The roof steams gently in the sunshine. A month of rain has left it damp even after three clear days. But the heavy rains are still to come. Ribbons of tar seal snake across the surface, joining and parting like a crazy jigsaw puzzle. In one corner of the parapet are gathered a crow's chattels: the skeleton of a small bird, a cork disc from a bottle top, a frog's leg. The crow swoops at Brij's head as he approaches the collection; he retreats, feeling exposed and helpless. He turns away, touring the roof, testing for cracks with the toe of his shoe, conscious now of the back of his head, where a beak might go in.

He comes to the far end of the roof, where the dish is. Here the view is along the cemetery wall. His own house is visible above Everest's boundary, among the auto workshops that blacken this end of town. Raju will be there, working with his father. Brij stands a while examining the dish. The air is full of signals that wither on its surface. No TV at Everest, he knows. He looks across the city rooftops with their scribbling of antennae and cables and home-made dishes of wire and tinfoil. Spots the dish his father rigged up. Brij is not a keen watcher; his favourite is an American beach show where the women wear very little. Mother always gets up and leaves the room, Father following reluctantly after taking in his quota; the brothers watch it through, giggling nervously at each other. It's the one thing that unites them. Afterwards they go to their cubicles and shut the doors.

Brij can see his window. Often he has looked across at Jed sitting here. Now he sits on Jed's chair and lets his eyes drift up above the antennae to the mountains. Straight ahead is a gap in the high blue wall of the first range, and there he sees against the clear blue sky a white peak. He stares at it, that anomaly, then returns to inspecting the roof cracks. He's squatting on his hams for a closer look, reading with his fingertips, when a voice makes him jump.

'Will you buy a bottle?' Ritu is holding the painted label towards him. 'All proceeds to charity,' she says, smiling.

'What is it for?' His hand is already groping for his wallet. He will buy two bottles, *three*.

'Mosquitoes. I made it. Thapa and I. It works, you know.'

He unscrews the top, sniffs and wrinkles up his nose. He would prefer something sweeter.

She shows surprise. 'I think it's heavenly.'

'Oh, it is,' he agrees, 'it is. I'll take two bottles. How much?'

'Twenty. But there's only one bottle left. And since you're my first customer you get a trade discount of five rupees.'

'Have you tried Jed Saab?'

'He took three. But he says it's his oil. They're his trees.'

'That's true. We're on his roof. Do you have change?' He flushes at the harsh commerce of the transaction. Give it all to her. What's fifty rupees? But he holds back: fifty rupees is a T-shirt at the Tibetan market, and Brij likes his clothes.

'No change,' she says, and hands him the bottle. 'Here, you can have it.'

'No, no!' He presses the note on her, but she steps back wagging a finger.

'It's a gift.'

Now he's truly mortified. 'For two bottles, please,' he says, holding out the money.

'But there's only one,' she repeats.

'You said it was for charity.'

'This is a sample. So put it in your pocket and say thank you.'

He obeys, crestfallen, stuffs his hands in his pockets, finds something there. A scallop fossil he carries, a small ribbed shell. He gives it to her in mock payment, a cowrie.

'I found it on the hillside near our village.'

She examines the purplish ribs that give it the look of a miniature Japanese fan.

'Imagine a seashell up there,' she says, looking at the mountains. 'That was all under the sea once.' Then, embarrassed by her teacherly tone, she looks down at the cracks in the roof.

'How is your seal working?'

'It looks all right from up here, but I'll have to check downstairs.'

'I heard the sailor complaining.'

'I'll do this part again tomorrow. If it doesn't rain.'

He squats there balanced on the balls of his feet, looking for something else to say. But nothing small presents itself.

'This charity,' he says abruptly. 'Why do you do it?'

Ritu is some time considering the question. He means her vocation, she knows. The other day, lying on her pallet, she wondered, was it like the apeman's thumb, was it the next step, into light?

'Because,' she says at last, 'it's the only thing that matters.'

'The *only* thing?' He is taken aback, not one for extremes, but flattered that she takes him seriously. He admires seriousness in a person; it suggests periods of solitary thought, tensions of a kind he can never sustain.

'What do *you* think matters?' she rounds on him.

'*Me?*' It's his cue for jokiness usually, but he senses that won't do today. 'I don't know. My friends, my parents, my brother. Akashkhand.' He shrugs with every guess.

She sits down on the edge of one of the tubs and looks up at him. 'What about people you don't know?'

'Why should I trust them? They could be anything. They could be building a dam to drown my village. The world is full of dangerous people.'

'The world is full of people. The danger comes from a lack of charity.'

'Maybe. But in the meantime you have to protect yourself. And your family and your friends.'

'And your valley and your hills and your country.'

'No, no,' he laughs. 'That's too big. Maybe the valley. And the hills.'

'A hill state would satisfy you?'

'More or less.'

'And then you can trust the strangers in it?'

'I don't know all that. There'll still be dangerous people.' He risks a shrewd look at her. 'Who aren't content with charity.'

'You don't give people everything they want. You see what they *need*.' She stands up and points at the bottle of eucalyptus oil in his hand. 'That was not charity, by the way!'

They cross the roof towards Jed's room. Just past the abandoned stoves the crow returns. It makes straight for Ritu, pulling out of its dive just short of her head. The beak, the claws, the sudden flapping wings out of nowhere; she screams and instinctively ducks down. Brij steps between her and the circling bird, waving his arms. Before he felt helpless, unarmed; now he could destroy the crow, lay waste its house.

'Are you hurt?'

'No. It just gave me a fright.'

He stands facing her, but cannot look in her eyes. She has never seen such confusion on a face, and can't be sure it's not reflected in her own.

'It's his lunchtime,' she says and goes in to Jed.

Thapa swings his other sword.

He is clearing the tall weeds in the walled garden, taking advantage of the break in the weather. He uses a light curved scythe that he swings with one arm, back and forth, cutting with both strokes. He works bent over, his free hand behind his back. It's a harmless sword compared to the kukri; once in a while he sharpens it on a whetstone in the garage.

With every stroke a tuft of cropped weeds flies up into the air like a sprung partridge, then flops back down, its flight aborted. He works his way up one side of the fountain, taking pleasure in the swathe he is making, adjusting the length of the stroke when the blade strikes brick or stone. The sun falls on his back as he works; the sweat drips off his forehead onto the cut grass. When he is done he will sort the grass and save the choicest tips for his buffalo. Succulents, wild irises, pampas grass crowd what was once seeded turf. A glory lily has spread its tendrils over the top of lantana, showing tongues of orange flame. The scythe cuts through stems and reeds, leaving a rough stubble that loses another inch on the return stroke. A frog, disturbed, moves stiffly away, pushing deeper into the standing weeds. Thapa is glad to see it out of harm's way. Which is why he stares in horror when, a minute later, his scythe cuts a grass snake in two. He frowns at the twisting halves and wipes his blade on a tussock. Then he leaves the walled garden without finishing the job, although only one swathe remains. He returns the scythe to its place in the garage and retires to his room.

It's bad luck to kill a snake; anything could happen.

Night. A blue beetle crushed underfoot releases its bitter draught into the dark. Ritu is in her room, under a sixty-watt bulb, staring at her parents' photograph.

Thinking of what Brij said on the roof. Keeping your family safe, protecting those you love. 'If anything should happen to you!' she says, speaking to the couple posing in front of a drop sheet with swans and marble columns in black and white. What would she do without them? Her rootstock, her mirror, her judges, her life. She is staring so hard the photograph begins to break down into its composite grains. Her icons, dissolving.

Cecelia comes in, stands beside her bed. Her feet wide and wedge-shaped, each toe a wooden chock.

'Your parents?'

'Yes.'

'How old are they?'

'Fifty.'

So. I could be your mother, thinks Cecelia. She says, 'My mother is seventy, my father would have been seventy-five. He died last year. And that?' She is pointing at the other photograph, Navin as a cadet.

'That was my brother. He died in the Army, in an accident.'

'I have six brothers outside,' Cecelia offers. 'Some in Poona, some abroad. But no photographs. When we enter the convent we leave our families behind. The world offers enough distractions. We must concentrate on God and on our fellow man.'

She holds out her hand. Ritu places both photographs in it.

'They'll be safe in the office.'

Cecelia looks about the room. The books! Ritu thinks, looking at her botany texts. But Cecelia finds nothing else amiss. 'Is that your painting in Mr Jed's room?' she asks.

'Yes. It's a moon lily. He asked to keep it.'

'You know he was a seed collector?'

'He told me.'

'Told you what?' Sharply.

'About collecting in the mountains.'

'He has his stories. Don't believe everything he says. He likes to shock. A great one for beauty when he was a young man, Miss Sampson says.'

'She knew him then?'

'She knew his wife. That's her photograph in the library.'

Ritu has stood before the bird-like creature and tried to imagine her life.

'She died young,' Cecelia adds.

Ritu nods. Something, some indefinable air in the subject, looks completed. The harvest already in her eyes.

'How's the fighting in Estonia?'

Miss Sampson never looks at the sailor when she addresses him.

'Latvia,' he answers, smoothing his napkin at the next table. 'Fine.'

'Nehru would have called in the Russians.'

'Russians, yes, Russians.' The Latvian has been extending his English.

'Rural electrification, that was his goal. Do you have electricity in Estonia?'

'Cities, yes cities.'

'You know, he said to me, "Miss Sampson, may I call you Rose?" And I said, "Mr Nehru, do I call you Jowar?" And he never tried that again. Always "Miss Sampson this" and "Miss Sampson that." Coming up close – oh yes – but never again Rose. In the end he said, "I won't wear my heart on my sleeve, but I can wear it in my buttonhole." And he did.'

She tickles her mongoose under the chin and glows. Cecelia, passing through on her way to the pantry, where the nuns have their table, wishes the old lady wouldn't bring the creature to the dining room. Today she says so.

'Only on holidays, dear,' decrees Miss Sampson, who's known Everest longer than Jed himself. 'And today is Independence Day.'

She looks up at Ritu, who's waiting for Cecelia to pass, and beckons her with a bony finger. 'You watch out for him,' she says pointing up at the roof. 'He may be ninety – so he says – but he's a devil, he is. And you look like her come back.' She cups a hand over her mouth and lowers her voice so Ritu must lean over.

'Not that he touched *her*.'

'This God you . . .'

Jed stops. The spoiling mood is on him because he wet his bed last night, but the needle skips. It's happening more often now, so his hearers are pressed into a cloze game.

'This God you . . .' he starts again, and is once more brought up short.

'Serve?' Ritu is peeling the linen off the rubber undersheet.

'Serve,' Jed repeats. It's not what he wanted but it'll do. 'I don't mean *me* – I mean the one above me, the Quartermaster. Does he keep track of all this linen? Does he tot it up? So many sheets washed, so many Brownie points?'

Charity again! Why does it bother them if it doesn't bother her? The sheets are nothing, she'd like to say. This is routine. She's even worked out a better system of washing for the rains, when things take longer to dry and smells hang about. She simply drops them over the edge where the handpump is and she and the goongi take turns at the washing. The sheets hang on a separate line in the back verandah until the first sunny day. They're kept apart, never get put away in the press.

She bunches them up now and goes out. When she returns he's chanting. He has a bottle of pills in his hand and is swinging it like a censer over the stripped bed. The pills rattle with every ceremonial shake.

'*In nomine Patris*,' shake, '*et Filii*,' shake, '*et Spiritus Sancti*.' Long shake.

She takes the rubber sheet out to a tub, not his tub, and dips it in the collected rainwater, then pulls the plug. Flops it on the line in the weak sunlight. Then fetches out the spare, but lets the bed air while she goes about making breakfast. She has already got him sponged and changed, and he wanders about the room in fresh pyjamas looking for mischief.

'Music.'

He stops in front of the gramophone and winds it up. Energy in that stroke; can't be ninety, Ritu thinks. He selects a big band record from among the survivors of the avalanche, blows on it and puts it on. Its tired thumping fills the room, thirties spry, like an old dog scratching himself. The crackle of dust and static drawing a curtain around the music, so now the instruments scat voices.

'Dance?'

Ritu is at the hotplate. 'Miss Sampson told me you were a great dancer. She said you won trophies.' Mouthing the words so he can lip-read over the music.

He frowns and freezes. One arm out, the other about an imaginary partner. Abandoned as he turns and snaps, 'Miss Sampson? What does *she* know?'

He stops the music, takes the record off and looks for something else. Spies a dog-eared jacket.

'Ah! *Salve Regina*.' He holds the record up but doesn't put it on. 'O Sweet Virgin Mary!' he sings at Ritu, on key. 'Do you know,' he says, 'the composer wrote this when his lady love forsook him to enter a convent?'

He slips the record back into its sleeve. Holds it before him like a breastplate and comes up behind her.

'Tell me, is it true that you have a wedding night when you

take vows? With special lacy knickers from your trousseau? I read it somewhere. Your parents send you a special slinky nightgown for the big night?'

'Porridge.'

She puts the bowl on his bedside table and walks out.

'No?' He stands looking at her departing back, breasting the waves of silent reproach in her wake. 'Pity. It was a good story.'

He empties the bowl ceremonially, spoonful by spoonful, on the floor. Then he puts the record on and sits down on the stripped bed. The music flows slowly over him, like memory. He hears around the curtain of static, through any earthly disturbance. She could switch it off and he would still hear it. He knows every bar. Cell by cell its bitter honey gluts the comb of his head.

When Ritu returns, the needle on the record has reached the blind track at the centre. The chrome armature is doubling back and forth with idiot persistence, the only movement in the room. He's sitting there staring into the heart of a continent suspended in the air, so real she must step around it.

Brij has an idea for the fountain.

In fact he has, when he comes to think of it, a pump. Somewhere in that backyard given over to machinery is an old desert cooler whose fan was borrowed years ago as a kitchen exhaust; the pump, he remembers, was left in its cage. He will get it going, borrow it for the sisters. For her.

'Very industrious today,' his father observes. Usually he hears the monotonous thud and clink of weights as Brij works out, the thump of home-made dumb-bells, grunts, heavy breathing. Today he's tracked down a gritty mouse-gnaw to Brij's cubicle and stands in the door contemplating the fine swarf of rust on Brij's white shirt cuff where the vein bulges.

Brij refolds the sandpaper and goes on working. He has kerosene-scrubbed the holding nuts, and brushed and emeried the terminals, petrol-swabbing the sickle-shaped one back to a high gloss, though he knows the thing will sit in a sump behind a brick wall. Now he's scaling the assembly out of old habit, learnt from this man in the doorway. And his father smiles approval. *Dirt forms a path for the current.* Brij imagines Ritu dipping her fingers in the live bowl of the fountain and almost shouts, *No!* So goes on sanding, though he's done it once, down to the oiling.

'Why didn't you think of it in the summer?'

'It's for a fountain,' Brij says, spinning the vane with one finger. He turns the pump upside down and watches a drop of oil slide down the spindle. As a boy he could lie awake feeling sorry for the table fan. Took it apart once and reassembled it and had one nut left over at the end.

'A fountain,' his father repeats, 'now why didn't I think of that?'

He casts his eye over the car hulks that addle the backyard, weeds grown past their mudguards. In front, the monsoon has churned up the oil-black mud, and cars brought for servicing leave deep soft ruts when they back out. The ruts have criss-crossed till the surface looks cancelled out, rejected. Only the old Fiats and Ambassadors come here; the new cars go elsewhere.

'It's for them,' Brij says, tossing his head towards Everest. 'We're not using it. It's been lying here for years. I had Himmat rewind the coil.'

'We can use it next year.'

'But we have two coolers.'

'We'll have two and a half,' his father rules. He turns away and goes out onto the terrace.

Brij remains seated, spinning the vane. In a little while his father returns.

'All right, take it. But one of these days you ask Jed Saab about the Packard. It's no good to anybody just sitting there.'

Brij takes the pump across, using the cemetery shortcut. Thapa is in the walled garden, working under the ape's gaze.

'Take a break,' Brij chaffs him, but Thapa bends to his task. He is scooping out the humus from the ground basin. It's rich soil, the leaf mould of half a century, and his spade goes in easily. There's a line Ritu has drawn as a guide, six inches from the carved rim, but here and there his spade has crossed it and grazed the fluting. No deeper than a span, she warned him after a preliminary dig, and left a cut-off stick measure that he has yet to use. Now and then he strikes bottom with a sandy clink.

Behind the fountain wall Brij gouges away the plaster with a screwdriver to locate the pipe. When he does he must trouble Thapa for a wrench. Thapa holds his hand up and goes on with his job. When he's finished he takes up his tools and goes to the garage.

'How long has this beast been standing here?' Brij asks, stroking the Packard.

Thapa says nothing, but rolls his head and shoulders back to indicate a long time. As if he has been here for ever himself and didn't come with Major Bakshi. On the running board of the Packard are set two empty glasses. Thapa frowns and picks them up with one hand, his finger and thumb meeting halfway down the insides. He sets them roughly on the floor against the wall and reaches up for the wrench. Brij borrows a piece of hose for the bypass then goes home after all to fetch some hose clamps, a plug and a tester bulb; the old wiring in the walled garden might still be working.

It is. The pump howls a high empty howl and he yanks out the naked wires from the old socket. He couldn't find a plug to fit. Now he must wait for the ground basin to be cleaned and filled. The pump is safe in its niche; nobody comes in here.

The goongi is worshipping at the anthill.

She has strewn champa petals on its crest and is standing there in mute adoration when she hears that dry retching howl from the walled garden. Her pupils shrink in sudden fear. The ape! Her head twists in his direction, then turns sharply away. Once, before the walled garden was cleared, she strayed into that enclosure. Was creeping along the nearer side when she saw him through the tangle of vines. She backed out carefully and has never gone in there again. Nor has he troubled her, until now.

She appeals to the anthill for deliverance, for a protector, but the fear is mounting in her and she pulls away. She will hide indoors, seek out Perpetua. She hurries along the path to the house. A monster like that could fall on you like a tree and pin you down. She breaks into a run and blunders straight into the arms of the ape.

'*Haay!*' she screams and shrinks back.

'*Arré, arré*, what's the big hurry?' Perpetua laughs, reaching out. But the goongi is shrinking back from her as the trusted face warps into simian horror. Lips stretched, black gums, yellow teeth bared, twisted hands reaching for her.

The goongi turns to flee, but as she does she sees Brij coming out of the walled garden. A prickling runs up her calves, her legs giving way under the weight of this new betrayal. The visitor she adores because everyone at Everest has time for him, because when she dreams of a wedding the groom looks like him, the man she will sometimes follow like a puppy, this man – coming out of that place! All her night fears come crowding in under the sun. Churails, two-headed boys, flying foxes that collect earwax, blouses that eat flesh.

Tsering, looking out of the pantry door, sees the fit coming on. She comes hurrying with a teaspoon that she forces between the goongi's teeth to keep her from biting her tongue. The albino head is rolling in Perpetua's cradled hands, the old reptilian brain in upheaval, a turbulence older than the species. Brij stands there helpless, a screwdriver in his hands, struck dumb by the ancient spectacle. Returning awe for awe, because there are times when he catches the goongi gazing at him as if he were a god.

'Why an apehead?' Ritu asks.

She has been scrubbing down the marble of the fountain basin, washing and putting back the pieces that have worked loose from the inlaid pattern at the centre.

'Why an apehead.' Jed must now repeat every question put to him, inspecting its facets before his brain can address it. This crumbling beastly brain. He shuts his eyes. 'Ramapithecus,' he mouths, quoting the cell to which he has gained miraculous entry. Another day the results might be quite different, but today there are bulbs lighting up all across the board. 'Dryopithecine of the Nagri formations of the Miocene beds. Pilgrim 1910. Lewis 1932.'

'An ape man?'

'Or man ape. He lived in these hills some millions of years

ago. And died and was buried and was dug up by my wife, among others. They called him Ramapithecus in honour of the god.'

'Was he the first true man?'

'Hardly. But he represented something new, the way his thumb was coming around. To let him grip a tool or weapon. So he not only used tools but made them, using his hands because he'd learnt to stand upright. Misusing them, too. The team unearthed evidence of a massacre, an organized slaughter – and maybe cannibalism – of other ape men.'

Ritu looks out at the hills with a new eye, a long sliding focus that takes in the whole range and zooms in on a single bone in a sandy cleft.

'Was she an anthropologist?'

'A palaeontologist. Or a student of palaeontology. But she did actually dig. And kept back a bone for me.'

'Really?'

'Yes.'

'That wasn't very professional.'

'Strangely enough, she was. But I required it, as proof of devotion.'

Ritu smiles. 'You call yourself a scientist.'

'I never have. Certainly not to you. I was a collector, I collected. Rather like her man ape. Hunter and gatherer.'

'You still have the bone?'

'It's somewhere down there.' Jed rolls his eye down to the bowels of Everest. 'Lost to science.'

'What part was it?'

'A part of the thumb. Where it joins the wrist. They were more interested in the teeth, but she left the team after that. Lewis wrote to her. I have the letter, too. But she never went back. Dug in the garden, made her rather romantic head cast. That was how the fountain started.'

'Would you like to see it again?'

'It's jungle now.'

'Thapa cleared away the jungle. I've been cleaning up the fountain.'

He looks at her with mild reproof, shading into admiration. Her fountain, after all.

'Thanks.' He taps his forehead. 'I have it in here.'

It's not the stair; it would be like exhumation. The last time he went down it was to the cemetery, by the shortcut. Circling, as always, vulture-like, that grave, then succumbing. Shambling up to ogle, to feast.

'It's empty, anyway,' Ritu says. 'One good downpour would fill up the basin.'

'You might be lucky,' he says, looking out at the soft grey light. She helps him up and out onto the roof, where he shakes her off and leans on the parapet. Fay made a nunnery of her garden; this one will make a garden of her nunnery.

Just then the puzzling cry sounds, long and strained, from the terrace with the underwear.

'What is that sound?' Ritu asks.

'Mrs Puri. And her cock. She's – how would you put it – vocal in lovemaking. So she keeps the creature as a cover. Actually keeps it covered, I'm told, day and night, until she has a visitor. During school hours, of course. Hard on the caller, though.'

Clouds have come up, bringing the gift of breeze. There are five kites in the sky, dancing, duelling. One serious fight in progress: a grass-green one tackling a black-and-yellow. Now that takes him back. Mad about kites, his always the first up after school. The number of times he cut himself on fight string. Powdered glass, sharper than a razor. The number of spools he collected. String enough to fly the moon.

'Yama Raja.'

Jed turns. The boy could be himself, he sometimes thinks. That wiry hair, the build, without the height. He beckons royally. Brij knows that wave. An errand.

'I say, Nachiketa. Let's fly a kite. Before it rains.'

Brij is delighted. Just this morning he went past the kite lane in the heart of the old market and felt a stab of pleasure at the display. After lunch he's back with a red kite and two reels of string, one from his own flying days.

'Plain string,' Jed sniffs as Brij hitches old to new, but he's not flying. He takes the kite in both hands, holding it delicately by the wing tips. Brij backs across the roof, watching for pipes, unwinding as he goes. When he reaches the middle he stops, reels in the slack, tightens up and waits for the hoist.

'OK,' Jed calls. He's been bowing the kite impatiently, strangely aroused by the rustle of its fine taut skin. 'Go!'

The kite lifts off, climbing steeply, then dips. Brij backs up again and makes a series of short tugs, letting it buck. Then pulls sharply crosswise, sends it veering, loving the tremor the rip sends along the string as much as that fierce gas-flame sputter of stretched kite-paper. Lets it hang bobbing, then, just as it's drifting out, hauls in four rapid arm lengths and watches it knife straight up. Jed looks on. The boy flies good kite.

In minutes there's a challenger from the roof next to Mrs Puri's, but Brij pays out and draws away over the cemetery. The wind catches up the kite, hauls it over the tall silk-cotton and carries it up among the low-circling hawks. Now there's a tension to the string and Brij milks it with his free hand while the other arm crooks the reel shaft. Then he loops finger and thumb around each end of the shaft and lets it run free. The reel spinning like a bobbin, faster and faster, till he's inclined to brake, but doesn't. Now he's past the join, onto old string, spooling out all the time. He wants to go higher than ever before, wants to be with the vultures. He wants to fly a speck in the sky.

Jed hasn't taken his eyes off the kite. Now it's up, a red blur, he taps his way across the roof to where Brij stands mesmerized in the crow's corner, pulling with the whole reel. He's reached the end of his string and wishes he'd bought more. Something in that deep smooth traction binds him, roots him to the spot. Here is the balance, that true measure of control and release, lacking in his life. Jed sees the look in his eye and contents himself with plucking the string once and stepping aside. The weight of it moves him, too, its vibration unlocking messages stored in his bones these eighty years. Swamping him all at once with discontent.

'You have a go,' he says to Ritu, who has come up from lunch. And goes off to crumple on his bed.

Ritu stands beside Brij, looking up at the red patch he's stitched on the sky. A low front of cloud has moved in from the east, lacquering the grey so the kite string cuts a hard clean arc across it, like geometry.

Brij finds her beside him in Jed's place and at once offers the reel.

'No, no,' she backs off, afraid she'll let it slip. But he insists, gripping the middle of the reel so she can take the handles.

'Just feel the tension,' he urges.

She takes the thing, holding fast. Unprepared for so charged a weight. It pulls like a magnet; she lets it draw, then pulls back down, delighting in the smooth resistance. Astonished, because a kite was a child's toy, not this exquisite sentient creature. She turns to say so to him and finds him looking at her. In a presuming way, and yet she can't find fault with him, even when his hands return to grip the reel over hers.

Brij cannot imagine where he's found the courage. He's staring pointedly at the kite: let his eyes stray a fraction, he thinks, and she'll break away. She doesn't. She's still there, in some pain as his hands crush her fingers. It could mean nothing, she's thinking, but supposing it's intended, that pressure, can it really be wrong, something so comforting?

The kite decides. It's been straining steadily all along, but ever since the rain clouds came up the wind has been leaning on it. The string snaps at the spool end, springs into the air and sails away, drifting across the cemetery, carried clear of the cemetery trees.

He's let go, his eyes still carefully on the kite. She hands him back the reel, her eyes on the vanishing red dot, too. But for days after, what she will keep seeing is the line as it was snatched away, the darting and slackness coiled in that moment.

B HADON, *August–September. Heavy rain. The dark month. Black nights, lit in flashes so a night-riser has the impression of lurching from moment to moment. Thunder like the rending of mountains. Thapa's buffalo calves in the middle of the night. Thapa dances in his room at the open window, a wild manikin.*

Sunrise in a black sky, red in a young crow's throat.

Grey days, moist and cool and heartsweet as water chestnuts. Perpetua buys a kilo off a passing cart at the gate and Neha peels them in the kitchen. Pricks a finger on the vicious thorns while shucking the leathery purple skins. Devil's fruit, she always calls

it, from its baleful horned aspect. But slips a smooth white heart

into her mouth.

Ritu with a bowl of peeled water chestnuts.
Appears in Jed's room a moment sooner than expected and catches him smiling in the mirror. Her step has changed, too, he notices, grown lighter.

'Have you seen the mountains?' she says.

'*Can* you see them?'

The high mountains, he means, the snows. His chair is out there still, facing the gap, though he hasn't sat in it for weeks. The wood is sodden, but he won't let it be brought in. The cane is black with mould, the same mould that has begun to appear on Neha's onions in the kitchen, under the dry outer skins.

She leads him out there, sets the bowl down on the balustrade beside his dentures, and waves an impresario's arm at the blue range. There is even a cone of white in the gap for him.

'Beautiful,' he agrees, looking across the wretched rain-soaked, moss-blackened rooftops. 'Do you hear that rustling in the undergrowth?'

She cocks an ear at the hills, then smiles. He's teasing.

'Leeches.' He worms a finger at her. 'Marching. You think jackboots are frightening? Not that you would know the sound of those. Well, you haven't heard leeches on the march. One minute the jungle is quiet, not a sound. Then it starts. Like gentle rain. And in a little while the undergrowth is quaking all around you. They've smelt your blood.

'We were coming back from Siloni once . . .'

He leans on the dish pedestal. Already there's a crack in the cement; it wasn't properly wet down after the job. The dish is still not hooked up. He'd like to push it over the edge, preferably as that jackal of a cousin is passing down below.

'It's like a eunuch in a harem,' he grins at her. 'Sees but can't do. They used to tear out the tongue, so he couldn't tell either.'

'You were coming back from somewhere.'

'Yes, from Siloni, when we ran into a storm. One of the coolies said he knew of a cave where we could spend the night. So we ran straight down the scarp into the jungle, following him. The leeches were waiting for us. They drop off the trees onto you, spring from the bushes. On the way down, the coolie who was guiding us twisted his ankle and had to be carried to the cave. When we got there we lit a fire across the mouth of the cave and stripped to pick off the leeches. I must have taken fifty off me: scalp, eyelids, anus. We used enough salt to pickle a man. After dinner we lay in our sacks and told stories. The coolie with the ankle said he couldn't sleep so he'd stay up and tend the fire. He was still sitting there in the morning with his back to the jungle, smiling at the fire. I asked him, 'Didn't you sleep?' He didn't answer, just kept smiling. When I touched him he just rolled over, dead. His back was covered in leeches.'

Ritu, who has been staring at the mountains, shudders and turns aside. She knows about leeches, prefers his collecting stories. But even those are faded. She breathes a deep fresh draught. Here is the real monsoon. Then why is it so flat, unstoried? She feels again the anguish of having woken from the childhood dream, that world of primal colours bathed in light. She can never understand Tsering's dispassion. Her spirit goes trekking across terraces of washed air, longs to be snared by beauty, by some grace it hasn't yet known, but keeps returning to that moment when the kite string breaks.

Jed looks sideways at her. She'll waste her youth. He never learnt to value his till it was gone, vanished into this long dreary decline. He clacks the set of spare teeth on the balustrade. You never learn, no-one does; by the time you've mastered life it's time to die. He places a water chestnut between the perfect incisors and guillotines it. And *then* death plays tricks.

'Any news of our friend?' he asks and taps the dish with his cane. The sun has come out.

She shrugs. At first she thought he meant Brij, though he always calls him Nachiketa to her, as if to draw her into the cast. As if there were a role for her there. Heavenly women.

'No TV yet?'

'No.'

'Well,' Jed says, dragging his chair into the shade of the dish, 'it has its uses.' But he decides it's too damp to sit on. He leans on the balustrade and looks the other way, at her hills. 'What about Brij? Did you have a go with the kite?'

Her eyes drift down and she nods a slow preoccupied nod. That irritates him, he can't say why, so he leers at her. 'He didn't tell you the kite joke? This man whose wife can't get enough?'

She takes up the bowl of water chestnuts and crosses the roof, leaving him there.

'*More tail! More tail!*' he calls after her and cackles without pleasure.

She's about to put the bowl down on the bedside table

when Brij comes into the room. He looks at her as he did yesterday.

'Where's Yama Raja?'

'By the dish.'

He makes for the roof, then stops and comes back to her. If he doesn't now he never will. He says, 'Ritu,' and puts awkward arms around her. She still has the bowl in her hands. Her eyes bulge at the wrongness of it, but she lets herself be held, returns the clumsy kiss when it comes.

Then breaks away and hurries down the fire escape. Doors banging in her brain as her feet skim the fish-plates. She must leave now, after this. She's gone already. She will tell Cecelia and pack, no staying here now. The iron stair ringing in her ears like conscience. Till her feet touch the ground.

She can't. The shame, the complications, the uncertainty, the wrenching. Better, simpler, to make a pact, avoid him. She goes to the office.

'Jed?' Cecelia says, misreading Ritu's confusion. 'He's an old rogue.'

It's not him, Ritu wants to say, but can't bring her lips to form the words. Unspeakable turmoil.

'I'll talk to him. But he won't let you go.'

'Let Tsering have a turn of the roof.'

Cecelia contemplates the switch; no harm in it. 'Let's see,' she says. 'I'll ask her.'

Tsering doesn't mind. First floor or roof are the same to her, her look indicates. A look that always falls at a point between the eyes.

Jed feels it there and cannot think what it recalls. Then remembers a night above the snowline, alone. He enters a shelter, one of those huts used by shepherds and climbers, looking for a place to spend the night. Has begun to undo his pack when he feels a prickling in his spine. Turns slowly and sees, hunched in the corner with his hands on his knees, a little man covered in white hair. Head thrown back, eyes focused on nothing. Frozen. Jed sleeps outside, in the snow.

Autumn

KUAR, *September–October. The rotten month over. Mould, stinks retreating. Tiny forests of mildew wilt in one dry afternoon.*

New ripenesses. 'Smell the rice?' Perpetua asks the goongi, who grins. Fields of it ripening beyond the jail; on a still night Thapa can hear the ears shifting drily. Lightning without thunder, its cursive low in the sky above the southern hills. A warm breeze pours out of the east, and the script moves away along the range. 'Smell the rice?' Major Bakshi asks Miss Sampson, who replies with a paean to wheat. Ritu, breathing in the same air one floor down, remembers a song of her hills:

The rice is ripe,
The sickle stone wet,
O my love let the blade
Strike sparks in the night!

Brij comes every day to visit Jed, but Ritu doesn't appear. Down in the walled garden he tests the empty water pump twice, trumpeting like a bereft crane, but she doesn't come there either. He peers into her pharmacy; there's dust on the remaining bottles of Everest eucalyptus oil. Well, the mosquitoes are slowing down every day. He hasn't used the bottle she gave him, but unscrews the top and sniffs at it during the night. During the day he wanders through the city, calls on friends, attends political meetings, anything to keep his mind off Everest. His separatist colleagues meanwhile are having trouble keeping people's minds on Akashkhand.

Dashera comes, and Thapa plants two grains of barley with the peas. He can't forget. At night he leaves a brass bowl of water on the window sill to catch the moon, and in the morning cuts the standing water crosswise with a knife and drinks it down in one go. He has a sore throat.

Mrs Puri feeds by turns a crow, a cow, a dog, propitiating the manes. This is the season of the dead, when her husband will *appear in an empty chair, or leaning into the fridge. Or his eyes will open on her pillow. Still tormenting her with his goodness. And for the rest of the season the neighbours no longer hear that racked cry issue from the upstairs flat with the underwear on the line.*

Jowar the mongoose prowls the long grass at the anthill looking out for his traditional enemy, the snake. He'd like a change of diet from Miss Sampson's toast sopped in milk. The local dogs are on heat. In the sodium light of a street lamp two males and a female recline like public statuary. Under Everest, a tide of white ants streams through the dark, breaching the floor tiled with winter roses, tunnelling through damp walls, invading a bookcase to consume the early diaries of Immanuel Jed.

In the grapefruit tree by the garage hang huge fruit, green as planets.

JED TELLS TSERING THE FROZEN MANIKIN STORY.

Just to see. Collects the same unnerving gaze, with the trace of a smile. This collector who prefers his women showing teeth. Wearing today one of his cream cotton suits with a gentian-blue tie. Sick of pyjamas. Send for Ritu, he decides. Or rather, send for Cecelia to send up Ritu. Tsering agrees, goes back down the iron stair, the mild ambassador with the even tread.

But fifteen minutes later, Jed, dozing, wakes to jackboots. A woman on his threshold. Or else a human candle, the hair an orange flame leaping up from cold wax.

'Mr Jed?'

Not young, not old. Damn it, young. Everyone is. Run out of twenties, though.

Jed knows what she wants. Europeans don't come this way as a rule. Golden Triangle and out; the rest writing deep journals in Benares. Nothing for them in Drummondganj except the cemetery, so Jed, Hony Secy, hazards a sketch as she enters. Raj parents, or grandparents. Not India-struck: researching, not searching. Ethnomusicologist, teaching at a London polytechnic.

'I'm Inge Vogel from Berlin.'

Ah, *frigwit* Jed! The Germans.

'The pastor from All Saints Church sent me to you.'

'Not an ethnomusicologist, then.'

'Pardon?'

The hair misled him. Like punk postcards from ten years ago, when Jed rumbled about youthanasia. Now he loves the young, but can take or leave their fashions.

'Please.' He indicates the only chair. 'You want to see where your countrymen are buried?'

Forty-nine of them in the northwest corner, wartime internees.

'One in particular, my great-uncle.'

'The name?'

'Planke. Otto Planke, my mother's uncle.'

Jed shuts his eyes. 'Otto Planke. Born 1919?' Details like that come easily to him. At one time they won him admirers.

She is impressed. The dyed black eyebrows arch into a chain bracket.

'I have been secretary of the cemetery since 1946. I keep the registers. Padre Masih would like to get his hands on them so he can sell off a few plots. In fact there are only two left, and then we close Ever-rest for good. So the race is on.'

'You keep the key?'

Jed smiles. 'I have a key, for what it's worth. And there's a watchman. But the walls are down anyway. You could climb through a gap from our own compound.'

'May I?'

Jed spreads his hands. Just as Ritu enters, sent by Cecelia. Jed looks past her, an aggrieved look shot through with spite.

'In fact,' he decides, ignoring Ritu, 'I'll come with you, if I can have your arm.' He nods at his walking stick. 'That's German, you know. Linden. An old companion. I studied your forests at one time.'

'You were in Chermany?' *When?* hovers unasked, and Jed finds such delicacy irritating. At least the other one is not coy about age.

'So long ago it doesn't matter.' He raps a full stop with the tip of the cane and turns to go. Ritu remains where she is by the gramophone. She has not been introduced to the newcomer, but they smile a wordless greeting at one another. Then Jed is on the iron stair, leaning on Inge on his first journey down since the fall.

Still have my first edition of *Mein Kampf* down there somewhere, with ruled underlinings.

At the back, where the pipal tree straddles the broken wall, they meet Brij, taking his own shortcut.

'Nachiketa! Where have you been?' Jed swats away excuses. 'Never mind. Come with us. This is Inge from Berlin; Brij, from that house over there.'

Inge looks through the breach in the other wall, sees a lane, black with grease and engine oil. Brij follows her glance in dismay and is furiously occupied with guiding Jed across the uneven ground.

Gloryweed, fallen angels. And Jed come down in shoes that pinch.

'Shoebite,' he announces with a stoic air, and lets himself be taken. Carried almost, the linden hooked on his wrist and dangling. A ventriloquist's dummy, he obliges with show-time patter.

'The family Masterton in that Roman pile. Not one natural death between them. Reginald Masterton has two graves. His head is buried in MP, where it was lopped off by his incensed mistress when she learnt his wife was with child again. It was never found, but she swore she gave it a fond burial with full tribal honours. The wife Rowena drowned at sea – well, in salt water – minutes before she alighted at Bombay with her infant daughter, Rhoda. The little stone there. Another daughter, Ruth, married a civilian and was eaten by a tiger while out hunting. No body was ever found. The son, a boxwallah, took strychnine in Simla.

'One grandson, who bought a separate plot, lived to be a hundred and one.'

Inge is smiling the smile of one who understands, but imperfectly. Her hair intrigues Brij, who wonders whether it would spring back if patted. She has made no concession to India in her dress, and he finds that refreshing. Worn black jeans, white socks, black commando boots. Black lipstick.

'That one's a cenotaph. The drum major combusted spontaneously.'

Jed, whose gabble has grown frantic at the approach of a certain frangipani, falls silent when it is passed. He indicates the German plot and is propelled there between boots and sandals.

'Otto Planke,' he points and watches Inge squint. A small square tablet, name and date. The tip of his cane is burrowing into the mat of nim twigs and berries that obscure the date. 1916, he notices, and desists. Inge does not reach down to brush away the mast. She is at attention, head bowed, her arm raised in a fascist salute.

Jed moves away, making for the frangipani. Brij would accompany him, but senses he would like to be alone, so begins a cursory inspection of the other German tablets. Strange outcroppings of consonants jag an eye accustomed to English names.

Inge has not moved.

Jed, too, is stationary now under the leaning tree, but talking.

You kept back the bone, stole its voice. For me, thank you. Now you're the bone – I'm the old fossil. Not long now. Then I'm yours for ever. I was almost there, but she got in the way. Saved me. Truth be told, I don't mind now. She's a lot like you, you know. Too like you. Not playing tricks with me, are you?

Inge is fumbling in her jacket pocket, produces a camera. Stoops to clear the tablet, steps back and takes the picture. Then looks for Brij to take a picture of her by the grave. He comes over, holds the camera as if it were an exotic quail. Aims, presses the button she tapped with a black-painted nail, examines the neat little compact before returning it.

'You know Leica?' Inge asks.

'Oh, I like it very much.'

She looks to see if he's joking, but he's not.

'What do you do?' she says.

Brij looks at his bitten fingernails. 'I'm a teacher,' he says. It's an idea he's had since returning from the Gulf ten years ago. No-one here had heard of physiotherapists then.

'And what do you teach?'

'I teach . . . yoga. And what do you do?'

'I'm a printer.' She begins to walk among the graves. 'What kind of yoga?'

'Hatha yoga. What kind of printing?'

'I do four-colour printing for magazines, greetings cards, wrapping paper, wallpaper. For the book trade, art books, coffee-table books. One I have done of Indian wild beasts.'

'How long have you been in India?'

'Just two days.'

'How do you like it?'

'It is dirty.' She answers immediately, then looks to soften the blow. 'Is it all like this?'

Brij looks down at his feet. There, planted by providence, is a turd, yellow as a garter snake.

'Yes.'

They stop before a large sloping stone that commemorates the collective German dead. 'Who sleep in the Indian earth,' Inge translates.

She turns away. 'Your holy men,' she resumes, 'they deny the world. That is fine. But the others who live in the world, they don't mind the rubbish, the dirt?'

Brij is provoked into cliché. 'They see through it,' he says. But knows they look past it. 'Dirt is just ... matter.' His immaculate shirt gives him away.

'Matter in the wrong place, no?' She completes the dictum for him. Her jeans, he notices, are frayed; one knee shows as she walks. 'They see the gold in the dust,' she banters, 'they penetrate the world of appearances?' The black lips twist him a hard smile. Her toughness has always intimidated, and this one is in sandals. Bodybuilder, but she could crush those feet.

'It's true,' Brij offers feebly.

'And we in the West are trapped by the materialistic world, yes?'

'Maybe. Here you have to close your eyes to some things.'

'So you see them better?'

'So you don't go mad.'

'And close also the nose.'

'Yes!'

They come to where the new graves are, the stones crowded together after the spacious British lines. Here the lines are more irregular, no one tomb squared with the next, every tablet out of true. Whole rows meander, as if heaved up by a quake. Cement has replaced stone; one grave is decked in kitchen tiles. There is no statuary. What marble there is is in small white slabs laid flat and incised with crude capitals.

'DIXIT,' Inge reads from the bottom of a new memorial. The word is on every recent stone.

'Dixit,' Brij corrects her pronunciation. '*Sh*—' Sanskrit, not Latin. A name. O. P. Dixit. 'He's the old sculptor at the gate.'

'Not very good work.'

The black paint sloppily applied, even in the DIXIT.

'He's almost blind.'

'So, if I wish to put a new stone on the grave of my uncle, who can do it? I wish good work.'

'There may be someone in the city. I can ask. But Dixit wouldn't be happy. This is his territory. He's a brahmin, by the way. His community have ostracized him for doing cemetery work.'

'So they should. I could myself do it better.'

'You could try.'

'I will. You know where there is stone? I wish red stone.'

Brij is delighted. If he could set up a procuring agency he would do well. Now there's an idea. But he's easily distracted, and he's just scented an idea he'd like to track down.

'Why do Christians make such a fuss over the dead?' He sweeps an arm to take in the graveyard with its doleful urns and angels. 'With us the body is burnt and that's it.' He flicks open a hand, as if releasing a bird.

'I don't know. I'm not a Christian.'

He is surprised, but sees she's speaking of faith. He had meant Christians, the group. The rituals they are born to.

'But my uncle's grave, yes. It is important. He was a poet.'

Earth, leaf and air swim at the word. The marble slabs briefly leavened. Brij, who seldom reads, reveres those who write.

'Then you should not put a stone on him.'

She looks at him with interest for the first time. And he, looking back at her, notices a grace inside that black armour. Her lettering will be slender, grave, beautiful.

'Stones are for soldiers,' he waves his hand again at the Everest dead. 'For postmasters,' he reads off a marble book. A dove is crooning high up in the branches overhead.

'In fact, I should take away the marker that is there,' Inge says, returning to her bantering tone.

He looks hard at her and takes the plunge. 'In fact you should dig—'

He stops himself. Sidesteps to avoid a gravestone. Her boots have been cutting across everything in her path.

'You know,' he starts again, 'there are, there is a sect that believes you should make a wine cup out of your father's skull.'

One cremation rite haunts Brij, the elder son. Sometimes, when he sees his father from behind, he thinks, That is the skull I must crush.

They've come up to where Jed is waiting, seated on a low bowed branch of the frangipani that children's feet have worn smooth. Jed wags a finger.

'Don't you go filling her head with your tantric nonsense.'

'But I am interested,' Inge protests.

'She would like to put a new stone on her relative's grave.'

'Excellent idea. Dixit will run you up one, if you're not fussy.'

'She is. She would like to do it herself.'

Jed looks at her. 'Even better. Brij here will get you the materials, chisels and so on. He knows all the dealers. What he doesn't know about this city is not worth knowing.'

'He wants me to make a wine cup out of my uncle's skull.'

Brij grins at his sandals.

'He'll have you performing all manner of satanic rites.'

'But not that one.'

'I hope not. I'm secretary of these grounds, remember. You're staying in a hotel?'

'The Rex.'

'Then we're neighbours. That's it over there.'

Inge is flabbergasted. 'But the scooter rickshaw man brought me a long way!'

'Well, he would. We don't get many foreigners here. Anyway, Brij won't cheat you. And you can use our compound to work in.'

They go back up the cypress walk to the lych-gate so Jed can have a word with the chowkidar. The coffin truckle intrigues Inge. Machined elegance in a handcart: precisely wrought, mounted on leaf springs. What a contrast with the other vehicles she sees! She tests the suspension, then goes to join Brij, who is feeding the chowkidar's mascot: a big black billy. She's never seen a goat so big. Perched squarely on a tomb, after all those fallen angels. The head a mossed rock, the eyes grave marbles with transverse yellow slits, through which an old intelligence disdains the fallen world. She takes a little grass from Brij and offers it to the creature on her palm. Endures the nibbling lips, her own drawn into a tight smile.

K ARTIK, *late October. The buffalo calf romps through the compound as far as the cemetery, where the ground is firm again. Some days there is even dust, a light pollen of it, on leaves that have begun to thin and curl, losing their monsoon succulence. The heat is gone, the cold not yet come. Wildflowers throng the vacant lots, the graveyard: tiny blood-red stars, pale-blue morning glory, golden rod. Miss Sampson loves this time of year, the calms, the dews. The morning sun slopes down on old brick and plaster, lending more colour than heat. In her window, a yellow petal spins on spider silk. At night the thudding of grapefruit wakes Thapa.*

B rij's oil-soaked lane is passable again, the drains no longer overflowing. He can walk on the firmed cleats left by truck and tractor tyres and not soil his new shoes. The city streets have dried out, too; you are no longer marooned in shops by sudden floods of sewage, or trapped in teashops by bores who love the rain.

This morning Brij is looking for stone and chisels, but first there is the blind tin-whistle man at the corner to greet. 'We've seen the end of it,' the blind man says, scanning the sky. 'No more rain,' Brij agrees, 'but start knitting your jersey now. Here's someone who can help you with wool.' The noseless shepherd goes by driving his flock and yells a friendly curse. 'More goats than sheep,' the blind man calls back and pipes a snaky note at the stragglers.

Brij glances in at the gas agency window. The young typist

looks pertly back and gives her roller a twist. He smiles; she'll have to twist it back, he knows. At the Delhi taxi stand there are drivers he must greet. 'What news from the capital, oh ministers?' They gather around him, drawn like iron filings. At the courts his notary friends will not let him pass without a cup of tea. He leans back on his chained iron chair amid the starched collars and carbon paper and hordes of litigants and knows that this is what he should have done with his life. At the gate a trotter curry man tempts him with a mound of fragrant rice. He takes the plate. 'How's the cooking-shooking, Ustad?' The scoop returns to crown the gravy with a piece of tender gristle. 'Bone china,' the fat man brags. 'Now *you* tell me.' Brij tests it, mimes floating away. 'Never better, Eugene Saab!'

Then past the district hospital, with the nurses in stockings. He wipes the foam of sugar-cane juice from his upper lip with a dazzling handkerchief, and is already halfway across the Tehsil crossing when he calls back to the man, 'Tot it up.' He waves aside a row of apple carts. 'Make way, princelings!' But stops in his tracks at the green-rot dump, where urchins rescue stalks of coriander to peddle with their stolen lemons. He has remembered the reading room on Gandhi Road where he meant to look up something. So he turns back.

In the squat yellow-washed building with the broken windows the books are mostly novels of the 1910s. In 1958 came the Raja of Raipur's bequest, a collection of esoteric texts, and since then the library has languished on a newspaper allowance and one salary from the city board. The bookshelves are not dusted nor the broken panes replaced, but one section never gathers dust. Brij locates his book and finds a window seat. It is three o'clock before he looks up from Saxena's *Tantric Love and Its Curious Disciplines*, and then only because he feels the need of a pen. He can never remember to carry one, so he finds an unlikely cleft for Saxena deep among the lady novelists of Empire, and steps out into the world.

A friend calls out from across the road. There's just time for a glass of tea before the rally.

The Akashkhand rally! He'd almost forgotten. But there's something else nagging at him. Brij wipes his glasses. There's something he's trying to remember, something he's trying to forget. He tosses back the tea and follows his friend, not really listening to the talk of committee meetings and agenda.

They come to the parade ground, where a crowd is gathered. Police on hand, but not in numbers to flatter the organizers. It's a public meeting and the public are urged to speak. Brij is caught up in the flow and finds himself on stage, speaking of the dam, of his drowned village, the words pouring out.

As always the crowd pays him special heed. He speaks from the heart, simply, but with a rapidity and colour that captivate an audience already impressed by his build and his Batman T-shirt. Unlike the other speakers he uses no gestures, simply stands before the microphone with his powerful arms folded. His eyes, warped by thick lenses, have the unfocused look of a blind man's, but the head is working overtime, rocking, butting, jutted in interrogation, tossed at the mountains over his shoulder, while the face mimes every conjured emotion for the gallery. And then, just as suddenly as he started, he stops, jumps off the podium, and is off without waiting to hear the other speakers.

On the way back there are masseurs to greet on the lawns of the Gandhi Park, and the fried-fish sellers next to the courier service, where a lovely lady gazes out at the petrol-pump customers. By the clock tower he has a word with Titu the bootboy, shares a joke with the seed and seedling man and admires a pair of running shoes. The glow of discourse is still on him. It's hard to concentrate: the young women of Drummondganj have begun their evening promenade, but there's something he has to do.

Confusion brings him to a halt: have *done* with it all! It seems he knows everybody and nobody, least of all himself. Ever since childhood he's been attracted by accounts of hermits, forest sages. Yesterday he read of a Chinese pilgrim who lived for twenty years in a tree overlooking the place where the Buddha died. Pictured himself doing that, then imagined himself hankering after a piece of fried fish. Always the world returns with its chores and pleasures: queue for kerosene, tea with the lawyers. If he could be like the nose-less shepherd, complete in his duty. He sets out again, has fallen in with the rat-poison-and-pyjama-drawstring-wallah when a long sardonic jaw blocks his way.

'I believe the German girl has won your heart.'

Baingan coolie smiles his heavy-lidded smile. Brij folds his arms across his chest in mock menace.

'I believe your son took her for a ride.'

'Her or him, no-one can tell. It could be a pretty boy. But you should know by now. You were seen in the cemetery together.'

'My God!' Brij slaps his forehead. His Adam's apple bobs in the dusk. 'I was supposed to find her some stone.'

'Stone?'

'For the grave. She wants to make a tombstone for her uncle.'

'So that's what took her there. What's wrong with marble?'

'She wants red stone.'

'Well, you've come to the right man.'

'I told her there was plenty.'

Baingan draws a breath and releases it slowly. 'Plenty there isn't. But it can be had. You leave it to me.'

'I knew I could rely on you.'

'Cost no consideration? Deutschmarks, no?'

'Cost *is* a consideration, sisterfucker! I'll be checking around.'

They clinch the deal in the Muslim quarter with seekh kababs on a leaf plate. Brij takes a raw onion ring between finger and thumb, and bends it into an oval; just short of snapping it springs into his mouth.

Clink.
Metal on metal on stone.

Old Dixit hears the presumptuous syllable all the way down the cemetery lane. From over the Everest wall it strikes at his heart. It's gained in confidence since the first tentative tapping. He stands at his mesh door cradling a blank white tablet, stroking the surface, his nervous fingertips brushing off the braille of grit accumulated there. He's been away in Dehra Dun, and it was torture as he brooded over the business he might be missing. And here's the proof, ringing in his ears. Not that he would condescend to ask that worm of a chowkidar. Better to go and snoop for himself.

He takes his rolling parrot walk through the lych-gate, his tabby cat following at a distance.

Half an hour later he returns to his post disappointed. There are no fresh mounds at Everest the cemetery. Then why this maddening refrain?

Clink. Clink. Clink.

Perhaps he should call on Jed Saab, make discreet enquiries?

Clink.

Ritu has grown accustomed to the ringing. It's like the bell on the level crossing gate, but flatter and continuous. Monotonous as the coppersmith.

Clink. Clink.

Miss Chatterjee has found a new illness to add to her armoury: tinnitus. Cecelia, writing letters, is distracted by the sound. But to Jed it's music. Flinty, epic music, distant battle blows, each stroke an act of will. He crosses the roof to his accustomed seat, but doesn't sit; stands looking down past the walled garden at the shared pipal. Sees the goongi crouching behind the anthill, staring goggle-eyed at the flamewoman with the hammer.

The stone must first be dressed. The edges smoothed with a flat chisel. Inge has worked out a glancing cross stroke that shears without skidding. The first day she planes the edges, unwilling to tackle the top. The slab now lies on a platform of bricks, like a sacrificial altar whose surface changes with the light: mauve in the morning, oxblood at noon, and in the evening a mulberry shading into the puce of old liver. She sent the first one back, too thin, and blotched besides, but now wishes she'd kept it. By German standards it was cheap, and slab upon slab would build up into a stronger statement. No matter. She will send for more, if only to watch the carter back his cart up against the wall before unhitching it, steering the bullock by the horns.

Brij supervises. He helped lower the slab onto the bricks, brought a second chisel, a third. Baingan coolie has sent a stamp-sized bill, although he cannot write, and words will fly over the total. Inge doesn't care. She is daily amazed at how far the mark goes. Rupee notes she cannot take seriously; they seem childish things, their engravings unreal. In her second week the rupee falls dramatically; to her it simply means more red stone.

Brij is always there to take delivery, fussing over chipped edges that will be rounded off anyway. He helps, gets in the way, comes close to blows with the bullock-cart man over the absurd cartage fee. And always he's conscious of a gaze from Everest that isn't there.

Or is it?

Might she just look up from Miss Chatterjee's bedpan and see him there? But what would she see? Him with this amazon, whose uniform hasn't changed in a week. The talk of the town, with her studded jacket, her swastika nosering, and her spike of red hair. And pretty underneath, the women concede.

One gaze there is, but it's not from Everest. Brij feels it graze his shoulders, sees Mrs Puri hover behind her pot of basil, watering it to death. He's been up that stair, too.

And someone else is watching. Thapa is bent over a swale of congress grass on the city side of Everest, swinging his scythe. The daytime sword. Sometimes, when his ears have heard enough, he simply drops the weeder and returns to his room, takes the kukri off its nail and runs it over a leather strop to concentrate his mind. Then shuts the window and climbs into bed and tries to sleep.

KARTIK, *November. The screech owls are back on the wires; all night they ring like telephones.*

October's wildflowers are dead, but there is oxalis sprouting at the foot of the rain tree. A blaze of bougainvillea along the front wall. On the portico a second flowering of quisqualis, that yields a drowsy sweetness at night. The cassia seedstraps have begun to blacken. Downy new leaves on the mountain ebony; the old leaves crowded like camel hoof prints in the dust.How quickly the soil loses its moisture! Waterlogged just the other day, now it's packed solid. Where the pick goes in it crumbles like biscuit. The pick comes out clean.

A grave is being dug in the cemetery.
Miss Chatterjee, who in her life knew every disease, has found the universal cure. The tinnitus, real as hammer blows, carried her off, abetted by sleeplessness and melancholia and mutability. Her last confinement will be fruitful, going by the chowkidar's pumpkin vine, which rambles over the new graves putting out crumply yellow flowers and marbled grey fruit. There are no relatives at the burial, just the nuns and Miss Sampson and the Latvian. The goongi is terrified of graves, Major Bakshi is away and Thapa must hold the fort. Jed has sent apologies. He is annoyed, apoplectic: now one berth remains at Everest the cemetery.

All through the service Inge's chisel tolls. Its ringing glints in the dark cypresses, joined by Thapa's scythe when the gardener and chowkidar chips a stone in the rampant congress grass. (Thapa looks out for snakes; he offered a saucer of milk to appease the wife of the one he killed, but Dixit's thieving cat got that.) Old Dixit is in despair. He was hoping for a dowager or a dearly loved husband. There are Christians of substance in town who would want a decent slab – and here is a mango wood crate being lowered into the last hole but one. Life.

The clouds remain aloof, a flat white wadding rucked in the middle, but the mountains, so different from the flat plain of Miss Chatterjee's birth, have put on a gauze of mourning made up of dust and distance and the exhaust fumes of the traffic snarled around the Rex Hotel.

On the way home there is rain, a light sprinkling. Fresh autumn rain, rare and gentle: the sweetness of dust damped down. Two voices bring up the rear of the Everest squad.

'How's the fighting in Estonia?'

'Latvia, my dear.'

'That's what I said.'

'Of course. Here, take my hand.'

'Arm.'

'Arm, arm.'

R itu's load is lightened by the passing.
Miss Chatterjee was more trouble than the twins, even if she didn't regularly overturn her porridge bowl. As demanding as Jed and heavier in the turning. Death could not have chosen better, she considers, and dismisses the thought as ignoble. Is it? she asks, and finds that her imagined respondent is still Brij. She thought she'd unlearned that habit, sent him further away than Miss Chatterjee herself. And yet there are times when her step is unaccountably light, when she hums a tribal courting song from her girlhood.

There's a kite in the sky above the cemetery and she steps towards the window for a better look. Sees an answering patch of orange against the dry grass under the pipal tree.

The German woman, bending over her stone slab. And beside her, sniffing like a goat, Brij.

Ritu flaps her duster in the tainted air. Returns to cleaning and airing Miss Chatterjee's room. Afterwards, to escape its ringing emptiness, she takes a walk along Canal Road with Neha. They go as far as the riverbed by the burning ghat and turn back. The next day they repeat the walk, and in a few days it has become part of their routine.

The road goes away from the city, the opposite way from the Rex Hotel and the auto workshops, growing greener with every step. The canal has lost its monsoon roar, but the market gardens it waters are thriving beyond the jail. Tiny fish glitter in its eddies like splinters of glass. Past the last of the cemeteries, the lychee groves give way to standing sugar cane and wheat bordered with tall straight sal. Not long ago this would have been forest. Beyond the river is a marsh, where lapwings weep. On this side the bamboo clumps of Jed's *Via Mortis* peter out in sandy soil not far from the blank platform where Hindu bodies are cremated. Ash and bone and charred logs lie strewn about there. There is a broken causeway across the river, but the stream is dry anyway, a bed of smooth grey and white stones. In the monsoon a torrent from the hills will wash the yellow boulders a little further downstream, and there they will lie till the next rains, a staging post for smaller rocks.

Cecelia encourages the walkers; they show the colours, establish a presence. It's half in her mind that Miss Chatterjee's room be filled. She has heard of a brothel at the end of the road that serves the migrant workers' camp and thinks a woman might be rescued from there, an example set. The women are hill women brought down to plainsmen who prefer their lighter skin. But when Ritu and Neha pass their door the women snigger at this sober sisterhood whose uniform actually shows their legs. The two nuns stop at the river, but are curious about a colony of lepers on the other bank. It sits on boggy, unwanted ground just where the forest begins. Might something be done there, among people even the lapwings mock?

It's the nearest Ritu has been to the forest since leaving home. The canopy is less dense than in her jungle, but the fire-break just here reminds her of the gap at the level crossing. There are cattle grazing on the other bank and a group of women resting among their headloads of coppiced firewood. A woodpecker drums urgently, high up in the sal, but the scene is one of repose.

'You'll leave some trees for tomorrow?' Ritu ribs the wood-cutters, missing Perpetua's tone.

The women are embarrassed. These city strangers could be anybody, even police.

'It's all there,' the leader points. 'We just pick up the fallen wood.'

'Of course,' Ritu says, sorry to have spoken. 'Where do you live?'

'Over that way,' the woman waves cautiously. She begins to wind her headcloth, and at the sign her companions get to their feet, winding theirs. They lift their faggots and each one stands a moment, steadying her load: long branches, stripped and bound and carried lengthwise.

'In there,' the leader says, pointing with a flat hand and shouting from the strain, 'they cut down whole trees. They come in trucks and cut down trees.'

The women file away towards Drummondganj. Ritu and Neha stand absorbing the forest's murmurous silence. These are the low hills, the chain whose wooded slopes and dunce-cap peaks Ritu has looked out across from Jed's roof for months now. A short walk, hardly a mile, has brought them up close, the forest foreshortening the hills. Ancient alluvial strata buckled by continental drift and worn into grotesque shapes. Cowled with tall straight trees whose leaves are stirring at the top. *Shorea robusta*, her botanist tongue pronounces before supplying the common name, sal. So much for my humbling, she smiles, thinking of Cecelia. The bedpans have not erased that.

A deer barks deep in the forest, a high shrill cry, stifled almost instantly by the afternoon's torpor. Ritu stares into the barred gloom. Hears a shuffle in the fallen leaves, a footfall that becomes a loping. Sees a shadow like a grey pelt flitting among the lopped trunks.

Jed watches them returning, a hawk.

Two grey doves among the bamboos on Canal Road. He has been leaning on the parapet, looking out at the low hills for a change. Her hills, what's her name.

He's having one of his days.

And knows it. Knows that much. Knows the doves, too, but can't put names to them. Tries to put a name to himself, and can't. What he does know is that he needs one of those doves. She – he knows it's a she – is precious to him.

So like the other. What other?

There's a ringing in his right ear that he knows he should know but can't place. *Chunk, chunk, chunk,* all day, like that summer bird. What is it called?

Coppersmith! He claps his hands, hugs himself. Got that one. Nailed it good and proper. Coppersmith. Try taking that name away from me. Go on, God. Let's see. Let's *see*, you old sod!

Coppersmith, coppersmith, coppertea.

Cup of tea, yes. Oh, yes. Sell my soul for a cup.

What's the word again? The bird, the bird . . . come *on*. Gripping the parapet. Fear. Cold hard fear. What's the *frigging* bird?

Cuppertea.

Cuppertea.

God.

God help me. Help me. Brushes away angry tears. Help me, you bastard of a God!

Clink, clink, clink.

Grey nunspots blossom at the gate. Know that one. Little beauty. My cup of tea. Yes!

'Ritu, Ritu, Ritu!'

He's shouting. Knows he is because there are people appearing down there, looking up. Can name them. Thapa. Goongi. Cecelia. The old nun, never remember her name anyway. Perpetua! Nailed that one, too – I'm cured! Coppersmith!

'Ritu, Ritu, I'm cured!'

Tsering comes up behind him, takes both arms, steers him to bed.

'I don't want you,' he says, looking steadily up at her from the pillow. Hot childish tears welling up in those black eyes. 'Do you hear me?'

Tsering can hear him. She can take it. Her eyes are focused on a point between his, but she understands. She misses nothing, forgives everything. When he's dozing she goes down to Cecelia.

'He wants Ritu,' she states.

'I heard him,' Cecelia answers. 'The whole town heard him.'

'He needs her,' Tsering offers, and glides away.

Frost Time

AGHAN, *December. Early mornings cut like a chisel. Dawn an aluminium basin filled with sky-cold water. Fingers red. Perpetua's arthritis twists its knife. Mist from Jowar the mongoose's mouth filters through the sunlit mesh of the pantry door.*

Geese clank on the marsh where once the lapwing ruled. A single skein this year, down from Siberia. Frost-mottled pomegranates hang on the near-bare tree, guarded by thorns as fat as sacking needles. A blight has killed the new red leaves on the lychee trees; tonight the cold will kill the blighting fungus. A garlic bulb pushes up a new green tooth.

At night Thapa's whistle is more shrill than ever; his steel-tipped lathi strikes sparks from the Canal Road. Two clacks and a whistle, two clacks and a whistle. Inge, listening from her room in the Rex, takes him for a crane. When she asks Brij he says, Yes, it's the chowkidar bird, a bandy-legged creature with a clacking bill and mournful eyes.

The water-table is low, the mains supply down. Perpetua has resumed her hostilities along the Everest line ever since a tub of water in her bathroom emptied itself. One evening the miracle is repeated. The devil's mischief, Neha feels, but Perpetua sits with her wrench across her lap and ponders. Then stares: you left the tap on, Perpetua! *The hose is dangling in the tub, the water level is down to the end of the hose.* Suction. *She marches off along the line to Mrs Puri's wall, brandishing the wrench. Knowing it could be any of a dozen neighbours, but convinced it's her.* 'You haven't got a booster pump, by any chance?' she calls up at the pot of basil. Mrs Puri leans her well-fleshed forearms on the balcony and glares down at her accuser. 'What booster-shooter? You be careful or my lawyer will bring a case!' She has a lawyer, has several.

Perpetua returns to her succulents. Prodigies of conservation, breeders of symmetry, they sit on her window sill, sufficient, patient, consoling. They are putting out new leaves, smooth and cold as Everest plates. Beautiful, too, a secondary virtue, but a

chaste beauty. In the morning each leaf, engrailed and edged with
a thread of crimson, balances a liquid diamond.

'TYPICAL.'

Tropical perversity, Inge sniffs, listening.

Floating upside down with her camera in her lap. The flash indicator light is on, a firefly in her bush. Her feet are bare, small and smelly as a boy's, her boots stowed under the bed. The toes are slightly bent, like piano hammers.

'The Egyptians used crocodile faeces in the same way.' Brij is expounding Saxena.

Standing on his head, his weight distributed in a triangle whose other points are his elbows. He is comfortable in this position, falls up into it. Can shift weight onto his forearms so the flesh bulges there against the hotel towel he has spread on the floor. The towel will appear in all the photographs. 'Rex', worked in green.

A one-bar electric heater sheds its meagre orange glow on the terrazzo.

'If you're very poor you can omit the saffron paste.' Retailing the book he reads every morning now after tea with the dyer round the corner.

Inge, too, has fallen into a routine. She breakfasts on coffee and a dosa that reminds her of the potato pancake her mother makes. Won't touch the sambar. Then she goes across to Everest to work on the monument. After lunch she sculpts some more, grateful for the afternoon sun, which slips too soon behind the tall silk-cotton tree. Back in her room, she fills a sketchbook with drawings of the work in progress, using a dark soft lead. Drapery, an acanthus leaf, a rosette.

The gothic O. Fluting on a possible urn. Then coffee, butter biscuits with a sprinkling of thyme from the bakery down the road. Then she walks. Through the bazaar, stepping carefully, boldly, setting her face against the looks. Curious, unbending, but no longer stiff, as if she feared contamination. After dark she does her drugs and waits for Brij. Secretly she's begun to admire his casual approach to everything, even the politics that sometimes exercise him. But would rather die than let him know.

The photographs were her idea. His thirty yoga asanas illustrated step by step. Some two hundred shots.

'An instructor must have a portfolio,' she said one night. 'A dossier, no? I will make for you one.'

Brij sat considering.

'Black and white, not coffee table.' Inge held up a fresh roll of film.

So Brij got up, spread the towel on the floor, removed his glasses and squatted down cross-legged in one supple movement. Grew still, collecting his thoughts. Flexed each foot, the middle and third toes joined up to the second digit, lifted it onto the opposite thigh, the limbs drawing like elastic. Finally, took in a long breath and stretched out his arms, so each hand lay upturned on a knee. Thumb and forefinger touching, a butterfly at rest.

'The Lotus,' he said, lowering his lids. The primary position.

'*Schön!*'

The grace of his movements making up for his clumsy lovemaking. 'But yogis don't wear jeans.'

So Brij stood up and stripped to his underwear, still bashful. Accustomed to her bare body, its clean miraculous lines, but still reluctant to bare his.

Now he's lost that unease, undresses without a

thought. Down to his funny drawers. Orange sheen on swells of obedient muscle, joints ticking as sinew tracks across bone.

Click.

'*Schön.*' Softly, tenderly.

The gentleness opens Brij's eyes. Again he observes a sweetness in her barefoot person that leaves her when she's clothed. The line of the lips changing, too. A taut silent lover. Hanging there upside down. But there are moments in the hotel bed when that line will harden till he feels she could reach her whole arm into him and pluck out some vital organ.

'You've been neglecting me, Nachiketa.'

Brij bows contrition.

'How's the village? Covered up yet?'

He doesn't really care, Brij sees. But he doesn't pretend either. He himself hasn't cared lately.

'Been triangulating, have we?'

Brij twigs at once. She is all triangles: the wedge of red hair above the forehead; the widow's peak below; the face itself, wide at the top, pointed at the chin. Even the canines, sharp. Wide freckled shoulders, pointed feet. Red delta.

And no-one more aware of Inge's angles than surveyor Jed. Would map her himself.

Brij has brought his dossier for safe keeping. If his father finds it he'll want to know who did it, and then there'll be trouble. Mr Bhatt is a bear when provoked. Already he distrusts the foreigner. Mrs Puri has whispered something to Mrs Bhatt.

Jed leafs through the album, eyes pantomime wide.

'Very nice, Nachiketa, very nice!' Staring alternately at the photos and at the clothed man.

Brij smiles a pursed smile.

Then, by way of a signature, a closing photo. Not Brij. Inge herself, in colour, her boy's chest bare, her small hands composed in the lotus position. Red bracts of underarm hair. Lotus in flames.

Jed on fire. Gazes, grazes. Always liked them boyish. Would she, just once, for begging and pleading, for crying out loud, for an old man's kneeling, would she? He would give anything. Anything. His eyes beginning to focus: he would give her Everest, all his substance.

Over Cecelia's head. Over that sharper of a cousin. Over, it has occurred to him, Nachiketa himself. He looks slyly at Brij.

'I must congratulate her.'

Brij pushes out another smile. 'I'll tell her.'

'Now?'

'She's working.' Brij turns his head towards the proof.

Clink. Clink. Clink.

Jed cocks his head, too, but can't hear it today. 'Well, when she takes a break. Cecelia tells me she drinks in the garage.'

Get her all the Scotch she wants. All the red stone. The album envoi burning in his head. The wick is a triangle too, but it's been so long he can't be sure. Inflamed.

Look, Fay! See Jed burn.

'The old parrot was up here.'

Jed is talkative today, glad to have Ritu back.

'Parrot?'

'Dixit. Out-patient Dixit. The old man who used to do the Ever-rest monuments. Wanted to know why I, as secretary of the cemetery, condoned poaching on his preserve.'

'Poaching?'

'You don't have to repeat after me. The foreigner, he means. He thinks she's taking work away from him. Showing him up, too. She can sculpt, Brij says.'

Watching her as he drops Brij's name. She looks suddenly distressed, but it could be at his cruelty. Ritu has already heard from Perpetua how the foreigner knocked a piece off by mistake and turned the result into a clever scroll. It hasn't occurred to her that Jed may be jealous himself.

They're out on the roof. Nowadays Jed wants to catch the sun. His chair faces away from the mountains, backed up against the dish pedestal whose cracks winter has made a little wider. He has worked out a tuck in the quilt, so his feet, in three pairs of socks, are completely enveloped. A blanket lies across his lap. The dish, like a shouldered umbrella blown inside out by monsoon gusts, is now his shield against the cold winds that sweep down from the mountains. A dusting of snow on the highest peaks.

'You're cold?'

Ritu looks up. Concern from Jed? She goes on with rinsing the bedsheets. Blue blankets steam on the line, torsions where she has wrung them, like geologic heaves. Yes, she is a bit cold, up here on the roof in this northern town.

'You want to know what cold is?' Jed pauses. 'Fill up one of those tubs. Let it stand overnight. Tomorrow, before matins – do you still call them that? – nip up here for an open-air bath. Then let the wind dry you as you watch the sun come up. I promise not to look. And sip a little cold water so your insides don't feel left out.'

Jed back on form.

'So I know how you felt on Everest.'

Jed's eyebrows twitch. Let that one go, one to her. He left six toes above the snowline; what are a couple of pissy sheets? He swallows. So you know what it's like to spend a night without a tent at 25,000 feet. Says, 'So you understand chilblains.'

She half lifts a sheet out of the water. A white sail, blinding curtain of water; in that moment she's nothing, transparent. The morning sun shivers in the bamboos, making Jed squint.

'Have you noticed the bamboos are looking sick? It wouldn't surprise me if they flowered next year. Did you know that bamboos die communally?'

Ritu didn't.

'It's one of the mysteries of nature. Every thirty years all the bamboos of a district flower together — don't ask me how they know — and when they've finished flowering, they die. It's a kind of mass suicide. They flowered when I was thirty. At sixty I made a porridge of the kernels, like kibbled wheat. Now they must be getting ready for my ninetieth.'

'And then a hundred and twenty.'

'Ninety will do. The way seventy used to, when you made a will, bought a plot. But then seventy-one comes along and you're still there, and seventy-two, and all the years up to seventy-nine, and you begin to think it was premature, that alarm. So that eighty is positively invigorating, and off you go again. Until you hear the bamboos creaking. Do you ever hear them at night?'

'We shut our windows now. You should, too.'

'In case I catch my death of cold?'

'Miss Sampson has a fever.'

Jed rearranges his blanket. 'I had monkey fever once, for six months, on and off. My punishment for shooting a monkey. The villagers were so upset they would have finished me off themselves, but I grabbed the headman and threatened to shoot him next.

'I didn't set out to shoot the monkey. He just happened to be on the same branch as an orchid we'd been hunting for weeks. In fact, he led me to the flower. The kraken. A bit like a mimulus, but white with a green speckling on the hood. I wouldn't have spotted it if he hadn't moved. Sitting on the very branch. Refused to budge. Showing his teeth and carrying on like its guardian. I thought I'd wait him out, but as I sat down he calmly went up to the orchid, picked it and ate it. Six weeks of searching! I shot him straight off, by reflex.

'*Hell* of a ruckus among the other monkeys. When I sorted out the villagers we stood back and watched the monkeys come down from the trees and carry the dead one off. I tracked them for a mile down into a gorge and watched them lay him in a hollow. Then they covered the body over with branches and leaves and flowers and went away.

'And do you know, the flowers were all the same orchid, the kraken. It grew in just that square mile.'

Jed stretches out his legs.

'On the other side of the gorge the villagers will sell you monkeys' brains, like pickled walnuts.'

She's sitting on the balustrade, staring at his mountains with a look of wonderment. This Jed she could happily nurse.

'And the famous gland, of course. Cheaper up there. They salt it and sun it and pack it in bamboo culms. You could take it to Calcutta and make a nice profit. The merchants do. Now *you'd* have to be careful up there. They say those monkeys can smell a woman's period.'

Ritu never learns. She hops off her perch, looks at him

coldly, and is turning to go when he holds up an appeasing hand.

'If you're going down, could you . . .' He hesitates. 'Could you fetch me a book from the library?'

She stiffens.

He holds up both hands. 'No tricks, no *Family Law*. Just this.' He fishes in his pocket and hands her a note. Title and number, question mark. His first strained piece of writing in a year. At one time he could have dispensed with the question mark; he did the classifying, after all. But more lights are going out in his brain. He sees it happening, like a watcher at a window late at night.

She scrunches the note up in her palm. Let him worry for a bit.

Miss Sampson and Perpetua stand by the anthill. On either side of a small dead creature in the grass. The goongi, who led them there, has retreated to the anthill, from whose cover she stares at the remains of Jowar the mongoose.

'An animal wouldn't have done that,' Miss Sampson says, sorrowing but dry-eyed.

Jowar's belly has been slit along its length and the entrails pulled out. White tubes and corrugations glisten in the early sunlight against a dark patch of blood that has soaked into the earth. The stomach has also been opened, and its contents examined. A yellowish paste is smeared on the grass where the blade was wiped.

'But who would do such a thing?' Perpetua's eyes are wet. She could find relief in anger. 'Hurting a defenceless creature.'

'He may not have been hurt,' Miss Sampson points out. There are no marks of injury, no blood at Jowar's mouth. His fur is intact, unruffled; he has not been in a fight. No-one has seen a snake in ages. 'And he certainly wasn't defenceless.'

Perpetua looks squarely at the older lady. 'You mean somebody found him dead – and did this?'

'He was getting on. Poor old Jowar.'

Thapa has come up with a leaf broom. 'What's this?' he asks.

'Jowar.'

'It may not be Jowar,' Miss Sampson reminds her. 'It could be another mongoose. Though it does look like him. He disappears from time to time.'

Thapa squats down for a closer look, leaning on the broomstick. 'Oho,' he says, and stands up, 'somebody's been divining.'

'Divining?'

'Sometimes they tell the future this way. By opening the gut.' Then he frowns, as if an idea has occurred to him, and marches off towards his room.

Overhead a crow caws in the silk-cotton, a single proprietary caw. He has spotted the carcass and knows the humans won't stay. From the back verandah Tsering is watching the little group as she slowly shakes out a biscuit tin.

Clematis I collected for her.

A blue-gold that Unger overlooked. It took, got a smile. One smile. A tobacco tin of stamens from the saffron crocus. One smile. In those days you could find a whole meadow of

159

sativus with the pistils intact. You could walk along a snowmelt stream and see fifty kinds of primula. Top the rise and there was an acre of blue poppies. Mind you, *we* were looking for freaks: grey poppies, green cyclamen, black cosmos. The great age of collecting was over, the blue poppy was a catalogue number.

Jed lying there, thinking out loud. Aware of Ritu, half talking to her.

Azalea, *mein Gott!* The frailest pinks, luminous creams, madder, flame, Naples yellow. Once a dwarf red, just a mat of it clinging to a ledge 2,000 feet above the Pindar. It's the river's tiny crawling that makes you sick. I inched back with it, said, 'You almost lost Jed to botany.' The same slow smile.

I potted daphne for you. Scraped ferns from under waterfalls, took tree orchids ninety feet up. Hydrangea you loved: I crossed to China for a silver strain. Burmese edelweiss. Plain sorrel from behind that peak there. Conch lilies, yellow violets, spurge.

It wasn't all for you, of course. It was a job. And I suppose an indulgence, a habit. Your foot learns to step from scree onto a cushion of moss, and then it needs to. Has to. Falls in with caravans carrying ginger and turmeric, honey, walnuts, antimony. Dances in high lonely places.

I stayed longer than necessary, it's true. And you were waiting. Under your famous wistaria.

How to explain the hold of those meadows? Of those sepulchral forests? Of villages full of rhododendrons and syphilis. Women like China roses.

A boy will show you a chancre, rose red, a button for undoing flesh.

Jed stammers, shuts the notebook. Ritu has brought up one of his diaries to show him where the white ants got in.

Riddled from cover to cover: the boards eaten, the pages doilied, flaking.

And she's brought the book he asked for.

Gedichte, by Otto Planke.

'Bees to a honey pot, dear.'

Miss Sampson bats a straight hand and rolls down the fine blue shutters on her eyes. Cecelia is cutting the nails on the other hand.

'They couldn't resist him. Nobody could. Don't ask me, but he had a way. Wherever he went women just caved in. *Phut, phut, phut, phut*. Not just gentlewomen either. Village women, hill women. He got into so many scrapes. Threats on his life. There was a great big Pathan who hung about the gate here for ages one winter, but Jed was away. Lucky that way. Collector Sahib.'

Cecelia does the other hand. The nail scissors say GERMANY in minute capitals on one tine. The blackened steel could be as old as Miss Sampson. The old nails are still pliant, but nowadays Miss Sampson prefers them short. Her manicure case, veteran of many campaigns, lies in the almirah drawer. A cold fishy blue, the aqua of early Rexine.

'*Shoo!*' Cecelia flaps her sleeve at a lizard on the wall.

'He's all right,' Miss Sampson says. 'Keeps those horrible winged things off me. The cleanest creatures, lizards. They make an excellent pet, you know: don't need a cage, keep themselves clean. Seen but not heard. Good neighbours, anyway.'

'Until they fall into your milk pot.' Cecelia gets to tell her wedding banquet story. Seventeen dead.

'Well,' Miss Sampson says, 'we all have to go, one way or another.'

They go downstairs together to the parlour, where Neha has placed a pink-iced cake on the coffee table and made a ninety-one out of a dozen candles.

Stopped with a woman near midnight.
Stopped? Jed can't put a face to the lingo, let alone the woman. Now *there's* old age. You forget your own slang. He's reading his diaries, what's left of them. The earliest volumes suffered most.

Walked out with Maja W. Most frantic kissing.
The same day? Yes, April 17 for the whole entry. *And* there's Kitty, the American. Now her he remembers. All April 17. Slings and bleeding arrows.

Mid-April and Heidelberg is still cold. Deep snow in the forest. He should be measuring trees, taking readings for girth, bark depth, sap. He's rolling in a snow cave with Kitty Kline. Rangy Nevadan, foresters together. Climber, too. Dead now, or laid up in Mount Something or other nursing home in Colorado Springs. Kitty, Kitty, are you there? Somewhere? Thought goes in waves: Do you have a dish?

Useless bloody thing! He knocks Bunny's dish with his cane.

But what a year, that! Jed twenty-three, the century twenty-three. The mark 48,000 to the pound on January 10. *Bought a camera.* 65,000 to the pound January 16. *Bought a riding cape.* 100,000 two days later. *Overcoat, trousers.* By January 30, 180,000 marks to the pound! *Buying typewriter, binoculars.* 207,000 marks on January 31. *Gifts. Crystal bowl for the Finnish girl.*

Finnish girl?

Climbing the European peaks. Now that they didn't like. Caliper their trees, caliper their women, but keep off their peaks.

What's this?

Playhouse with Grete. Still April 17! *No headway.* Ah, that explains the woman at midnight. Dear woman, dear faceless woman, *where* are you? Never mind the who. I kiss you now, again, here and here. Is there ever atonement?

Tally for April 17: *102 trees.*

Calipers faulty, all work washed out.

From *Tantric Love and its Curious Disciplines:*

Both partners will by now be naked.
They must at once bathe, separately; she first, and, when the towelling is complete, the towel is taken and torn down the centre. One piece is dropped on either side of the bed. The bed may be a couch or simply a mattress laid upon the floor and spread with a cloth of cotton.

She who is Shakti or Energy will be seated between a tray of unguents and a libation jug. She may not move more than is necessary, unless it be to pass the adept a phial from the tray. If it is winter she may shiver, but on no account must fires, electric or coal, be lit, unless the bed be in a room on the top storey of a tall building at the north end of a city.

The adept, clad now in a garment of raw silk, open down the front, must hold himself in readiness, having already emptied his mind of futurity. He shall extend his right hand towards the seated Shakti and receive on the palm from time to time and by rotation a dish of scented oil. Here begins the massage.

With fragrant oil he massages the small of her back, with jasmine anoints the roots of her hair, with night jasmine the forehead, touching especially that part where the gatepost left a scar in her youth, with murraya the nape of her neck, with gardenia the nose and the nose jewel, with spider lily either eye, whose folds she has already lined with eyeblack, with maulsari the lobes of the ears, with lime (or lemon) the mole on her right cheek and the tender hairs growing therefrom, with Chinese orange her cheeks, with anise her mouth — what though the bottom row of teeth be crooked? — with supari or tobacco, or both, her tongue, with nak champa her upper lip, with son champa her lower, which may protrude like the lip of heaven, with raj hans her neck, with kadamba her narrow shoulders, with spikenard her small breasts, with magnolia her belly, with khus her navel, with lotus her hips, with mogra her buttocks, with tuberose her pubes, with chameli her yoni, with karaunda her thighs, with musk her knees and ankles, with dahlia her calves, which she will take greater care to shave in future, with sandal the soles of her feet.

Failing which, one oil may be used for all. Mustard oil will do.

When this is achieved, the censer is passed over Shakti's head and the oil lamp revolved before her face. Prayers of purification may then be offered. The adept next invites the protection of the goddess, as who should say, 'May the goddess shield my head, my throat, my tongue, my organ, my every other part,' the listing of which would be tedious. The process of translation has begun and the adept must take great care. Hazards attend the enterprise on every side; let him embrace his fate with courage and wisdom. His guru's word is with him, and also his sacred mantras, which he may wish to chant, invoking first the guru himself and then, when he hears the master's clapping, the vehicle of the goddess, and finally the goddess herself.

Adept and Shakti will now worship the goddess in their hearts.

When that is done, body worship may commence. The dish of cooked meats, including some shred of rotting flesh, or some excretion, may now be eaten, but not to the finish, some morsels being allowed to remain. A cup, which need not be a skull, filled with the blood of a creature newly sacrificed for haruspicy, is then held under the lips of the celebrants, who will ceremonially dip their tongues therein. Shakti will then rinse her mouth and pass a draught of cold water into the mouth of the beloved. It runs across the tongue like a freshet in the mountains. The adept will then carry the seated Shakti to the bed and place her thereupon, addressing the parts of her body, beginning with her feet. As who should say, 'I salute the great toe, Om. I salute the foot, Om. I salute the buttocks, Om.' And so forth, taking care to salute each breast separately and both breasts from the side as well as from the front, not forgetting the nipple and the hairs thereon. The adept will conclude his tour of Shakti's body with the following words, uttered with clear eyes, three times: 'If there be greater beauty in this world I have not seen it.'

Whereupon yoni worship commences. Uttering the given mantras, the adept offers sandal paste, scented oils, sacred water, wine and a drop of fresh blood to the Shakti's organ. She is now the goddess, not simply her vessel, and she in turn must anoint and worship the adept's lingam. He is now the god, not simply his vessel. All obstacles to their union have been removed.

But there remains the union of minds to conduct, and for this the couple, if couple they be, and not one already, must concentrate their essence upon a vision of fire.

Fixed on the horizon is a mountain covered in snow. The mountain is ablaze. It is the snow that is burning; red tongues of flame reduce it, whiteness dances in the gaps. Snow and fire consort in ecstasy until the mountain vanishes in an explosion of light. Here at last is the light of lights which consumes all impurities, all rotting flesh, all desire, the whole world and the shadow of the world.

'So, you can stand on your head.'

At once Ritu is sorry. She thought she could keep that note out of her voice. What is he to her? But the shock of the album remains, a faint persistence like the ringing of the stair.

Brij is also sorry. He remarks the note but he's too timid to hope. It's their first meeting since the kite and the kiss. Since that one time when he felt, holding the string, he'd found the control and release wanting in his life, found some kind of balance, even mastery. He hasn't regained it, not even when he loses himself with Inge.

He glances at the album on Jed's table. How one can hurt without meaning to!

She's dusting around it, a distracted wretched dabbing. Her eyes on the duster, a piece of flannel torn from Jed's discarded pyjamas. She knows who took the pictures, doesn't need to be told. She looked at the first few pages and the last. Not the same shock as with the other book. This body more innocent, open, yet somehow more naked. Brij laid bare, breathing betrayal, separation.

This dense column of flesh wrapped about itself. Yet desirable in itself.

And that last photograph, yes, the woman, desirable, too.

Custody of the what? She can hardly bear it. Let them go. Let them all go. Leave her alone. Custody of the self.

'Jed is out there.'

'Ritu—'

'Jed is out there.'

He turns away, goes out onto the roof. She feels the room

dissolve around her, the harsh winter light trickle through her lashes. Brings the duster up to her nose and stands there a while, balanced on nothing.

Jed's mask is looking down at her. Her moon lily shines behind glass, framed long ago by Brij. She wipes the gramophone lid, finds her tears have streaked the dust there. Wipes the streaks away. Wipes one by one each of Jed's old 78s, careful not to tear the foxed sleeves.

Winter

P USH. *January is an emerald dove in the silk-cotton tree. Tiny fruit on the mulberry, green, hairy. Red nibs on the bare willow.*

Snow on the whole range. One night the Latvian sailor leaves his window open and dreams of home. He is burying his mother under a tinsel jacaranda whose leaflets flurry into the open grave.

The goongi hunches on the fender of the Packard in the pale morning sunlight, greeting no-one but Perpetua, who merits a nod. Neha boils up water for the dishes against the rules; she could be making tea. Cecelia has a heater under her writing table. A note of boding has entered her letters to Mother in Delhi. Late at night she hears a single lapwing swoop over Everest and disapproves of its hysterical weeping.

Ramapithecus snuffles in a polythene bag that has reached deep into the forest. Major Bakshi darkens his rum glass till he's drinking neat Double Dog, bottled in Jalandhar. The label shows two terriers, one black, one white. He sits on the running board of Jed's Packard, holds his head in his hands, and stages once again the battle of Hili.

On the second day of the winter session the coalition government falls. Certain backbenchers have defected and tipped the balance. A snap election is called, and the Akashkhand issue, smouldering all autumn, flares up again. Brij attends rallies, underground meetings; women picket the post office. The police deploy extra units, sirens, spies. The armed constabulary are called in, the home guard called out.

Thapa is untroubled by the fall of governments. Leaf fall is his concern, and a headache for which he makes an infusion of hibiscus and buries a smooth stone. He exchanges his scythe for a broom and sweeps the leaves into regular heaps till the whole compound is hummocked in brown and yellow. In this way he can confuse passing ghosts and burn them to death. At night he strops the kukri, rinses the major's rum glass, and goes to bed. His window is tightly shut and remains so by day. On the sill stands his *collection of chisels: upright, shoulderless, bevel-headed, a row of*

cold totems.

JACKBOOTS ON THE STAIR.

Jed could come at the very sound, but must hoard his seed. Think of work. Collecting. Those endless dreary hours spent devising ways to pack his findings. None of these acrylic seed cases he hears about nowadays. Tissue paper, wax paper, Bromo paper, small blue envelopes, muslin, cartridge cases, pillboxes, tobacco pouches. Once, the barrel of a fountain pen. Delphinium, that was, a noble midnight blue. Five hundred seeds, and not one lived. Nor could he write, having poured away the cobalt ink. And Fay waiting.

Inge appears, the whole fire escape ringing behind her. Her orange tuffet azalea-bright.

Jed waves her to the only chair. 'I hear good reports on the . . .' The what? His tongue a foot groping for its slipper.

'Monument?'

The foot goes home. 'Monument, thank you. Your uncle would be pleased. He'll have two, now.' Jed checks himself: leave the book for now. 'He tried to follow Harrer to Tibet, you know.'

'Tibet?'

'It's just across those mountains. Shangri La. Nirvana? I can see you're not sold on it. I must say I approve. You're here to work, and I'm told you work well.'

'I have stopped work.'

'You need more stone?'

'I need my tools. Somebody is removing them.'

'That's strange. Where do you leave them?'

'In the garage. Behind your car.'

Jed considers. 'Well, next time leave them in the car. The key is in the fish up there. The ring with the leather flap.'

Inge holds it up. 'Thank you. I have almost finished, but too many chisels I am losing.'

Jed declutches, shifts down. In the Packard with his girl. 'Tell me, did you ever see your uncle's poems?'

'No. Neither did my mother. His friends in the camp told her about them after the war. They were not printed in Chermany.'

'Who would have printed them here? German poems!'

'I don't know. Maybe he was a—' She mimes a harp.

Jed returns the favour. 'A bard?' Strike *now*. 'Oh, they were written down, all right. I've seen them.'

She stares.

'Yes. I have a copy, possibly the only copy. You see, they were not printed, they were typed. Bound in cloth. And his line drawings were bound up with them. Indian ink. Fine work, better than the poems, if I can judge. A handsome volume.'

'Can I see it?'

'I'd have to look for it.'

'Shall I come tomorrow?'

'If you like.'

Another foot on the stair, the jackboots hardly gone. This one light. Known, but not lately.

'Jed Uncle!'

'Bunny!' Jed's heart is singing. He can even take this vile cousin, but will goad available flesh.

'Merry Christmas!'

'Too late.'

'I mean, compliments of the season.'

'The cake's all gone. We had fireworks, too. And as for Everest, you're just a few seconds late. I've left it all to her.'

'To who?'

'To the German girl.'

Bunny connects the departing figure. '*That?*' He rooftrees his fingers over a balding head. Inge's orange spike.

'The *Pickelhaube*? Well, that can't be helped. You don't look at the mantelpiece when you're poking the fire. But, yes, she gets it all.'

'Who is she?'

'Destiny. Dressed as Inge Planke. But he was on the mother's side. Inge Somebodyelse, then.'

'*Come* on, Uncle.'

'It's true, she gets everything.'

Bunny sits down, short of breath and happy to start all over again. Anger is not his failing; his sins are solitary and passionless.

'So. Where's the cutie who looks after you? I know what you get up to. Listen, the TV's arrived. They'll deliver it tomorrow. Where would you like it put?'

'I tell you, it's too late. And anyway, don't you dare come anywhere near this place between two and four.'

'Wednesday, then?'

'Not Wednesday or the next day or the next. Or ever.'

Frost on the ground at dawn. Sky stainless steel. Every blade of grass damascened. Returning to dew by breakfast, even in the shadow of Everest, when Perpetua's sandals print a double-dotted line across the back lawn. The dew gone by mid-afternoon, so

Inge's boots leave no mark, crossing the other way.

Jed watching. Hunched like a spider under his dish. He picked this hour because Ritu goes to the forest. Hurries back to his bed, shuts his eyes. Aroused already, under the long johns, but his hands composed, indifferent, on the blue Everest blankets. The linden laid beside him, a weapon. Hard with hard women. Fay was water, soft water. Lathered easily, found her level, went quiet before coming to the boil. This one is rock; ice will crack it.

The stair is cumbrous thunder: soldiers break step on a bridge.

Quickly: seedpods. Castanets, canoes, winged shields. Jacaranda oysters that spill out soap flakes. No, not that way. Burrs, prickles, kernels of diseased corn with a white cloud near the point, like a decayed tooth. Cashew seeds, gross, malformed foetuses.

'*Morgen, Herr Jed.*' If he studied in Germany.

'Good morning, Miss . . . Planke?'

'No, he was on my mother's side. Vogel is our surname.'

'I see.'

Silence. Inge breathes the changed air. Not the Jed she saw yesterday.

'This cold. You like it?'

'It's there.'

'Me, I like it.' Her eyes sweep the table, the room. Not there. 'You must get bored up here.'

'One's company, two's a crowd.'

'But the view is always' – she slopes a hand – 'down.'

'You get used to the foreshortening.'

'I saw you watching me from your seat just now.'

Jed is put out. 'I watch the world.'

What's his game, the old geezer?

'The book, you found it?'

'It's a big library.'

'And?'

'And there have been white ants this year. Some books the nuns threw out without consulting me.'

Inge is distressed. She looks for a chair, but Jed has seen to that. When Ritu left he dragged the only chair into the bathroom and bolted the door on it.

'The junk men have been circling like vultures,' he says, closing his eyes. 'But that's all right. They buy back books they sold me when they were young men. That's how your uncle's poems came to me. Do sit.'

He taps the foot of the bed with his cane.

She won't. Walks around the room instead, halts in front of the moon lily.

'Your work?'

He doesn't hear unless you face him, she remembers, so turns and points. 'Your work?'

'Long ago.'

'It's good. What is the mask?'

'A yeti. The death mask of the Abominable Snowman.'

'You found a yeti?'

'He found me.'

Inge turns on a boot heel, her eyebrows arched enquiringly. No ring in her nose. 'Yes?'

'I tracked him for years. Photographed his footprints in the snow. Even tried to shoot him once, but the gun misfired. I still have the bullet that was meant for him. To cull him for science. I bought enough yeti fur to line a great coat but it always turned out to be rhesus chin hair. And then, when I stopped looking, he turned up.'

Jed's eyes are on the ceiling. Inge sits.

'I was collecting at the snowline one year. My last year up there. On the way down I saw a geranium which the hill people use to treat rheumy pains. It was the middle of the monsoon and my joints were on fire. I dug up all the roots I could find – except two clumps, you leave two – and made handkerchief panniers to carry them. My haversack was packed with seeds. On the way back up the gully I slipped and fell. I must have slid forty feet before I hit a rock and passed out. I remember thinking as I fell, They'll see the hat. I wore a white astrakhan collecting. It was late evening. If I hadn't stopped for the ratijari I could have made it back to camp.

'When I came to it was night.' Jed shuts his eyes, sees again the black litter of gully sky, bright with stars. A small back-sloping moon. 'I couldn't move. I should have been cold but I wasn't. My stomach had risen grotesquely: somebody had heaped juniper branches on me. Crushed the leaves nearest my nose so my head spun. Slipped a pellet of spruce gum under my tongue. Wads of grass, saxifrage, under my head. No pain, except a crick in the neck because my haversack was still on. My hat was beside me on the ground.

'There was a cave, a kind of cleft in the wall of the gully. He was sitting there on a rock. Staring.

'Not at me, at the opposite wall of the gully. He may have been dozing, because when I stirred he was on his feet and away. I heard little showers of stones where he ran. Then nothing, just the wind in the gully.

'In the morning I woke to his breath. Sour berry breath, sad wrinkled eyes, two inches away. Looking to see if I was breathing. Red hair. Not quite your red, but not brown. Not rhesus chin hair. He sprang back as I opened my eyes. One sharp breath – *Hifffff!* – and he was gone. I never saw him again.

'They found me, but not by the hat. We had to look for that. It was in the cave. My ratijari was scattered at the foot of the gully where the gully opened onto nothing. A free fall.

'The rock had stopped me. It may have stopped him when he first found the cave. But the astrakhan I can't explain. Sometimes I see him in it, a sad caricature at the mouth of the cave. Or maybe the wind blew it there.'

Jed lies there, his eyes roaming the corrugated iron roof. Rain and damp have left stains there, white incrustations whose shapes have hardened in his mind: the pig, the fox, his father in profile reading the newspaper, spectacles on his nose.

What was he after? There's a woman on his bed, but all he wants is to capture a single sound: that inrush of air between bared teeth. Not vowel, not consonant; a bare fricative, wind in a crevice, rough sibilance of terror and discovery.

Inge is rapt. She missed some words, but caught the gist, was on the mountain with him, under juniper. Sits with one hand in her lap, one on the blue blanket. Away from the feet. Old men's feet she cannot bear. His are covered, one foot lower than the other. Brij has told her about that foot, the expedition.

A mummy, she keeps thinking. The one in the museum at home with the toes gone. She's heard of the mummied saint in Goa whose toe a woman bit off. Can't understand that frenzy, but wants to. Then remembers something.

'But the mask?'

Jed is sucking in air, hissing like a pressure cooker. Signs Inge can't read. In a little while he'll swing out with his stick at the Philistines. And rage at Death, wrestle him to the ground, savour his holds, taunt him, toss him. Then sit there justifying the ways of Jed to man. Feeling for the linden now, his face contorted. *Slay* them!

Inge jumps to her feet, stands back, dithering. But somebody is coming up the stair who knows the symptoms.

Ritu, back from her forest walk. She takes the stick away, nodding at the visitor, pats Jed's cheek, rubs his temples, grips the bridge of his nose. He loves that. Right on the saddle, oh, *yes*. A pinch of that's worth a box of tranquillizers. She feels the head sink down into its pillow, the neck unlock, the shoulders flatten. Rummages with the other hand in the fish for the clothes peg that will take the place of finger and thumb. Lined with cotton wool. Pegs him down.

Jed stilled.

Inge has been watching from the foot of the bed.

'Is he often like this?'

'Worse sometimes.'

'He was telling me about the yeti.' Inge nods at the mask. 'And then he just . . .'

Ritu feels a stab of jealousy. The stories are hers, he saves them for her. What's he doing sharing them with this outsider? Who's already stolen Brij. From him.

'Don't believe his stories.'

Didn't someone say that to her, in the same tone? *Cecelia!* Nettled. Suddenly Ritu sees the Superior in a new light. And herself. Is history repeating itself? Has it always been this way with Jed? Jed's women. She looks at him lying there, eyes shut, mouth half open. Laughing. Must be.

'He was a good painter,' Inge says. Back under the moon lily, her saffron crest tilted back.

Ritu looks across at her, still bitter. This body that she's seen naked in the lotus pose, and for some fraction of a second desired. And would like now to erase. She swallows the gall.

'Yes.'

Brij goes out to buy some tripe.

Sortilege by entrails is simpler this way. He's never been to a butcher's before; his mother will not allow meat in her kitchen. His father eats meat on the sly, and his brother will go to Muslim eateries. Brij goes everywhere, eats everything. But he's never ventured down the lane where the buffalo butchers are.

There's a fodder wheel at the head of the lane, its double blade slicing through bunched stalks of feed. The sound has always fascinated Brij, its steely succulence, one cut hardly done when the next blade falls. A shower of green, the rising heap of fodder by the roadside, a storeroom overflowing with fresh green feed. Then a gateway, a brick lane, and immediately the butcher's.

Carcasses hang from meat hooks, flayed horrors, hulks of rubied flesh. The bits and pieces down below. A thread of white tissue hanging off a bone. No fly screens on the poorer shops. Even in winter the smell is strong. Piles of offal steam on the floor, tangles of yellow tubes, violet membranes, a honeycombed sheet of sponge. Stripped knuckles, horns, hooves. On a slab, two kidneys with leaves of fat. A fissured brain. In one doorway a buffalo lies expiring. The drain runs red with blood.

'Come, sir!'

'Here!'

Brij hears the calls but his head is spinning. His hand goes to his pocket, pulls out a handkerchief, puts it to his mouth. His feet are scrabbling, tripping on the upedged bricks, carrying him away from this place.

The butchers don't smile at this apparition of a muscleman with a handkerchief. One man hawks, spits, feels demeaned; most simply flap at the slow winter flies and wonder how the dandy strayed among them.

Back on the main road Brij pulls himself together. Swallows the waterbrash, wipes his eyes. Stares at the fodder wheel and imagines his fingers drawn in there. Recalls hearing of a woman scalped when her hair was caught in the cogs. Breaks away and hurries down the street.

In the middle of the road he sees a severed buffalo head. It can't be; not out here, surely. Crossing to the median strip he finds it's a dented tar barrel.

'The Romans built roads, the Chinese built a wall. We build tombs. Temples and tombs.'

Jed is expansive today. Would be barmy, but Ritu checked the slide in time. The chair is still shut away. Inge sits on the bed.

'Only now do I see why my father burnt his papers. Letters, memos, everything. They were finished, done with. I saved every scrap of mine, and it's all empty talk. Boxes of it; a paper cenotaph.'

'You mean why am I bothering with a monument?'

'A tablet would do.'

'What should I do, then?'

'Forget it. Live. Love.'

'But I do.'

'Do you? Every minute of the day? We have so little time.'

Her look says, 'You've had plenty.'

'I didn't waste my time. That's the only sin, waste. Have you ever noticed how obituary photographs say *Dead*? Wasted. I used to be an obituarist, so I'm on your side actually, and Dixit's. I framed lives, turned life into art.'

Inge looks down, crosses her boots.

'You know,' Jed smiles, a shift of gear, 'I once designed

another sort of cenotaph. I sent an outline of my organ to a lover. In ink, on regular letter paper, amongst the other pages. She never mentioned it. God knows what she took it for. An express train? A dolphin?'

Inge twists her thin lips. Jed shifts under the blankets.

'It may never have got there; she may be dead. But I'd like to send a reminder half a century on. Would you help me?'

'I'd like to see the poems of my uncle.'

'You can. They're here.'

'Where?'

Jed shifts again. 'Here.'

Inge looks hard at him. Well, they could be. She reaches under the blanket.

They aren't. Jed's dolphin is.

She jumps up, whips off his blankets, all of them, and flings them across the room. Then storms down the fire escape.

Jed lies there uncovered, wet, trembling. His last conquest, and the taste in his mouth is of bile.

Bunny sits in the annexe, sipping rum and watching Thapa watch somebody.

The man is collecting firewood for the Lohri bonfire tomorrow night. He has taken the dead wood from the lychee grove and the leaf litter from the bamboos. Now he's tackling a large branch that has hung all year from the silk-cotton tree down to the ground. With every stroke Thapa looks across at the garage door, as if he'd like to deaden the sound of the hatchet. The babblers in the grapefruit tree keep up a shrill clamour.

A cockscomb flashes in the garage door, orange in the white winter sunlight.

The foreign woman. She bends to fossick in a toolbox left open on the garage floor. She was hardly gone ten minutes, so didn't lock it away.

Thapa has stopped his hacking and shrivelled into his khakies like a great horned owl.

Bunny puts down his rum glass, leans forward. This is the woman who is to inherit Everest. And knows it from the way she goes about hunting for whatever it is. The Packard could be her car, from the way she shuts the boot. She has the key.

But can't find whatever it is. Curses under her breath and sits down on the running board, where he and Major Bakshi still drink.

Where she drinks, too, apparently, going by the way her hand comes up with a bottle of Johnnie Walker. She swigs it neat. Bunny has never seen anyone drink Black Label before. Just the other day he found an unfinished bottle among the local empties and wondered how it got there. Even Red Label is for nobs. Major Bakshi drinks Kerala Scout when his half-price quota from the Army canteen runs out. Bunny drinks hooch. It's not fair.

Brij is in deeper than he cares to be, now.

Last night the he-goat; next she'll want a buffalo. Blood on his jacket, too.

He winces at the memory of it. The great black beast clambering off his perch, curious, even eager, as they led him away. Stumbling along in the dark to the far end of the cemetery, pulling ahead, rolling those satirical yellow eyes. Waiting, looking up at the last moment, as if he had something to confide, then seeing the raised arm and understanding what it signified. Disappointed in his fellow conspirators. Humans after all.

The chowkidar's family are aghast. Their loan sire, friend and pet, the cemetery mascot, found in two pieces. They sit on their string cots, stunned; the children snivel. The gamblers leave their cards on Isola Rattray's tomb and saunter across in a group to the paupers' corner to have a look. Here is stronger mischief than the knave's.

Balanced on the last of the standing tombs is the goat's massive black head, its horns curved up like funerary ornaments. Black clotted blood where the trunk was hewn away. Contempt lodged too deep in the eyes for death to glaze over.

The body is some ten feet away, another mound among the pauper mounds. Its belly has been slit open. The viscera have slipped out of the cavity but not been touched, as if some ritual were interrupted. They end abruptly, like a glacier.

On the tombstone are the imprints of two hands, in blood. They are both left hands, but one is smaller than the other.

The goongi puts one foot on the stair.

She's never dared to before: it's a twisting snake that could swallow you up. The foot is albino pink, cracked all around the sole, the toes thrawn, nails blue.

Cold. She jerks the foot away. But the pot is heavy and she must take it up to Jed. Summoned by God.

Jed, who was on his back an eternity, trembling, uncovered, the wet patch stiffening. His eyes shut tight, the dark stained with shapes, dots, shadows of possibility.

Till, out of nowhere, an idea. Jed grinning into the void. This is how God felt in the beginning.

'Show her,' he decided. 'Show her some pictures. Theatrical enough herself. Got up like a bloody dominatrix!'

Got up shivering, put on dressing gown and scarf, went out onto the roof, crossed to the back. The goongi was at her anthill, mumbling into the middle air, her head turned studiously away from the red-crested man-woman hammering like a demon today. Jed caught her eye.

No ants, she signalled.

Bugger your ants – come here!

Who, *me*?

Yes, you.

Where? Her eyes widening as she ran her half-toppling ape-run. Chubby pink ape.

That side, down below.

Here?

Yes, I want one of those.

These? The row of periwinkle pots. The ones he pissed in.

Yes, those. One.

Thapa builds the Lohri bonfire.

It's a job he likes, involving patience, selection, balance. Usually he's cutting down; here he's building. A fire tower, complete with staircase and balcony. It's a comforting ritual; there is solace in the round of the year. He builds it on the same spot each year; the grass is thinner there as a result, but to build it somewhere else would offend his sense of harmony, a harmony of cycles, not straight lines. He favours repetition, routine, army habits dying hard. He keeps a tidy garden, a neat garage. His tools are clean and sharp; he lops off branches that stick out. Now he sits whittling away imperfections in the wood, painstakingly dressing logs that will be ash by morning.

Cecelia comes up, tight-lipped. She doesn't quite approve of Lohri, the leaping pagan shadows it casts on Everest.

'Thapa.'

The man rises, preoccupied, a stake in one hand, a hatchet in the other.

'I need a hammer,' Cecelia begins, not going straight to the point. 'There's a nail in the office chair that wants knocking in. I can do the job myself if you're busy. Don't go now. Just leave it on the telephone table. Tell me, do we really need a bonfire this year? It might rain.'

'It's what *brings* the winter rain,' Thapa answers, and goes on whittling. What's it to her? She has her Christmas. When he gets, unfailingly, a muffler. And nowadays Diwali has become a rich man's festival. Lohri is for nightwatchmen, gardeners, peasants, men of the soil. Besides, it's when Thapa comes into his own: he's the master of ceremonies, fire-bringer, fire-quencher. Rainmaker wouldn't be far off the mark.

'Well, don't make it too big. We could use the wood in the salamander.'

Thapa nods. He likes this grave correct woman, has sometimes dreamed of her round orderly breasts. In a way she's taken the place of Major Bakshi, whose flesh he once encountered, and whose moving wreckage he observes with a mixture of censure and regret. The more the major drinks the less his former batman is inclined to. Since the corn crop fiasco Thapa has sworn off liquor altogether.

'Not too big,' he promises.

Bunny is waiting for Cecelia.

Sitting at her desk, in fact, the chair pushed back so he can lean against the wall. Half of him is watching, wondering where the other half has found the courage. But Bunny must speak the lines he's been rehearsing ever since Jed's revelation about the future of Everest. His brain is exploding, words, pictures pouring out. Yes, that's him talking – he recognizes the voice – but Cecelia isn't here yet.

How much can one woman pray? He steps into the hall to check. It's late evening; the chapel is empty.

Someone is standing in the shadows at the foot of the stair, looking at him. Bunny frowns at the spectre. Tall, moon-faced, implacable.

Bunny breaks into a sweat. Spins round and shuts the office door behind him, trembling. The timid half of him has absorbed that long malevolent stare and cowers, aware that he needs help. But Bunny's hand is already looking for a weapon, picking up ink bottles, rejecting them, brushing aside blotters, wicker trays, rulers. A paperknife falls to the floor. Sandalwood. He kicks it away, losing his balance. A bottle smashes on the tiled fringe, the last of the Black Label he brought with him, for support. Nothing heavy on Cecelia's desk except for the brass table lamp. He tries it for weight. The shade is awkward, but the base is wide, heavy. He grips it at the neck, wrenches the lead from the wall and turns to defend himself as the light goes out. The door swings open.

Cecelia. Standing there, a hammer in her hand.

Her cold eyes focusing.

She recognizes him, then takes in the chaos. Screams and runs into the refectory.

'Thapa!' she shouts. 'Thapa!'

Neha comes running out of the kitchen, half an eggshell in each hand.

'Bunny's gone mad,' Cecelia breathes, pushing her back into the kitchen and slamming the door. Then she calls again through the window, '*Thapa!*'

Neha unbolts the service door and they hurry out into the night.

But Bunny isn't following. He's in the hall, tackling the spectre. Which hasn't moved, except below, where the legs would be. A leaden rocking there, mechanical, relentless. Bunny swings the lamp. Glass, shattering. Time spilling out, ending on the floor. The next blow dislocates, nicks Bunny's wrist. Now the mechanism jangles to a halt, chaos returning to the works with every blow. The rods clang and tremble: Bunny is striking six. Seven on the moon-face, eight on the hands. The grandfather clock has told its last hour.

Bunny turns, trips but keeps his feet, the hall revolving around him, the marble stair rearing up with Tsering's head dangling at the landing. He tosses the weapon back at the office door, meaning to return Cecelia's lamp. But he's all turned around and lofts it into the chapel instead. Then runs at a squat figure that's blocking the front door and knocks the wind out of Perpetua. In the portico he stands for ever – time suddenly expanding to infinity – considering whether to turn left or right. Right is safety, the annexe, his instincts tell him, but the garage is that way, too, and danger. The Packard, something about the Packard, and then there's that moon-faced Gurkha. He staggers off to the left, his feet ploughing up the gravel of the drive. That's the gate ahead, these are Cecelia's rose bushes that are raking his legs. He falls among the thorns, gets up, but pushes on through the beds. He must bite off one of those splendid blooms, must make the wall, smother himself in Thapa's dahlias, there's one as big as the rising sun, take it home, and the sweet peas, black, white and grey, only those can help him, take them all, the whole row, the string, too, that might come in handy, and why not a handful of grass, the dew will save you, take as much of it as you can, lick it off the blades of grass, spit out the dirt, undo these buttons, hooks in the flesh, wrap yourself in the blue sheet of stars, pillow your head on this brick, never mind.

A yellow beam, lengthening, contracting, swivelling in the dark.

Thapa finds him by torchlight, swathed in his sweet peas. Drags him, roughly now, to the annexe. Puts him to bed, watched by Cecelia.

All next morning Bunny sleeps. In the afternoon he slopes off, leaving Everest behind. He'll never touch Black Label again.

Nine o'clock.
Thapa puts a match to the serrated edge of a newspaper egg at the heart of the woodpile. The flame passes shyly to the other eggs nestled there, then swarms through the kindling. It's away. Thapa steps back to admire his engineering. The splintered bits from the old toilet seat will catch next, then the jujube brambles, and then the inner scaffolding of dead bamboo with its staircase of petioles. Thapa smiles and goes to fetch the puffed rice.

By half-past nine the silk-cotton branch is crackling and the eucalyptus logs have begun to spurt.

Major Bakshi is sober tonight. As Thapa's sometime officer he is obliged to preside, but he likes the festival anyway. Lohri awakens childhood memories from Patiala; his eyes are soft with them already. Later he can drink a sentimental toast to those days, but for now there are the guests. Chief among them, Mrs Puri, in a white sari whose crisp lines define but cannot contain her; nor will her shawl. Robed with flesh she greets the major with a special smile. Since the death of Miss Chatterjee he's been especially attentive, and she likes a military man. Five fat children of school-going age cluster around her, made in her image; the skinny sixth wedges himself between her thighs. Last year a falling log showered sparks on him. Her children were a surprise at first; they always are. Their clothes hang on another, lower, line.

From the cemetery lane, rolling his parrot walk, comes O. P. Dixit, red-sweatered and olive-jacketed, in trousers that show the whole length of his nylon socks. Trotting at his heels with loyal disregard is his cat, which he has never bothered to name. His hands, from enforced idleness or some other infirmity, have taken on a life of their own, twitching and jumping in a manner unlikely to win him the tombstone contract he still covets. He flops into a moulded plastic chair and sits there glowering. Now and then he lifts murderous eyes above the flames to see if she is there.

She is, but in the shadows.

Inge sits on her pile of masonry by the pipal tree, watching the bonfire from a distance. She is waiting for Brij, who should have been here half an hour ago. Indian Standard Time, she curls a lip. He taught her that gibe. She has come by the main gate this evening, doesn't use the cemetery short-cut after dark. She carries the garage key, but won't be needing her hammer and chisel any more. Today she finished the inscription on the tablet, with the last word in gothic letters: *Dichter*.

Tonight she wants a different set of tools.

She should be pleased: the monument is complete and simply wants assembling on the grave. Instead she feels empty, emptied of the work which filled her mornings and afternoons. Already that time has begun to stretch away into nostalgia, an emotion she detests but can entertain. Swamp fever. And there is still the question: who, what, was Otto Planke, poet? A ghost her mother lived with, his photo on the radiogram. She's never proved him, fleshed him out, and nothing in the inscription convinces. So, what's she left with? A heap of red sandstone, lighter than air: ghost tomb for a ghost poet. Nothing of the man, Otto Planke.

Bone, hair, a tooth would anchor it. A skull is solid.

The he-goat was real enough, fine hot blood. Perfectly weighted, the kukri, good grip to the hilt.

Thapa comes over with a basin of puffed rice. He smiles conciliation.

To eat? She gestures.

No, to throw into the fire.

She takes a handful, getting up, and accompanies him out of the shadows. The Puri children are eating and throwing rice by turns. She tosses her handful, watching the grains flare up.

'Randi!' Mrs Puri hisses behind her. 'Wa-hore.' And smiles as she passes a cup of cardamom tea. Inge finds a seat. She understands the look but not the words.

Major Bakshi returns with a bowl of peanuts. He's beginning to hate the sickly child. The other children race around the fire, cracking peanuts with their teeth, tormenting Dixit's cat with firebrands; this one burrows deeper between those generous thighs.

'Peanuts,' he offers Inge. 'At least one you must have. It's the custom. These are old traditions – the fire, the nuts, the rice – part of Indian culture.' When the major speaks of culture his eyes grow soft as the dross of the present falls away. It is something fixed, outside time. He seems inclined to elaborate for the German girl, but catches a glint off Mrs Puri's eye which could cut glass. So widens his ambit and says, taking her in, 'We are all Aryans here.'

Inge looks at him and looks away. Is he joking? She feels the air harden around her and looks again for Brij.

Presently Cecelia leads the nuns out of the chapel to the bonfire. To stay away would be ill-mannered; better a measured participation. She congratulates Thapa on his work, lets the younger nuns throw rice into the flames. Neha has lost her little frown; her black eyes shine as she stares into the fire. Outnumbered, says Major Bakshi's Aryan glance at Inge. Tribals, he means, but it's lost on her. Shortly Tsering and the goongi appear, wheeling the twins in old Everest bath chairs. Perpetua does a circuit, greeting everyone except Mrs Puri, who resolves to turn on her suction pump the minute she gets home. The goongi glares at Mrs Puri, too; she resents her hold on the major, another candidate for bridegroom in her fitful dreams.

Halva?' Ritu offers Inge, who's still glancing around for Brij.

Inge takes the little stainless-steel dish. Raisins and nuts in a semolina pudding. Rich, sweet.

'Lohri sows the seeds of spring,' Major Bakshi is explaining to Miss Sampson as he pulls up a chair for her, 'in the heart of winter.' Miss Sampson has come down on the Latvian's arm, looking uncommonly fit and full. It's the firelight and the winter clothing: shawls over cardigans over sweaters; somewhere at the centre of the swaddling moves the drooping flesh of ninety-one winters.

'In Vedic culture,' the major goes on, 'fire was sacred. Some sacrifice had to be made to it.'

'I know that, Major Bakshi. I was born and bred here. And Quetta is *much* colder than this, by the way, so I know a thing or two about fire.' India was never divided in Miss Sampson's mind. 'I spent a whole night trapped under rubble in the great earthquake. And that was the middle of winter. No bijli for a week after. It's at times like that you appreciate it. Townspeople take it for granted, but Nehru didn't. Rural Electrification,' – Miss Sampson thumps her chair – 'that was his watchword. Good fire, Thapa!'

Thapa bows. Tonight he will drink.

Miss Sampson glances at the German woman behind her. English on her father's side, she can't help an atavistic spasm. Her father died in the Great War. The Latvian sailor, seventy next year, bears a more recent grudge.

Inge has no ally, has never felt such a weight of unspoken hostility press down on her. Where can Brij be? He hates the cold, but a little spadework will warm him up. They won't be disturbed. Winter midnights, he says, nightwatchmen sleep.

And where is Jed?

A loud bang, a shower of firecracker sparks, and there he is against the smoking sky. Sure-footed as a chamois once, now leaning on the parapet, firefly lights in his shot-silk dressing gown, the dish a magus turban. A wind up there, freshening, so his beard lifts, the gown ripples, the tower of pomegranate sparks leans. Jed knows how to steal a show, has left little to the gathering clouds. He spreads his arms in malediction and disappears. He will not be coming down.

Cecelia, finding an opening, sniffs and rises, wishes all a good night. The nuns follow her back to the chapel for a cleansing round of beads. 'Or was it the middle of summer?' Miss Sampson wonders, thinking back to the earthquake as she and the Latvian leave. The twins are wheeled away, lolling over the arms of the bath chairs like broken dolls. At length Mrs Puri gathers up her brood and Major Bakshi escorts them home. The fire is burning down. Thapa, who has kept a small pile of firewood in reserve, now tosses irregular shapes onto the flames. Then he goes to fetch a pitcher; he and Dixit plan to drink.

Dixit's jumpy hands snatch a pouch from his padded person; they could be the hands of someone behind him, a pickpocket or a conjuror, but there's nobody left. Just Inge, staring at the embers, and Dixit fishing out a piece of betel-nut. His jaws have been working all evening; his mouth is stained red. Dracula, Inge is thinking idly; she knows him from his forays into the cemetery. Brij has pointed him out: the DIXIT of the tablets. Who abruptly breaks the silence.

'Twenty thousand rupees,' he accuses her, out of the side of his mouth. The venom bubbles up through hoarded betel juice. Dixit can go hours without spitting. *'Twenty thousand!'* A screech the second time, shredding on ruined teeth.

Inge looks up. He's staring evilly at her under the white thickets of his eyebrows. The figure he quotes matches a total she scribbled just this morning. Now the work's done. Twenty thousand rupees, give or take a hundred. So Baingan coolie has been boasting.

'I charge ten,' Dixit says. He would have saved her ten. 'Materials five, me five. Ten thousand. *In toto.'* His forehand slashes a line in the air; it could cut a throat.

At last he spits into the revived fire, and finds room in his mouth for repetition.

'Ten thousand rupees you throw away.' It's a staggering sum for an old man. Who's lost five, by his reckoning. His due.

Inge watches the ball of spittle hop as it shrivels, crimson on gold on ash. Dixit's nest egg gone up in smoke. She spent ten, she knows. The second ten was the market's doing, not Baingan coolie's or anybody else's. Or else everybody's. The rupee fell, the Deutschmark jumped. Where do you pin the blame? Her grandfather was ruined when the Führer pegged the mark artificially high. Good for Germany, bad for him. Money flowed back from conquered Europe – just when he'd been persuaded to speculate on Dutch guilders. Serve him right, she always thought, or learnt to think. Now she doesn't know. Currency flows are a mystery to her, how could she ever hope to explain them to this old man who knows only notes and coins? The mark is a whole people's will. The rupee is a whole nation's fate, not one man's. And he sees just his notes, disappearing.

She spreads her hands and shrugs.

Thapa returns with the pitcher and glasses, sets the tray down on the table. Stoops to push the unburnt ends of logs into the fire's empty centre. Dixit stirs the liquid, pours shakily, spilling a little. Inge casts a last glance around for Brij and gets up to go.

'Try some,' Thapa gestures. He's brought three glasses.

She turns.

Why not? What the hell.

Midday. Rain spots on the window pane.

Inspector Bisht, tall, sallow, neat, morose, would like to ask a few questions. He sits in the parlour with Cecelia, who has never looked so distressed. Neha is trembling as she sets the tea tray down on the latest *Tablet*. There is no plate of coconut biscuits.

The inspector waits till she's gone and asks, 'Did anyone at Everest harbour a grudge against the foreigner lady?'

Cecelia considers, her upper lip resting on the tips of her folded hands. None of her nuns, of course. None of them ever met her, she points out, except the one on duty with Jed. They might greet her in passing, but that was all.

She herself only spoke to Inge once, on the first day.

'So who *did* she meet?'

'Well, Mr Jed. He's secretary of the cemetery. She had to get his permission to put up a monument on her uncle's grave.'

'Could Mr Jed have had a motive?'

Cecelia allows herself a smile. 'Mr Jed is ninety. And he never comes downstairs.'

'And the nun on duty with him?'

'Impossible.'

'The other inmates?'

Cecelia runs through them: Miss Sampson, Major Bakshi, the Latvian, the goongi. Absurd, unlikely, unlikely, absurd.

The inspector sighs and puts down his cup. 'Sometimes,' he says, in the table fan drone that Mrs Bisht has learnt to endure, 'people take bhang at Lohri. They make a milkshake with some cannabis in it. Was there any drinking last night?'

Cecelia frowns. 'Not in my presence.'

'But perhaps away from your presence, there was?'

'You should talk to Major Bakshi. He knows I don't allow alcohol and all here.'

'How was the festival celebrated here?'

'There was a bonfire, some guests – neighbours.'

'Everybody at Everest was present?'

'I think so. Except Mr Jed.'

'Is there anybody you haven't mentioned?'

'Thapa, of course. He's our chowkidar and gardener. The bonfire is his business.'

'The guests?'

'Mrs Puri and her family from next door. And Dixit, the old stonemason from the lane.'

'Was the foreigner lady known to them?'

'They may have been acquainted.'

'There is a Mr Puri?'

'No. There are several children.'

'The stonemason was alone?'

'Yes.'

'He works at Everest?'

'Dixit used to do the tombstones for the cemetery.'

'A Dixit!' Bisht raises slow eyebrows.

'Yes, he's a brahmin.'

'Did the foreigner lady come here often?'

'She worked here – in the compound. She was making a tombstone for her uncle's grave.'

'She was a sculptor?'

'She was a good sculptor. The monument is still here, at the back.'

'She worked alone?'

Cecelia hesitates for the first time. She has just realized that one regular visitor was missing last night. A face she normally looks out for.

'No. She had a friend.' Cecelia's speech slows down, grows guarded as certain implications crowd in on her.

Bisht has been in the CID long enough to detect subtler hesitations.

'Who was it?'

'A young man who helped her get the stone and all. He lives behind Everest.'

'Oh, that loafer from the National Auto Works. We've picked him up already.'

Cecelia's face expresses incredulity.

'*Brij!*'

'Oh, Mr Brij is not guilty in this case. No, no. He has the perfect alibi.' The inspector produces a scented handkerchief and coughs delicately into it. 'You see, Mr Brij was not at the Lohri celebrations last night because he was already in custody.'

Brij walks out of the Kotwali cell.

Rubbing his cheeks. He looks scruffy, wants a bath, a shave. Also he's hungry. His friends go straight to the sweet-shop across the road and eat plates of reheated samosas. They wear the slight bravado of political detainees. Brij goes straight home, where his father is waiting.

The thrashing goes on and on. *Shame-bringer, layabout, terrorist.*

Brij submits. He got off lightly at the police station. In the end his mother intervenes, scolding in her own way.

But it's his brother who delivers the final blow. When Brij is bathed and changed, Raju comes and whispers in his ear.

'She's dead.'

Inge laid out on the slab. Cold, clean, pointless. A warrior, from the slash that all but severed her right thumb.

Inspector Bisht looks at his watch.

'Can you show me the garage?'

Cecelia is glad to get up, be doing. She leads the inspector through the verandah door to the portico and along the front of Everest. He notes her rose beds with approval: the edges are nicely done. But someone has barged through a whole row recklessly. Bisht shudders as he thinks of the thorns, a dahlia man himself. His double yellow won second prize at the YWCA show last year.

They turn the corner on gravel and Bisht's scented hand-kerchief appears as they step around the cesspit with its scummy grey bubbles. The drive goes down the south side of

Everest. A row of periwinkle pots, the ones Jed pisses into when mad, brightens the drab wall with splashes of pink. A circle of rain-pitted earth shows where a pot has been removed.

'Your gardener lives on the premises?'

'Thapa's room is behind the garage there.'

'And this?' Pointing at Bunny's quarters.

'That's the Everest annexe.'

'Does anybody live there?'

Cecelia is relieved to say, 'Not now.'

They come to the garage, padlocked this morning by the police. The key is now with Bisht, and he opens the lock as if it were he who was showing Cecelia around. But allows her to help with the double doors. They stand a moment looking in at the car. A heightened vibrancy attends the place of death. The polished Packard, the chrome mudguard-mounted headlights, the very tools on the tool rack in the shadows beyond the car, wear a patina of inside knowledge. Not telling. Some enormity pinned on the air like still music. No matter how often he comes on such a scene Bisht can never shut out the thin high trilling in his ear. He's always dismayed to find himself turning loud.

'Who found the body?' he calls as he walks around the car once without touching anything. The brash voice bounces off the back wall where the tools are. A row of empty whisky bottles on the floor there.

Cecelia, no further than the door, is about to answer when a voice from behind her says, 'I found her.'

Major Bakshi has come up, freshly shaved, timid at the prospect of interrogation. His epic moustache, dyed with henna for Lohri, is no comfort; with his moist eyes and worried frown it gives him the look of an abject demon. The eyes are the malt brown of Kerala Scout, and bulge with a sincerity that Bisht, coming face to face with him on the driver's side, cannot doubt. Cecelia introduces the major.

'When did you find her?' Bisht begins.

Bakshi looks as if he'd like to lie but cannot. 'At half-past five this morning,' he says, looking hard at his watch.

'You are an early riser?'

Now Bakshi must lie. Mrs Puri cannot be compromised. 'Yes.'

'What brought you to the garage?'

'I was going for my morning walk when I noticed the garage doors were open.'

'An early walk, in winter.'

'Fairly early.' There are walkers on Canal Road by six.

'What did you do when you discovered the body?'

'I woke up my batman, Thapa.'

'The same Thapa?' Bisht turns to Cecelia.

Bakshi answers for her. 'The gardener and chowkidar. He was my batman, formerly. In service. His room is just here. When we found she was dead we woke up Sister Superior. She telephoned the police.'

'Did you touch the body?'

'Thapa felt for a pulse.'

The two men stare at the empty driver's seat, dark with Inge's blood. Cecelia remains by the garage door.

'You found no weapon?' Bisht asks, leaning into the car. The keys are in the ignition. He takes them, reluctantly, in his handkerchief.

'No. We didn't do a search. The police came in half an hour. We waited in the verandah.'

'Was the car door open or shut?'

'It was half open. She had one foot on the garage floor. The police took photographs.'

Bisht ignores the querulous note and tests the other doors.

All are locked. 'There was some drinking last night,' he says, kicking the tyres.

'When I left,' Major Bakshi raises one hand, 'there was just tea. Sister Neha brought the urn from the kitchen.'

'Who was the last to leave?'

'That you must ask Thapa. The bonfire is his baby. He's waiting outside.'

'These are your bottles?' Bisht waves towards the back of the garage.

'Some of them may be. Some of them were the lady's.'

'She used the garage?'

'She kept her tools here.'

'Her tools?'

'Her hammers and chisels and so on.'

Thapa is not outside, but in his room. Seated on his string bed with his face buried in his hands. He is trying to shake off the stupor which has returned to claim him now that the morning's activity is past. Also he's shivering, not from the cold. He has hung a weaver bird's nest at the door, trodden on a split thorn and sprinkled a line of flour across the threshold. It should be barley flour, to placate Masan, god of cemeteries, but he hasn't any.

Bisht stoops to enter the room. He is almost twice as tall as the gardener and chowkidar. Thapa springs to his feet, salutes.

'You are Thapa?'

'Sir.'

'You saw the foreigner lady's body in the car this morning?'

'Sir.'

'The major tells me you looked for a pulse.'

'There was none, sir. She was finished.'

'When did you last see her alive?'

'Last night, sir, about midnight. She had a drink with us, sir.'

'Who else was there?'

'Dixit, sir. The stonemason from the cemetery lane.'

'What did you drink?'

'Bhang, sir. Not much.'

'Did the lady know what she was drinking?'

'I don't know, sir.'

'You didn't tell her?'

'I did, but she may not have understood.'

'Those bottles in the garage, were they hers?'

'The foreign ones, sir. She drank there sometimes.'

'Where did you get the bhang?'

'It grows in the compound, sir. I picked some and made up a drink.' He indicates the floor where there's a mortar and pestle. Also on the floor, washed and upturned on a tray, are three glasses and a pitcher. A plastic basin with a few grains of puffed rice at the bottom sits in the corner among Thapa's cooking things.

'How much did she have?'

'One glass, sir.'

'Did she finish it?'

'Yes, sir.'

'And then?'

'She sat for a while – two, four minutes – and then said thank you and good night.' Thapa uses the English words.

'Which way did she go?'

'She went towards the pipal tree at the back wall. I think she was expecting somebody.'

'In the middle of the night?'

Thapa drops his head and says, 'It was not the first time.'

'She met people here?'

'There were some strange happenings, here and in the graveyard.'

'What happenings?'

'Somebody was practising sorcery. First they killed a mongoose and spread out its intestines, the way soothsayers do. Then they killed the cemetery goat. You can see the handprints on a gravestone still, in blood.'

'And she was involved?'

'I can't be sure, sir. But she went that way last night.'

'What's at the pipal tree?'

'She used to work under it. She was making a tombstone, sir. And there's a gap in the wall there.' Thapa points through the small barred window. 'The cemetery is on the other side.'

Bisht looks around the room. The iron roof slopes away from the door where he has been standing. One corner of it is black with soot. On a crude shelf in that corner are tins of provisions. Thapa's steel trunk is on the floor under the bed, his army roll number still painted on it. There is another shelf, lined with newspaper, which Thapa's toiletries share with assorted trinkets, among them a child's pink plastic doll. At the centre of the shelf, in an electroplated vase, are the remains of incense sticks. Behind it, leaning against the wall, are framed pictures of goddesses. There are other holy pictures pasted directly onto the wall above or hanging from nails, calendar gods, but in the centre, under a prominent nail, is a blank space.

'You are also a stonemason?'

'No, sir.'

'Aren't those chisels?' Bisht points to the row of iron totems on the window sill.

Thapa closes his eyes. He cannot believe he left those there. After taking care of everything, down to the rings left by the glasses on the running board.

'Sir.'

Bisht stands there a moment. 'Go and call Dixit,' he says abruptly, and turns on his heel, ducking under the lintel.

Cecelia and Major Bakshi are waiting by the garage door.

'Would you please lock the garage?' Bisht asks the major and becomes busy with a notepad. But waits to see it done. To Cecelia he says, 'Maybe I should see the rest of the compound?'

Cecelia walks him through the lychee grove towards the back wall. Bisht admires the various trees, mature specimens such as one doesn't come across in the newer suburb, where he lives, at the other end of town. The towering silk-cotton, a sombre jackfruit with one sundered fruit hanging like a green lamp, a magnificent tree of heaven, some fine teak, a little crowded together. An old frangipani with strange slashes on the outermost branches. Past the anthill they come to the monument, and stand in silence on the carpet of red stone chips, considering Inge's work. The component pieces have been assembled but not joined: the broken urn, the drapery, the fasces, the border panels of laurel wreaths, the top slab with Otto Planke's brief history. There are blood spots on the stone which will want analysis. Leaning up against the monument is a spade; another spade lies on the ground beside it, blood on the handle.

Spades? Bisht wonders. Cecelia, too, is mystified.

'See that nothing here is touched,' Bisht says and turns away towards the walled garden. 'And what is this?'

'This was Mrs Jed's retreat. She died many years ago. It was overgrown, but Thapa cleared it and Sister Ritu has restored the fountain. She uses it sometimes to botanize.' A word she learnt from Ritu, who prefers its amateur implications.

'Can we go in?'

Cecelia leads him through the arch and along the pillared gallery cabled with bare wistaria. They pause to take in the wall fountain with its apehead spout and empty basin. The pool beneath is full of wet eucalyptus leaves. At the end of the corridor is Ritu's workplace, once Fay's glory-hole.

A single window, the view split by a smooth grey eucalyptus trunk that would not have been there in Fay's time. To the right of the trunk the cemetery wall with the straddling pipal tree; to the left the stone pile where Inge worked. At the window is a wide sloped desk; whoever sits here sees without being seen. Pinned out directly onto the desktop is a piece of stretched cartridge paper with faint pencil lines on its surface. A vase sits on the level top edge where the inkwell would have been. It is empty. Bisht brings his long yellow nose to within an inch of the paper and still can't make it out. His hand gropes for and finds the latch of the hinged lid and lifts it by degrees so the light falls better on the paper. He is half expecting to see a sketch of Inge at work, but as the lines clarify he sees another ghost. It's a plant. The ghost of the plant that stood in the vase, of course, and one that looks oddly familiar. In fact, he's just seen it somewhere. Bisht lowers the desktop slowly as recognition dawns.

It's the pink periwinkle in the row of pots by the garage.

The inspector moves once around the room, taking in the contents. A leaf press. A box of watercolours, a jar of brushes, saucers, spoons of various sizes. A water goglet. A narrow shelf of bottles that haven't been touched for some time. He unscrews the caps and sniffs eucalyptus oil, a clear odourless liquid, probably glycerine, a perfume like violets, a small pot of balm.

Bisht leads the way out, pausing again by the fountain to admire the marble inlay.

'The nun who works here,' he says, stooping unnecessarily as he passes under the arch, 'can I talk to her?'

Cecelia has a way of suddenly narrowing her eyes. She

looks at her watch and says, 'She'll be at prayer, but if you stay for lunch you could talk to her afterwards. She has half an hour then, which she usually spends here.'

Bisht is unhappy about the lunch, about any lunch eaten away from Mrs Bisht's kitchen. He's meditating on an excuse when he sees an old man approaching from the gap in the back wall. Thapa is with him, so this will be Dixit.

'You are the stonemason?'

'I am the sculptor,' Dixit glares. 'And I didn't kill her.'

But I'm glad she's dead, incised in the air around him.

'No,' Bisht agrees, burying his toe in the soft ash at his feet. He wears Quo Vadis sandals that show his long finger-like toes. They are standing over the remains of last night's fire. The morning's light rain has pocked the surface of the ash without sinking in. So far Thapa's rainmaking skills have proven only indifferent.

'You may not have killed her,' Bisht says, and marvels at the transparency of the man's hatred, unmuddied by the errant silts of revenge. 'But you can help us find out who did.'

Dixit dips his head and goes on chewing his betel, a fleck of red on his white moustache.

'You could tell us, for example, where she sat.'

Dixit walks around the ashes like a trick parrot and stops, stamping a foot. 'She sat here.'

Thapa, who has joined the small group, looks doubtful. He would have said here, and coughs, crossing to where he thinks Inge's chair was.

'So she drank her glass of bhang sitting there. And then?'

'And then she left.'

'Straight away?'

'More or less.'

'Which way did she go?'

'That way.' Dixit points towards the garage.

Now Thapa is plainly agitated, but says nothing. He takes a few steps towards the monument, as if retracing Inge's true route. Bisht turns his back on the man, addressing Dixit.

'And you never saw her again?'

'No.'

Bisht turns to Thapa. 'Can you show me the handprints in the graveyard?'

Thapa leads the way through the gap in the wall to the far end of the cemetery. Bisht, Cecelia and the major follow; Dixit goes home, followed at a distance by his stiffly trotting cat, whose upright tail reveals a dark star at the sphincter. The small group make their way across the humped ground of the pauper section and gather round the last of the headstones. There's a smear of blood at the top of the stone where the goat's head was, and spidery trickles where the blood ran down. Underneath are the two handprints. Cecelia stares in horror; the major twists his moustache. Thapa stands back with an air of exoneration. Bisht bends and lays his hand over the smaller print, taking a rough measurement, and appears satisfied. Then he turns and leads the way back, looking distressed, as if he would like urgently to wash.

B isht nibbles at a green chilli.

He glances around the dining room. Rice tastes different, poorer, off a spoon; it was meant to be caressed. Miss Sampson, at the next table, has introduced a fork into the spooning operation, and the Latvian sailor uses chopsticks.

The nuns are in the refectory at their own table, eating in silence. Bisht can't tell whether this is the rule or the result of the morning's discovery.

'Do you know, Inspector?' Miss Sampson says in a stage whisper that says, I know death is serious, but, 'when Nehru was in jail here he started a little garden?'

Bisht was not aware that Nehru had spent time in Drummondganj jail. He is not aware of Nehru's views on rural electrification either, Miss Sampson can see, and means to fill the gap.

'Imagine! The hand that signed the instruments of independence grubbing for radishes behind that wall.'

She points through the window and Bisht looks at the jail wall with new eyes.

'Not that that's all he planted. Oh, no. The first thing he put down was a rose bush. "Whenever I tended it," he said to me, "I thought of you."' Miss Sampson leans towards the inspector with a smile that says, Don't get up, and mimes shaking his hand. 'Rose Sampson, how do you do?'

Bisht pushes his chair back a little and bows, leaning right over his plate. 'Inspector Bisht,' he mumbles.

Miss Sampson presses on. 'He used to say, "My dear, you mustn't shake this wicked hand, and you mustn't break this fickle heart."'

Bisht finds his cue and smiles the smile that says, Well, this is very pleasant, but. Pressing his handkerchief to his lips, he rises, bows once more to Miss Sampson, and slips out into the hall. He's got no sense out of the Latvian, and Miss Sampson's stories aren't going to pay the rent. Something tells him the case is slipping away.

He'd like to look again at the pink periwinkle, so he ducks out through the portico and around to the garage end of the house. He's pacing along the row of concrete planters when he stops. On the gravel walk is a cake of green soap. He picks it up and sniffs it. Neem. And new. But there are toothmarks in it: a neat semicircular bite. He hears footsteps approaching around the corner and slips it into his pocket. It's Cecelia, and with her the nun who paints.

Immediately he's disappointed. A little bird-like creature. Not frail, but hardly the build for moving concrete planters.

'You knew the foreigner?' he says to her.

'I met her once on the roof.'

'On the roof?'

'Sister Ritu looks after Mr Jed,' Cecelia explains. 'His room is on the roof.'

'And you use the room near the fountain?'

'I work there sometimes.'

'You are a botanist, I understand?'

'I studied botany. Now I botanize a little.'

'You were drawing, I think, one of these?' Bisht's long fingers caress a periwinkle. Tsering, watching from the window above, notices the tawny nails.

'Yes.'

'What is it?'

'The pink periwinkle.'

'There are other kinds?'

'A few. There's a blue, and maybe a white.'

'Does the pink have any special properties?'

'It has medicinal uses. It's used in treating cancer, but it can cause hallucinations. The roots are poisonous, and the leaves. The butterflies love it.'

'And you picked a stem for your painting. From this very pot perhaps.'

'No, from the one upstairs.'

'There are more?'

'There's one on the roof.'

'Could we go up and see it? Anyway, I should meet the great climber.'

'Mr Jed is not very well today.'

'But we can go up?'

'I think so,' Cecelia puts in.

They walk round the back to the other side of Everest. The goongi is sitting by the water tank chewing a stalk of grass, on duty. Minding Perpetua's pump, which whines dismally behind her. She has on her rough sari today, as if in mourning.

'How is the water supply?' Bisht tosses at her, adjusting his tone, and receives a frightened animal look.

'She's a goongi,' Cecelia intervenes.

The goongi whimpers. She'd like to help, would give much for a little comfort. Today her head is full of ghosts and moon-blood. Bisht notices her powerful arms, looks searchingly at her and gives up.

They climb the iron stair.

Jed hears them come, a group. Three footfalls, one new. How is he disposed today: mad or not? He can decide. Mad, then. He slips into madness, this hair shirt. Sitting up in bed, singing softly to himself as he waits. What can be keeping them? Pop in the teeth.

The periwinkle stands just outside Jed's door, serene in its planter.

'This is it?' Bisht frowns.

'Yes.'

Bisht considers it without bending, then nods and goes in after Cecelia. Ritu pauses, puzzled, then follows the others in.

'Mr Jed. Inspector Bisht would like to meet you.' Cecelia's business voice.

Jed leaves his eyes shut, goes on singing to himself, smiling. Cecelia taps him on the collar bone.

'Mr Jed, the inspector is here.'

Jed leans forward with a start, eyes staring. 'Inspector who? Inspector who? Whoo? *Hoo hoo hoo*.' His eyelids roll down. He falls back on his pillow, cooing *hoo hoo hoo*.

'Inspector Bisht,' Cecelia repeats.

Jed allows his eyes to open again, focuses on the man. 'Inspector,' he says, 'the drains are disgraceful. Stinking. Really, you must send your men regularly. Regularly. *Hup hup hup.*'

Bisht moves away from the bedside, looks at the gramophone, the records, the mask, the moon lily on the wall. He wanders out onto the roof. Rooftops he likes, especially on big buildings: the emptiness, the sudden abandonment of pretensions, an odd feeling of transcendence. Treetops, the horizon, the sky.

He takes in the row of bathtubs, the clutter of what look like boilers and pipes. Hears water running into a tank from the goongi's pump. He crosses to the other side, to a row of flowerpots ranged along the parapet. Dangerous place for pots, he thinks automatically. Nervous as a child, he still sees danger everywhere, and his job has not helped. That bride who brained her husband from the balcony with a pot of portulaca. Or was it geraniums? These are. He peers over the edge, sees the periwinkle in an answering row below. His gaze sweeps the compound.

The garage. Thapa's lean-to, a buffalo tail swinging just beyond. The lychee orchard, the bonfire ground with its circle of ash, the red pile of sculpted sandstone. From here the walled garden is hidden, so he follows the parapet to the back of the house, Cecelia trailing behind.

A satellite dish. Bisht has never seen one at close quarters before. A few houses have them and they always manage to look slightly threatening. Still, the country's opening up. He'd like to touch this one but imagines it would shock. Gives it a quick tap; it gives back a dead clang. Something about them at once open and cryptic; this one he feels could tell him something, but won't.

'You get a good reception?' he asks Cecelia.

'We don't have a TV,' she says, virtue sneaking into her smile.

'No?' Bisht raises his eyebrows.

'The dish was installed by Mr Jed's nephew, but he never got round to the TV.'

'He might still?'

'I don't think he'll be back soon.'

'No?'

'I hope not. The last time he was here he went completely mad. He occupied my office, threatened me, smashed up our clock.'

'Just like that?'

'Yes. We never provoked him.'

'Had he been like that before?'

'No. He would get drunk sometimes, but he never threatened us before. He pulled up Thapa's corn once, but that was all. This time he was like an animal.'

'When was that?'

'Just the night before last.'

'Where did he stay?'

'He has the annexe. It was a kind of guest house before he took it over. He keeps the key.'

'He drinks alone?'

'He drinks with the major, I think. I come across their bottles in the garage sometimes.'

Cecelia's narrow look has returned, but Bisht looks away at the mountains. The clouds have cleared there, and there's a gap in the range that he's never noticed before. Through it he sees a single snow-clad peak.

So that's that. Now he simply needs to wait for the post mortem report. He picks up the bottle of vitamins on the parapet and examines it idly before putting it down. A glass of water there, with a limy scum. Dentures. He knows the toothmarks will fit. He turns back towards Jed's room.

'Is he really . . .?' Bisht lays a long finger along his temple.

Cecelia smiles. 'Some days he's daft. Other days he's just a bit deaf. He's a bit of a trickster.'

Jed is in bed conducting Mahler. Ritu is making onion soup.

Bisht and Cecelia pass through the room without disturbing the occupants. At the door Bisht bends to check the periwinkle. The soil in the planter has not been disturbed, and, yes, a stem has been taken. Nuns don't lie, he's pleased to see. The plant confused a layman at first. The ones downstairs were covered in pink flowers. This one is simply green, a deep dark green.

The report comes in at night.

Bhang. Cannabis, pure and simple. And traces of tea, semolina, peanuts, rice. Among the drugs found in her room, the report notes, Serafin, alongside its euphoric effects, inhibits clotting of the blood. And the blood on the stone matches.

Bisht goes back to bed and makes a cocoon of his quilt and dreams of bats. Nibbling at his ears. He wakes with a start, lies there quaking. It's all right; you're grown up now. When calm returns, his mind drifts back to Everest and he begins to review the case.

Two cases, almost. That's what had him confused: where they crossed over, and yet didn't. The one sidetracked by chance, the other overtaken by chance. No intent to kill, or he'd have used the root, and the soil was undisturbed. He picked all the flowers; petals make a simpler tea, which can be decanted into the bottle of Black Label that the goongi fetches up from the garage, blending nicely. (She carries up the planter first, of course; with those arms she could pluck up a mountain.) But along comes nephew, sneaks foreigner's Scotch, goes mad.

The joker's upstairs. Stupid, though, supposing something had happened to the nephew. Too old to care about consequences perhaps. But some motive with the woman. A quarrel? Disappointment, jealousy, a score, real or imagined: always a motive, even at ninety. And then chance intervenes, a random crossover. But for the satellite dish he'd still be chasing periwinkle. In the wrong stomach. The other stomach, the nephew's, bubbling away somewhere. Hallucinations returning till the substance is wholly expelled. It was the rosebeds that misled you. No scratch marks on her, but the nephew's legs, now, must have taken a beating.

Suppose she had taken a swig: would that implicate the old man? Does the bhang implicate Thapa?

No. She died of bleeding, not bhang.

So, back to the thumb.

There'll be a kukri, naturally. Perhaps at the bottom of that foul cesspit. See Thapa.

Question: was she left-handed? No lefties at lunch. The major used his right hand to turn the key in the garage padlock. Thapa right-handed, too. So what? Bisht yawns. So the major goes there for a topping up on his way back from wherever he spent the night after the bonfire, finds the body. Wakes up his batman: together they remove any current bottles, glasses, wipe down the running board, the whole car perhaps. Then wake Cecelia. That much is fairly plain. Unless Thapa knew more than the major and hid the weapon.

Bisht sinks into turbid dreams.

He is roller-skating, the way he never could as a boy, the way his classmates did effortlessly at the rink up the hill. Skating around Everest, round and round, breezing through the case. Flying.

He sees Inge leave the bonfire and walk the way Dixit said she went, towards the garage, where she sits a while on the fender of the Packard and waits. She is depressed, hallucinating mildly, aware of a larger disappointment than that of being let down by Brij, depressed by the job now finished, by the enigma of Otto Planke, by some deeper loss of faith. The lights have gone out at Everest, though there is one resident who never sleeps. Inge picks her way by moonlight around the house and comes to the iron stair. Go up to him? But he would fob her off, want some complicated revenge. So she simply sits down on the bottom step and watches the front gate. Brij might yet come.

Bisht circles the house, a widening ripple in Inge's eye, which has begun to admit the strangest shapes and fancies. On the other side of Everest the fire is dwindling. Dixit grunts and goes home by the front gate. Inge watches him leave a hundred times. The bhang has gone to work, on top of the Serafin. The moon is a giant clockface and all the stars are eyes. Thapa has picked up the tray, kicked apart the logs and made for his night-duty cot on the front verandah. He gives a perfunctory blast on the whistle as he turns in.

Now Inge is alone. She returns unsteadily to the garage for a set of digging tools, even though she knows Brij is not coming tonight. Something has happened or he would be here by now. Still, she will wait at the monument till her head clears. She can think, if watching every thought coalesce over aeons is thinking. She thinks of their last midnight meeting under this pipal tree, the night of the he-goat. That last quarter moon hanging from the branches like one of those weaver bird's nests lit up. A thought that troubled her then returns to torment her now: a suspicion, even before the goat, that this trail of blood is leading nowhere. And more. That her pursuit of purity, the black uniform, the blind salutes, fared no better than this impure chase. And still more, that both quests might be one. She jumps to her feet, kicks out at one of the spades; it rocks back, then tips over. Even their spades are crooked. She can't hope to dig up Otto Planke alone. But must do something to redeem this unsatisfactory night.

Besides, she has not marked the finishing of the monument, this altar where she sits.

She finds herself making for Thapa's room, where the kukri hangs, feels for it in the dark, carries it back to the stone. Unsheathes it, and sits there waiting.

Here is the table, where is the feast?

Bisht circles Everest on his skates, his dreaming eyes wide open. Inge, too, is looking about. The goat was good, now what? Half the night sky is full of clear light. The stars are scattered evenly, all equally dimmed by the moonlight. Pixels on a backlit screen. A gauze of cloud is spread over the rest of the sky, with one bright edge that might be the milky way. Silence, broken only by the clink of the buffalo's chain.

The buffalo!

Inge absorbs the bolt. No. Too big, she couldn't do it alone. The calf, then? She fastens another button on her jacket; moisture on that wind. Yes, the calf. She leans back on her hands. All right, then. No hurry. Work it out.

The wind chafes a half-burnt log, which the fire has fretted into a row of charred teeth. The teeth glow red, with black gaps in between, so when Dixit's cat circles the ashes Inge sees its outline flow against the light and dark.

'*Hier, Mieze!*' Inge calls.

The silhouette freezes at the voice. Relaxes when it sees

the colleague of its lazy afternoons. It comes over, purring. What is the outdoor companion up to now? Over the past weeks Inge has watched the cat lie beside her in the winter sun while she worked. She has sometimes talked to it, and been answered with a look, but has never felt the need to touch. Nor has the cat, a creature of consummate assurance, who can dismiss her with a glance, not even stirring when she leaves. Remaining there some evenings long after Inge's gone, its stomach gently rising and falling as it absorbs the heat stored in the stone. Now it jumps up beside her and sits. Inge runs her hand along its fur, starting at the rough dry snout, thumb and fingers parting at the whiskers, dropping to tickle the pouchy jowls, then combing back the lashes at eyelids that close with each stroke and open again, then the ears, which flatten and stand up again, then the crown of the head, the whole skull, the neck.

They sit a long while staring at the last of the embers. Till Inge stops her stroking, knows what is to be done. Not the calf.

She scoops up the cat, holding it from underneath, between the front legs. Feels the dark wind from its eyes. Holds it out above the stone, and aims the kukri. The knife flashes, but the creature pulls back, and Inge feels the sharp edge of the steel shear through flesh and bone. Throws back her head in a silent howl of pain as she spins around and doubles up, the hand folded between her legs. The cat leaping away and racing off into the night. Inge sits on the sandstone, winded, wide-eyed, tingling. Hallucinating still, not sure whether this is real. The kukri is at her feet. She picks it up, holds it close to check for blood. The blood is there. She sucks in cold air through clenched teeth. Drops the kukri on the stone, wraps the hand in her scarf.

Bisht sees her stumble towards the garage, the muffled

hand rammed into her chest, the good hand fumbling for the car keys. Sees her collapse in the driver's seat. Goes skating through the sublunary world of Everest, his hands tied behind him, finding inmate after inmate asleep. Not a soul on the midwinter Canal Road; the very owls have gone home. Pools of impassive yellow lamplight, mist scrolled along the canal.

And the car mounted on bricks all along.

At four o'clock he hears Thapa's whistle as the man swings out of his cot for a last round. Must have a clock in his head. Thapa does a circuit of Everest, finds the garage doors open, discovers the body. Hunts desperately for the kukri, finds it just before dawn. Is scrubbing it clean when Bisht feels a pummelling at his side.

His wife is elbowing him. Roll over, she commands, and goes on levering until he does, and the snoring stops. She once sewed half a tennis ball into the back of his nightshirt.

In the morning he lies there pining for the vanished dream, looking for crumbs of inspiration. The spades, for example. But it's gone, and with it those tantalizing revelations, promissory glimpses, intimations of complete knowledge.

Who can say exactly what happens? he asks the dahlia that is his morning comforter. Nobody, certainly not the detective. It's why he's stopped reading detective stories, and he has a shelf-ful. He can't bear their omniscience any more: an unsleeping despot rules over that exhausted land. Bisht never read one that satisfied, he thinks now as he mounts his Luna moped.

Not one, ever.

Only the cat, padding through the long grass, nursing a slashed paw, and still slightly fuzzy because Dixit gave it a saucer of bhang, knows.

Thapa breaks down on the second day.

She borrowed his precious kukri, and not just once. For the mongoose. For the goat. And then this time. The cemetery chowkidar still blames him for the goat.

'But I didn't kill her.'

Bisht nods. Now he remembers the slash that did. Was she imbalanced? The young man would know but wouldn't tell. On drugs anyway.

'When I found the kukri I scrubbed it many times and wiped it carefully and hung it back up. Then I took it down and threw it in the cesspit. Then I got it out and buried it. It's under the custard-apple tree.'

'You'll have to dig it up,' Bisht says, 'but I'll see that you get it back.' He stares at the nail where the weapon hung. 'How did you know she'd been borrowing it?'

'Oh, she was careful to clean it up. But it was always hung up this way.' Thapa's hand does a dancer's backward twist under the nail.

Bisht nods and turns to go. 'And the chisels?' he says, looking back.

Thapa gives a foolish smile through his tears. 'I could never sleep with her racket. She worked all through the afternoon, *tung, tung, tung*. The afternoon is when I sleep, after lunch. So I took them.'

Bisht remains bent over, reflecting. 'Maybe she found out,' he says, 'and thought it was a fair exchange.'

Thapa's face falls. He sits down on his bed and cups his

face in his hands. So much trouble that kukri has brought him in this life.

In the portico Bisht pedal-starts the Luna. Today he feels gloomier than ever. It's always like that at the end of a case, but this one hinged on a trifle. And so did her life: without the Serafin she'd still be alive. So, an accident. Should he go and see the young man? But he would hardly be communicative.

There is somebody else he should see. Cecelia is out; he can telephone her.

He lets the motor die and goes round to the iron stair. Climbs up to Jed, who's lying there reading the roof iron.

'Did you find her beautiful?' he asks when Jed's eyes climb down.

'She did her best to look ugly.'

'She was a good sculptor.'

'He was a so-so poet.'

Jed picks up a yellowed cloth-bound book of poems on the bedside table and reads a few lines.

'Sah ich dich, Heimat, auch nur in Gedanken,
Mein Glaube am Führer läßt mich nicht wanken.
Stolz bin ich auf dich, deine große Macht,
Die, wie nichts, das großte auf Erden vollbracht!

'Naturally it was confiscated. The British released it after the war, but he was already dead. A good illustrator, though. Look at the drawings.'

He passes the book to Bisht, who leafs through it, stopping at the pen-and-ink sketches.

'Yes . . . *yes!*'

Bisht has come across one of a garden, the wicket-gate open. Hollyhocks along a stone wall and, in the beds on either side of an arch, dahlias. Bisht feels the sting of sudden tears: that is where he'd like to go, through that gate. Even if it meant never returning.

He plucks up courage. 'Excuse me . . . could I . . . keep this book?'

Jed looks surprised, caught off-guard.

'No,' he says at length, and shuts his eyes.

Bisht goes down the iron stair, holding onto the serpentine rail. Now he's thoroughly dejected. He'd like to go away. Not far, but away. He's always wanted to travel: Bhutan, Kerala, Mauritius, anywhere in the Arabian Sea. The rest of the world he'll take on trust. But where's the money?

He could go home and play his flute. Or take Mrs Bisht to bed. But it's mid-morning and he has to be at work. She would be shy anyway, shutting windows and carrying on. He could read, but he's stopped the paper: there was nothing in it. Except noise and murder mysteries, and he's had enough of those. He should sell his collection to the kabariwallah. How could he have gathered so many, despising them as he does? Addicted. No, inured.

After all, there are people who do crossword puzzles.

He'd like to write. A paper on lizard aggression, his theory of toes and character-formation, that letter to the editor of the *Horticulturalist*. But where's the time?

He stands at the bottom of the stair and sighs. He feels a wave of weariness flow over him as he feels in his wind-cheater pocket for the Luna keys. Mrs Bisht wants him to pick up a tin of mustard oil on the way home. Yesterday he forgot; today he has on his person three separate slips that read, 'Mustard oil!'

Well, back to work. In Delhi, in Bombay, there'd be another body; in Drummondganj they're still rare, thank God. It'll be a quiet day, writing up his report.

Hang on to one of those slips. He feels in his other pocket. His hand closes on something smooth and waxy: his blood freezes. Not the thumb! No, no – it wasn't severed. Then the shadow of a smile crosses his long tallowy face.

The cake of soap! New, too.

Well, some perks there have to be. He likes neem soap.

Spring

PHAGUN. *February is a mob of babblers in the cassia, fluffed out, screeching, pecking one another dry. The black seedpods add their shuffle to the din: the whole tree is in uproar. Its wet black branches jog, bare except at the tips, where new green dances.*

The horror of the lately vanished is on everyone. Like the warmth of a newly vacated seat. Ritu torments herself with the knowledge that she felt a flicker of desire for that absent body. Beauty now coming apart, but the memory still bites. The goongi mopes by the anthill, Miss Sampson meditates on untimely deaths. Everest the cemetery is one body richer.

Deep-blue skies, their depths unnerving. Naphthalene moons stare at the risen sun. Sharp mornings, smoky dusks. Heavy dews on the crabgrass, blossom on the peach. One day, on their way back from the leper colony, Neha and Ritu detour into a pea field and pick a few pods. Green sugar in the smallest peas! Perpetua intercepts one and pops it in the goongi's mouth. The goongi smiles her first smile since Lohri.

In the old tile-kiln garden lizards have begun to stir, but the weeds around the compound are still dormant. Thapa has not used his scythe in weeks. At noon the gnats begin their sunlit mote dance over the compost heap. Mosquitoes return to patrol the swampy ground by the gate, big slow black ones that leave a fossil shadow on the skin when smacked. Cecelia hates the soft skidding of their legs when they touch down.

The rooftop air is sharp and clean, uncomplicated with perfumes. Jed breathes deep draughts of it and looks across at his mountains. The beginning and end of winter smell the same.

BRIJ SITS AT THE WINDOW IN HIS NARROW ROOM.

The man who could never be still for two minutes together sits motionless. There's a white kite in the sky. Beyond it black specks wheeling 10,000 feet up. He tries to imagine what it's like up there, but his mind keeps slipping back into the groove it has cut for the last two weeks.

Dead.

Dead and gone. Not here, not there. Nowhere.

The kite jigs, but he's looking through it. The vultures wheel endlessly: he's looking through them. Brij is looking through the sky. Across, away from the world that keeps turning and turning with its surfaces. Transparencies laid one upon the other. Distracting him from something that's not there.

His eye falls on the roof of the Rex Hotel. He flinches, as if he'd looked into the sun.

Not there. Not at Everest. She's nowhere.

If only. What? She's dead. Now he knows he would have, should have, given up everything. Home, family, the ones he always meant to keep safe in a treacherous world. Given everything up and gone. Where? With her. Would she have agreed? Yes. Love inside that loathing, ridiculously tender feet.

Dead.

He could cry out, is crying out in some room, in all the back rooms of himself. Has lived for two weeks in a state of choking, tormented by an absurd simplicity: Inge is dead.

She walks through his head. Her boots are under the bed. She has a camera in her bush. She is leaning over red stone. Turns to face him, talks without a voice. Cannot hear him. Hears nothing.

He jumps up. All his movements now begin with a jerk, then slide into the same slow consciousness of futility. The sorrow glazes every object: faces, a doorway, a pelmet board. He hears an engine raced, picks up without trying the hunting of the pistons. Goes downstairs, along the lane. Past the typist at the gas agency. She looks up, a ghost. He avoids the taxi rank, the law courts. Looks away from certain teashops, feels eyes on him. His friends annoy him, he is angry with total strangers, his family are suddenly just people.

Back at his window. The kite, the vultures gone. Nothing there.

What can have possessed her? Simple anger? He imagines her waiting for him, her impatience, her rage. Thapa's kukri coming down. Her lips moving. This'll teach him. Or was there more? He'll never know. She hid her heart, and his is always on display.

His mother comes in, this person. Has brought a glass of hot milk.

Thapa is sweeping up leaves.

Under the camel hoof, bent in half, the varnished dome of his head probing the air as he goes. He has put away his army surplus stockings and his cocoa-coloured sand-shoes. He wears khaki shorts and leather chappals that show his delicate feet, the toes like macaroni. The leaf fall has been heavy this time round after last year's long monsoon. He has a fire going at the main leaf pile by the guava and adds to it from lesser piles roundabout. The smoke blows now towards the gate, now towards the house. He is ruminating as he works, a small intense man become his task.

Late afternoon sunlight slants through the smoke, its red-gold lighting up the blue. The air is rare and soft.

He's fetching another basketful of leaves when he sees her. Stops dead. How long has she been there?

Small, still. Neat as a new broom. Four spans high, maybe less. Standing a short way off, staring at the flames. A broom with a head.

Thapa shakes the leaves out of his wicker basket, looking across the fire at her. He goes to say something but changes his mind. Let her watch. He goes about his work.

When he looks up he expects to find her gone, but she's still there, staring at the flames as if something of hers were burning there. Thapa goes around the fire.

'What's the matter, child?'

She starts, the thread of her gaze broken. Looks up at the man.

Thapa bends towards her. 'Where have you come from?'

She smiles, looks down and says nothing.

Thapa squats down on his hams. 'What do you want, little girl? Where do you live?'

She smiles and looks away.

'Whose child are you?' he persists, but she makes no answer.

He looks at her. She is wearing a white frock, washed but not pressed, a navy-blue hand-knitted sweater and blue plastic sandals. The middle toe on each foot is hardly there at all. At her wrists are yellow glass bangles. She is carrying a polythene bag of what could be toys. Her hair, cut short, with a fringe high on the forehead, is freshly oiled.

Pinned to the frock with a safety pin is a note which Thapa fingers doubtfully.

Writing.

He stands up, dusts his hands over the fire and looks down at her with a worried smile.

'Come,' he beckons. Then shyly puts out a hand.

The girl smiles back and takes his fingertips. Thapa raises his eyebrows; a grip on her. He leads her to the house and rings the bell. Neha comes to the door, runs a puzzled eye down the girl.

'Sister?' Thapa says, meaning Cecelia, and Neha goes to fetch her.

Cecelia comes out, frowning a little. She was in the middle of a letter to Mother. Her eyes narrow when she sees the girl, taking in the situation at once. At least there's a note on this one.

Neha switches on the verandah light and smiles at the girl, who is smiling all round, even at the flowerpots. Cecelia bends and unpins the note, then takes it under the verandah light. Low voltage in the evenings. Frowns again and holds her head back to focus. The note is crumpled: the girl has been tugging at it on the way in. In blue ballpoint: LOOK AFTER HER. NO CHILD SHOULD SEE WHAT SHE HAS SEEN.

They go in to dinner.

Ritu is seated across from the girl, who still has not spoken but continues to smile and eats with an appetite.

'What do your friends call you, then?'

The girl looks up at Ritu. There's a blank moment before the smile comes on. Food in her mouth, which she continues to chew. Absent, Ritu thinks, looking steadily at her through her own smile. Not there.

'Your friends?' she repeats, but drops her gaze when she feels it grow too keen.

The girl has stopped chewing and is considering a point in the air just above the tablecloth. She could dissolve into tears but is not going to let herself. Ritu sees the resolve and waits admiringly for the smile to return.

'Who is your best friend?'

The smile deflects that easily. Her fingers have found the napkin ring.

'What does she call you?'

Chewing.

'What do you call her?'

The smile is armour.

'My name is Ritu.'

The eyes shine. She takes the hand Ritu is holding out across the table and squeezes it.

Perpetua hobbles around the table and sets the dish of potatoes with cumin seed in front of the child. The smile drops away, replaced by a look of disbelief. All for her? Perpetua spoons out another helping, and leaves the dish there.

Cecelia is looking levelly at the girl from the head of the table. Three. Maybe three and a half. Healthy, not malnourished, but hungry. Bathed, so she's not from out of town. But then they might have bathed her on the train before they brought her to the gate, carrying that polythene bag that's still in her lap. She'll let no-one touch it. Her treasure. A mystery, like her name. Like her.

Nobody's child. Everybody's child.

'She mustn't sleep alone.'

Ritu speaks up as she clears the table.

Cecelia returns a look that says she's considered that. 'She can have the other bed in the twins' room. Tsering is next door.'

'She must have someone with her tonight. Let her have the other bed in my room.'

Cecelia frowns. Can the lay-religious divide apply to children? It can. But should it?

Perpetua, swinging the key to the linen press on her bent index finger, catches her eye and shrugs.

'Well,' Cecelia allows, 'for a couple of nights.'

What place is this?

Mummy? Where are you? The light is coming the wrong way. The bright square should be *there*. The window's in the wrong place. What is this white net hanging over me? Sister? I think I'm going to cry. The pillow is already wet. Have I wet the bed? Don't leave me.

Breakfast.

Neha has made parathas especially for the girl, who is wearing her frock and navy-blue jumper and clutching her bag. She has a way of swivelling her head and drawing her whole smile along so it plays like the beam of a torch.

'So, are you going to tell us your name?' asks Ritu, who is pleased to see the smile return. She found her crying silently in bed this morning, washed her face, helped her dress, and sits beside her now.

'Is it Lalbuchi?' The crimson velvet-backed beetles of childhood.

The girl smiles and shakes her head. The nuns look at one another. So at least she understands.

'Lillighori?' The piggyback crawlers of the rains. A rapid shake of the head, a deep gurgle. The first sound she's made at Everest.

'Well then, what?'

A whisper into the lap.

'What?'

'—sha.'

Ritu leans forward. '*What?*' Soft but sharp.

But the girl returns to her smiles. Then stops smiling and eats determinedly.

'So Miss —sha,' Perpetua jollies her along. 'Some more scrambled egg?'

A vigorous nod.

'Could be Asha,' Perpetua supposes, watching her eat.

'Or Ayesha,' Cecelia reminds her. Muslim or Hindu, she will have to be reported to the police today.

'*Arré* – Ayesha, Asha, Tamasha – how does it matter?' Perpetua wants to know.

'Why not Shama?'

Neha's voice is always tentative. She has a friend with the name. Shama. A little light, a small flame. But also, with the first vowel stretched, a songbird.

The girl looks up at the new voice and smiles.

'Why not?' Cecelia agrees. They have to call her something.

South Col under his eye.

Snow lining the ridges, packing the hollows. Dazzling where the light bends, the mountain folds. Bluebottle shadows, a mountain of flies' wings. Sunlight fizzing on the rim, wind keening, snow whipped off the crest. Curling up in slow sheets against the sky. The whole mountain smoking.

Jed's eye roves over the wrinkled sheet. The pillowed eye closed.

Hell is hot? Give him flames any day. The cold has got into his bones, will not leave him now, in spite of the long johns, the blankets, the electric heater brought out when everyone else is putting theirs away.

And who said Everest was white? It's black. Black rock stuck like a great raven's beak into the sky.

My mind is going, I know. I know I don't know: things I

knew yesterday. Lights going out in my head, and I dread the dark. Also there's a new whistling in my ear, like an A flat chord of three piccolos.

But Everest I'm sure of. Or am I?

Sherpa Dorji toiling over the folds in the bedsheet, slips into the rough blue crevasse of an Everest blanket. The wind whistles, snow stings his cheeks like sand, and Jed watches him go, helpless. A hundred yards of line going with him, unravelling like blanket stitch. Gone.

Go up alone. This mountain, any mountain, can fall to one man, you always said. You don't need 10,000 porters. A short sharp thrust, with luck on your side.

Jed, three days from base camp, half snowblind on the beak. Two telegrams in his pocket, one from Nehru in prison: THE NATION WAITS ALL INDIA HOLDS HER BREATH, old mealy mouth; one from Rose Sampson: FAY SERIOUS COME AT ONCE.

And Sherpa Dorji gone. Or hanging there?

Which way?

Jed goes up. Into the blue sky, Lady Luck with him, the new Swiss crampons, a lesson learnt on the Weisshorn, and the dire Jed will.

Jed on top of the world. Down every way from here. Wind ripping into the handspun flag.

And then the lady blinks. Clouds ship up, dump snow on the whole north face. Jed stumbles, spends the night in an ice chimney belayed to a piton. Head imploding, feet on fire, as Fay, pruning the wistaria beside him, looks on.

Or no?

Dorji finds him in the morning. Dorji, who was saved by an ice shelf, who pulled himself up, now half drags, half carries Jed down to base camp, where they remove six toes with a penknife. Jed stretchered to safety in one long delirious march of bandages and pus and flies. And porters. Paid in red chillies. Waking up on clean mission hospital sheets.

Enough foot left to hold a shoe, just.

Cecelia has been to the police.

There is no little girl reported missing. Shama can stay.

She has taken to patrolling the house, her polythene bag clutched at her side like a briefcase. She steps briskly through the hall, nodding at herself in the mirror, going somewhere. Turns right at the portico and marches round to the garage where she sits on the fender of the Packard. There she soaks up the morning sun and considers the day's business. Sometimes she will slump and stare, interrogating the empty air. But then she will stir herself and make for the walled garden, where she's discovered the fountain. The apehead could outstare her if she let it, but she keeps her head down. What intrigues her is the basin of dry leaves.

'Leaves,' Ritu pronounces, coming out of her studio one day. She holds up one. 'Leaf.'

The girl tilts her head, dog-like, suddenly serious. It's the first time someone has named something for her in this place.

'Leaf,' Ritu repeats, handing it to her.

Shama takes the leaf, turns it over. She *knows* what it is, her look says. It's what you just said.

Well, then? Ritu's look replies, with an expectant shake of the head: *say* it!

But Shama doesn't follow, or is too far ahead. It's enough that the leaf is there. That all these leaves are here. She runs her fingers through them, scoops up a handful. The ones underneath are wet.

Wet, she wants to say to her best friend, and holds out her hand. Droplets of water, running together, trickling down. A eucalyptus leaf, long, narrow, stuck to her palm. She wiggles the hand to show Ritu. The leaf is stuck, can't fall. See? Peels the leaf off, sticks it back down. Wet, she wants to say, and sees the problem. Her confusion shows: there *was* a way of putting it.

Her tongue is making a hundred journeys in her mouth; tremors run up and down its length as it probes the dark.

Wetness.

Water.

It's at the tip.

Ritu waits, bends close to her. Then scoops up her own handful of leaves and holds out her palm.

'Wet,' she says.

Yes, *that*. Shama's eyes are sure. She goes to speak, but only air leaks out. She knows she's failed because tears damp down her smile. But not for long. Leaves and water win her. She takes double handfuls and throws them in the air, laughing silently.

Fay is sitting under the wistaria.

In the walled garden, doing nothing. From where she sits she can see the top of the silk-cotton tree, where a hornbill is perched, quietly surveying the valley. The casque on the beak is not pronounced; it's a young bird. It turns its head to left and right unhurriedly, as if wondering which way to go. A slight lift to the bill, the thrown-back head add to this look of contemplation.

As Fay watches there's a puzzling intrusion. The top of a bamboo pole has entered the picture. It inches up from below, stealthy, steady.

And suddenly she knows what is happening.

The bird remains looking about mildly, the keel of the casque a knife slicing the blue sky.

The birdlime edges closer. At the bottom of the pole there'll be a man, his eyes fixed on the bird's undercarriage, his mouth straining open, windpipe taut. Hardly breathing. Every muscle of the forearm tense, the wrist bones agreeing among themselves on minute adjustments of rank. The bamboo halts under the bird's chosen branch, moves sideways by calibrations that verge on instinct. The hornbill's tail is cover. Rudder for the bird, cover for the hunter. Little by little the bamboo tip creeps back, skirting the claws.

Fay watches, rapt. She wants to cry out, warn the bird, but the wires to the voice box have gone dead, the strings in the box hang slack.

Clap, then.

But her hands remain frozen to the chair arms. Legs crossed at the ankle, one wedge-heeled shoe off, lying on its side in the grass.

Jab.

At the anus, for surprise, but near enough the tail to catch on bigger feathers. Twist and smear in one action. The bird fluttering wildly, gathering more lime.

Fay watches aghast, her fingertips now gripping the chair. All of her willing the bird free, except some weird weight at the tail of the brain, dragging it down.

'Did you see that!'

Rose Sampson comes running through the arch. She's been watching from the back verandah. 'Poor thing!' she says and flops down on the grass. 'What a shame!'

'I thought it was quite cleverly done,' Fay says, still staring at the treetop. 'It doesn't usually work with bigger birds.'

Miss Sampson looks at her friend. The gooseberry-green eyes are serious; they always are now. And this is the girl who made a Dutch bed for Sister Bettina at the infirmary. Wore lipstick to communion. The parlour boarder we envied and imitated. Swept off her feet by Immanuel Jed, collector.

'Are there any letters?' Fay closes the subject of the bird.

Miss Sampson swallows her pique and answers, 'No.'

Fay looks away. When she was newly married she kept a diary, put everything in it. She put a daisy in the margin the morning after they made love. The book was a bank of daisies. Until he began to bring her flowers.

Fay's eye rests on the fountain. It's never worked. The basin fills up in the rains, then the water evaporates, leaving a murky scaling that hardens like a grievance. He promised to get it going, but summer surprised him and he had to be up in the mountains. Collecting. Or it was autumn collecting. The species he brought down are bedded about the garden, returning to seed. The daphne in the corner won't survive another summer. Only the wistaria persists, spiked with that cinnamon that saves the sweetness from cloying.

'We marry our fathers,' she reflects. But knows the old blowhard was not driven, unless by his wife. Cyril Popescu was happy piping cakes, raging at the kitchen staff, assaulting waiters. Madeleine, handsome in a florid way, with narrow wrists and large raw hands, ran the Everest. 'Or do we marry our mothers?'

Miss Sampson, who married nobody, inherited nothing, is here to nurse her friend. She was always in love with Fay Popescu; all the juniors were. Beautiful, clever, rich Faizy. At one time, for a whole term, she dreamt of dying for her friend. Now she likes to picture them growing old together, once she's put the colour back in those cheeks.

The head gardener comes to the arch and coughs.

'What is it, *mali?*' Miss Sampson asks. She gives the orders now, the servants know.

'The papaya, memsahib.'

He cradles the fruit in one gnarled hand, then turns it over. 'A crow has put its beak in.'

'Take it to the kitchen and tell the khansama to have it served here in twenty minutes.'

Fay may or may not have heard. She is staring at the top of the silk-cotton. That is the branch the hornbill was sitting on. Sky there now.

At four o'clock the papaya arrives on a silver service. The family never used Everest dishes. Miss Sampson spoons papaya, pours cream. Cream she simply adores.

Fay takes her plate mechanically. A luscious yellow cube is poised for an eternity on her fork, but passes eventually to her mouth with its drip of cream. Sweet. She nods approval at Rose, who glows so bright it hurts. Nurse Sampson would give anything to feed her, but helps herself instead. Fay eats, almost with appetite. The tip of her tongue sneaks out and searches for a drop of cream that settled on her chin. Nice.

You could almost forget you were dying.

S tay with her, stick with it, Ritu tells herself. Pretending it's duty.

'It's coming,' she pleads with Cecelia. 'Let her stay a little longer.'

Cecelia thinks the mothering has gone on long enough. It's time the girl went up to the twins' room. Tsering is cooler, more balanced.

'Anyway,' Ritu says, 'the stairs would be dangerous for her.'

Cecelia has no answer to that. The girl's a wanderer.

Stick with it. Water will wear down stone, will weary iron.

But Perpetua is putting away the blankets; Shama has seen the spring out and still not spoken. The heat is coming too quickly this year.

'It'll build up and then break,' Perpetua predicts, looking at the sky, where by teatime the thunderclouds have begun to herd together. Ritu sees how their fretful milling sends the vultures soaring. The thunder has the hollow sound of a giant milk can opening. Then rain, just as Perpetua forecast: she knew it in her knuckles.

It pours down on the roof, spouts from the gargoyles. There's a waterfall pounding the row of periwinkle pots.

And there's Shama catching raindrops on her tongue, dancing wildly in the spray off the portico roof until her new frock is soaked, running from jet to jet under the gargoyles till her hair is plastered down, feeling the water drum on her skull, shouting for all to hear, 'Rain! Rain! Look! Look at me!'

Wondering why the nuns have come out into the portico and are standing in a row, open-mouthed.

CHAIT. *March is the first hawk-cuckoo. It hasn't been away; it simply fell silent with the cold weather. Up and up the call goes now, as the heat mounts: brainfever! brainfever!*

Ever since Shama found her voice the house has come alive. Cecelia is not quite sure she approves of the new regime. It doesn't help that the air is semeny with mango blossom. On the lychee trees new pink leaves are spread like watered silk. Sparrows throng Everest, putting up their scruffy nests; Cecelia has a shock of crabgrass cleared out of the verandah meter box. Large rain-drops clatter on the plastic sheet Thapa has rigged up as a tent for Shama to play in, but now the rain will come to nothing. It's hot in the tent.

She is everywhere.

Released, rediscovering Everest. In the kitchen, too near the gas stove, but Neha won't chide. Upstairs with the twins, forbidden territory, chattering to them, pinching their calves or gravely watching their heads roll from side to side. The goongi plays hospital with her, patiently fetching serum from the tank, submitting her arms to the needleless syringe. Ritu has taken Shama to the doctor for immunization. Perpetua has found a miniature glazed teaset in the market and must pay the price again in cups of tea when she gets home. Thapa fetches down his pink plastic doll for her. He lets her ride the buffalo calf, walking alongside as she shrieks. Or he conducts her around the compound: there are still corners to explore. She grips his finger and leads him, her walk still a waddle. The bamboo culms are shedding long brown riverboats; Shama seizes one and launches it in the air. Any pile of leaves is good for kicking down, but Thapa is less patient there.

'*Shama!*'

She likes the sound of her name, will repeat it to herself endlessly: *shama-shama-shama-shama.*

The guava trunk is pink marble, mottled, cool, smooth on the cheek; the silk-cotton has curtain-like roots you can hide

243

in. There's a brown toad lurking under the monument; talk to it. Discourse with the cat, heckle the babblers. Big black ants are marching down the anthill in an endless line. Order them about, break up their ranks, and when one fastens on your fingertip, scream till all Everest comes running.

'Well, she's found her tongue,' Miss Sampson notes drily.

It's the opposite of death, Ritu considers. She's come out of nowhere fully formed. A magic mushroom, a button, sealed and perfect.

The leper colony agrees to give Ritu's class a try. But no alphabet, Lakhi the elder stipulates, no longer than half an hour, and no later than nine, because then the burnt-out cases take their aluminium milk cans and go out to beg. Lakhi has a watch and would like to be able to read the time. Also, he's sure the grocer across the bridge is cheating him. Numbers he needs.

'One,' Ritu calls and writes the figure in chalk on a slate. She's not sure she wants to be doing this, but Cecelia has plans for the colony. It's a kind of barter, for Shama.

She feels a little foolish at the start. Neha has pulled out, pleading kitchen work, and anyway two teachers would be confusing. Cecelia has talked to the local literacy committee, who have a volunteer programme and a target; they have also provided the slates.

One. She draws it again.

'It looks like a snake. With one eye. Standing on its tail.'

Laughter from the class, who've never even watched their children write. The children live away: this is a colony of adults.

'Try it.'

How to hold the chalk is a problem. For those with stubs for fingers there are the gaps between the stubs. For those without there is the fold at the top of the palm, along the life-line. One man, with arms that end at the wrist, presses both stumps together. Several women are using their feet, but grumpily, to show that they wouldn't be doing this but for their husbands. The husbands are not sure they would be there but for Lakhi.

Ritu goes round the outdoor class assessing the ones. *Laugh.* Perpetua would. She does, holding up one effort where the squiggle shot off the slate. The woman doesn't mind, is shaking with laughter herself.

'Here. Like this.'

Ritu draws the eye, the body, the tail. Then tries the hold the woman uses, the fold in the palm, and fares worse. More laughter.

They get as far as three. Lakhi is well pleased, having discovered a talent for writing. He appoints a widow to gather up the slates while discussing the finer points of three with his neighbour. The result is predictable: those who made most progress are keenest to continue.

Ritu walks home along the forest track. Lakhi's role in this is vital, she knows. If the numerals work well he might be persuaded to try letters.

A stand of white teak abuts the riverbed, the leaves now turning yellow. Where the bank falls away a single flame tree leans, scarlet against the smoky mountains. On either side of the path is poor marshy ground where the river regularly overflowed before the embankment was built. Mosquito-ridden, unproductive, good enough for lepers. Here, screened off by the teak, not quite in the forest, but not in town, the colony measures out its days.

Brij is looking haggard.

He's stopped working out, can't bring himself to eat more than a mouthful at mealtimes. Yoga he cannot even contemplate.

His mother suggests a trip. Her brother's family live in New Mandia, the township built by the government to replace the old town behind the dam. There are still people living in the old Mandia, where the waters have not yet arrived, but many have already moved into the smart pre-fabricated houses high up on the overlooking hill.

Brij finds himself on a bus, toiling up the mountain road above old Mandia. The lake spread out below.

Somewhere under that expanse of water is his village. He's trying to work out where, idly, when it rolls over him. Nausea. He's in the old house, under forty feet of opal water, walking. In slow motion. The lids of his pink-rimmed eyes flaring with every step. A handkerchief rising slowly to his mouth, this handkerchief.

A girl across the aisle smiles. Delicacy in a muscleman!

Brij sees the smile, the bus, the house, swamped. Sucked under. He's walking against stacked water, straining towards black light, the dark high wall of the dam.

'Blow it up.'

Out of nowhere, that voice. Inge's sitting cross-legged in the drowned room. It's the old house still, not the Rex. A pale-grey lotus rooted to the waterlogged divan. Bubbles when she speaks, stretched quicksilver bubbles, trapped in black glass.

'They destroy your village, you destroy their dam.'

Brij turns his head slowly, stares at her. He's not used to such simple solutions.

The girl on the bus looks away, annoyed.

Yes. He will act. With Inge's boldness, with that

decisiveness he always admired in her. He will reach out to her, and strike back at them – two birds with one stone. Yes. He'll prove himself.

But where would you plant the bomb?

'You never touched her after that.'

Memory fogs Miss Sampson's eyes. She's staring at a motive half a century away. Light travelling from an older star, and the event cloudy even when new.

Jed looks hard at her. Knows he should know her. Knew her. What's she doing in his room?

Miss Sampson has climbed the stair. Borne up by the goongi, but her own feet working, paddling the fishplates. Her own hand on the rail. Past the periwinkle pot at the door, where the goongi leaves her.

'Why?'

In a younger woman it might have come out as a scream. Miss Sampson, still looking off into the distance, repeats, 'Why?'

Jed knows now. Sister Sampson, nursing sister. Always in the way, if he remembers, but still can't fathom the event. Too much water down the canal. He's staring, too, now, following her gaze through the same crack in the wall.

Fay.

O my sweet Fay. Tears welling up, so the light in the crack spangles.

Miss Sampson sitting in the only chair; rocking in an upright chair. Resigned as always to the likelihood of not being loved. Somewhere on the wall the dry *cluck cluck* of a lizard waking into summer. Quiet up here. The air sifts car horns from the Rex corner, the whine of a raced engine, a panel beater in one of the workshops, so the sounds arrive faded.

Jed's mind is focusing. Nothing concentrates like guilt. *Guilty*: his own verdict, and yet, and yet. Innocent! he wants to shout.

Who's guilty? The first whore, the first sailor, the first student? The spirochete treponema? In Crete they've found skulls riddled with tiny holes, like sponge fossils. A whole civilization brought down, not just one man.

Collector Sahib. Beloved of many women. Cured of his collecting. So he brought her flowers instead. Daphne. Chinese wistaria. The flower of waiting.

Miss Sampson is waiting. Fay is, too, for an answer.

'Here,' Jed says, and holds out his hand. This will hurt.

Let it.

Miss Sampson stops her rocking. He wants her hand, the old devil.

'Here,' Jed repeats. The fingers beckon.

She gets up, puts her hand out, lets it be taken.

'Look.' He takes the soft olive fingers, draws the hand towards him.

She's waiting for the kiss, but her hand is drawn up past Jed's mouth, over the celebrated forehead, to rest on the roof of the skull.

Sponge.

She snatches her hand away. Looks at him. Sits down and begins to rock faster than before as the truth sinks in. Then draws a deep sob and grows still. So old a grudge cured so simply.

The leper colony is seething. Today it has no time for slates.

'Just look!' Lakhi says and leads Ritu to the edge of the colony. The residents follow their visitor, this teacher from the world of the whole, who might help them against something more menacing than numbers.

Some twenty trees, half the white teak on the riverside knoll, have been felled. The logs lie stripped, waiting for the trucks. The screen between the colony and the town is thinner now, that isolating screen which the isolated have come to cherish.

'They return tomorrow to cut down the rest,' adds another man, a dwarf who has lost part of his nose to the disease.

'Where are they from?' Ritu asks.

'They say they're Pyare Lal's men.'

'And who is he?'

They stare at her. 'The MLA,' Lakhi says.

Pyare Lal is the member for Drummondganj, a former quarry owner with many business interests, and a history sheeter. The charges pending against him, including three murders, will never come to court.

Ritu surveys the remaining trees, a mature stand, fifty years or more.

'Get your women to chipko,' she says. 'Isn't this where the movement began?' She waves an arm at the hills.

A generation ago, in these same forests, village women showed the world you could resist a far greater force simply by putting your body in the way. 'Chipko,' they cried, 'Cling to the trees!' and defied the loggers.

'That's what I told him,' a woman breaks in, Lakhi's wife.

'You shut up,' Lakhi snarls and looks down at his feet. Toes missing there. 'Our women are not that sort,' he mumbles. 'We're decent folk.'

'And these men of Pyare Lal's?'

'They're scum. I'll stop them myself.'

'Listen to the hero,' his wife taunts. 'Fine job you did yesterday.'

'Woman, I'll break every—'

Ritu intervenes. 'That's one day's work left, Lakhi,' she says nodding at the remaining trees. 'If you can't stop them tomorrow there'll be nothing there. Let the women try. What have you got to lose? They write as well as you.'

'Yes, but who's stronger?'

'You, you.'

Next morning the trucks come early.

The logs are sorted and loaded by ten, when the saws appear. The women of the colony shrill a collective 'No!' Then they rush down the slope and up the knoll to the remaining trees, shouting the famous war cry of the hill women, 'Chipko! Chipko!'

Ritu, coming along the forest path, hears their cicada cry, sees their silhouettes race among the standing teak. One by one the figures latch themselves to the trunks and stand there waiting for the saws. Lakhi's wife has no fingers but can imagine the cut coming at the wrist. She grips the tree with such force it looks as if she's buried her lost fingers in the trunk. The dwarf, who's found a vacant tree, has his whole nose sunk in wood.

Pyare Lal's men put down their saws and stand bemused. Their leader spits in the dust and starts a discussion with Lakhi; the discussion grows heated. Some of the sawyers drift up the knoll to the trees, where they begin to talk money with the women. But the attempt breaks down into jibes and abuse and one man returns to the truck for an iron bar. He comes up behind Lakhi and assumes a look of exaggerated innocence that puts fear into the men of the colony.

When Ritu arrives the balance shifts again. A townswoman, educated, a nun from the look of it. And hanging from her shoulder, a camera.

Lakhi turns to her. 'Sister, you explain to them.' His faith in education is touching; she will clear it all up.

'What has she got to do with it?' the leader snaps. To Ritu he says, 'You live here?'

'I work here.'

'We have to clear these trees.'

'On whose orders?'

'The Big Sahib's.'

'But this is public land. The trees belong to the public.'

She unbuttons the camera case. The man turns instinctively away, but she gets a picture of Lakhi and the man with the crowbar behind him. The leader calls his men aside. Emboldened, Ritu photographs the trucks, then goes up the knoll and photographs the women. The trucks start up and Pyare Lal's men jump in.

'We'll be back,' the man with the iron bar calls, and the trucks drive off.

Laughing, trembling the women come down from the knoll. Ritu, trembling, too, takes a victory photo of the whole group. Lakhi is staring at his wife as if she's a new person.

It's on the way home that Ritu remembers Perpetua looking out of the window at Shama and the goongi yesterday and saying, 'Now *there's* a picture. If only we had film in our camera.'

Thapa is cutting back the squirrel's tail.

At the portico, watched by Shama. Nipping the corded new shoots, tearing away frizzy hanks of old growth where the last red berries glow. When there's a shout from the front door.

'Come quickly!'

The Latvian running back indoors. Shama gives chase. Into the hall, where there's a small heap of clothes at the foot of the staircase. Miss Sampson.

How to pick her up is the Latvian's dilemma. She's fallen from the landing, despite the devil's long arm, and broken every bone in her body. Her chest is trembling. The shivers pass into the rest of her body and linger there before subsiding. Her eyes open and shut unseeingly, a wounded animal waiting for the end. Thapa, who knows that look from the battlefield, would leave her where she is so the last minutes aren't clouded with further pain.

Miss Sampson is aware of feet around her – Cecelia's have just come up – but the faces she sees are of ghosts: Fay, Nehru, her rescuer the morning after the great Quetta quake. How different Fay's death, which she missed, from this indignity! Fay rang for tea at noon, drank it when it came, and lay down and died. *And I*, Miss Sampson is saying when the last black wave swamps her.

Thapa stands back, at attention. Death has put in the beak.

She's buried in the last plot at Everest, has outrun Jed. She had no money, none for the plot, much less a tombstone that would satisfy O. P. Dixit. Not that Dixit has been idle: as the mourners file down the cypress avenue they notice the new tomb in the German section. Red sandstone. Jed has paid to have Otto Planke's monument installed. The stone has been set askew – Dixit's work – and the cement has hardened. And Dixit has even inscribed, in shaky squarecut capitals, an addendum for Inge, also interred there.

'All flesh is grass,' Padre Masih reads over the open grave, 'and all the glory of man as the flower of grass. The grass withereth and the flower thereof falleth away.'

The nuns stand in a grey huddle. The Latvian shakes his head and sighs, 'Estonia.' Then Cecelia picks up a clod and drops it on the coffin in the grave. Shama hears the hollow knock and wants to drop a clod of her own. Go on, Ritu nods, and the girl does. A big one that goes boom.

'Will she get up now?' she asks. 'Has she finished being dead?'

Books for Shama.

On Ritu's shopping list. She hasn't been to a bookshop since she came to Drummondganj last year; hasn't been to the shops much at all, so is happy for a chance. Everest is full of books, but none for children. And she knows Cecelia finds Shama loud.

Perpetua takes her to where the school bookshops are in Patel Chowk. Twenty bookshops side by side with nothing in them. Stationery, yes, geometry boxes, ruled sheets, chart paper, but nothing to read. School texts, of course, and cribs and keys. Even keys to keys. On wretched paper, badly printed, poorly bound. Shoddy, shoddy, shoddy. Mirrors of the country, hardly books at all.

They walk on, past the clock tower and up the broad road to the better part of town. Two bookshops here with foreign books and foreign prices. A girl in denim wants Milan Kundera. The nuns browse in the children's section but can only gape at the prices.

'There's the Soviet Bookshop,' the owner says, grasping

the problem. 'Try there.' He points the way.

Soviet books! Perpetua frowns. But Ritu cheers up: she's used the Delhi shop for science texts, Russian novels. Hardbound, handsomely printed, without the American gloss to the page, without the Indian wretchedness. And cheap.

They come to Amarnath Place, find the familiar drab shopfront: cataract in the glass, dour jackets pinned out and fading in the window. No customers, just a grizzled shopkeeper and his rows of dismal texts. Declamatory titles, lumpish words, like a shout that died in the mouth. Chekhov biding his time. A whole poignant shelf of Lenin's *What is to be Done?*

But on the floor in bright stacks, the children's books. Lev Tolstoy's *The Three Bears*, five rupees. *Hic Hac Hoc*, by Yuri Nosov, seven rupees. *How They Live*, by Y. Charushin, five rupees. One called *Little Masha*, whose watercolours glow with a child's wonderment.

Ritu takes one from each pile: ten Moscow books for the price of one from London or New York. Scoops up two more for good measure.

Once home, she rations them, two at a time. Let the words come later; for now there are the pictures. Pictures Shama gorges on, her eyes roaming the page with an avidity that almost frightens Ritu. Riding a blue whale, picking brindled mushrooms, stroking the leopard's molten coat.

Her favourite is *Little Masha*. Masha is two, a year younger than Shama, but Shama sees herself there, in that bedroom washed in violet shadows, in that garden wild with blackberry canes. She is rummaging in that giant chest of drawers. *Shamashamashamashamasha*. The book is soonest dog-eared. By the time it's lost its cover Ritu has already begun to call her Masha.

Major Bakshi objects.

'Masha is a foreign name.'

'The potato is foreign,' Ritu answers.

'*Alu?*' the major says, horrified. '*Never!*'

'It is. We got it from Europe. Where it was foreign, too.'

'But what did we eat before!'

First there's gelignite.

Brij knows that much. Then he's lost. He goes to the library: nothing there. He goes to the technical bookshops by the Iron Bridge, but comes away bewildered. Then he enters the Soviet bookshop, but chokes on the word *explosives*.

A light comes on in the bookseller's eye. A fellow traveller whose plans came unstuck twenty years ago, Sandhu is trying to run the shop on reformist lines, strict profit and loss, but can't in conscience put the prices up. He's installed an old photostat machine, but can't keep up with the competition.

'Explosives,' he repeats, and twinkles at Brij. 'As in bomb?'

'No, no!'

'Just explosives,' Sandhu nods, giving the word a softer, theoretical cast. And frowns. 'I had a book, a pamphlet really. No, not a pamphlet, a small book. Let me see.' He wanders off into the back of the shop while Brij looks around at the stern hardcovers, the stacks of children's books on the floor. He feels the man's eyes on him from the shadows. 'No, it's not here,' the bookseller calls. 'But I think I know somebody who can help you.'

He takes a sheet from a blank letter pad, folds it in half, then quarters, eighths and sixteenths, running a dead thumbnail along the fold each time. Tears off a corner piece the size of a visiting card and writes the name and address of a travel agency on it in pencil. Then holds it up for Brij to read. Not to take: when Brij reaches for it he withdraws his hand a fraction.

'Read it again,' he offers. And when Brij does, he repeats, 'and again.' Then he tears the card up into little pieces, puts some into his pocket and drops the rest into two separate bins.

Brij thanks him and leaves. Sandhu sits back down and watches him through the shop window and pats himself on the cheek several times. Leans his chair back and pokes at the books on the bottom shelf until all the spines are flush. Then picks up his keys, bolts the back door and locks up the shop.

Brij wanders down the road to the clock tower, repeating the address to himself. If he knows his town it should be behind the bus depot. He turns down the lane beside the skewered chickens of the Shere-e-Punjab and asks directions of the leather belt specialist, where the lane forks.

'Along there past the electricals, last shop,' the man says. 'You need a belt?'

Brij comes to the agency. 'Sonam Travels' reads the green and gold sign. Two identical posters of an alpine pasture are taped to the glass as a blind. He goes in and stops in his tracks.

Sitting at the only desk in the room, with his hands folded on the blotter, is Sandhu.

Ritu is on her way to the leper colony.

She crosses the riverbed, enters the forest. The passage from light to dark is always a relief now that summer is approaching, but also it evokes a forest childhood whose disappearance she still regrets. It's not the retreat of childhood that troubles her but the dying of its memories. Of certain heightened moments when the world was transfigured, when it seemed she was truly alive. Every day there are fewer left. Some mornings a fragment will return, glowing to bewitch her as she wakes, more a feeling than a memory, and leave her mourning its loss.

But here is another forest path, strewn with fallen leaves. The gumhar is shedding. These are the trees she helped save. She picks up a rumpled leaf, large as a dinner plate, and strokes the underside as she walks. Hundreds of short hairs bending under her thumb make up that one sensation. She examines the cottony pubescence, looks at the dark straight trunks.

There is a figure behind one of the trunks ahead.

A man.

She walks on, still carrying the leaf, though her instinct tells her to stop. To go back, to run.

He is shearing with his sickle the slender twiggy growth at the base of the tree, but without conviction, not working but waiting. For her, she's sure now. Because as she approaches his concentration tautens, till at last it breaks and turns, on her.

She recognizes him. She took his photograph. The man menacing Lakhi with an iron bar. Now dropping his sickle and making for her.

He takes two steps towards her and smacks her hard across the chest. The other hand grappling with her head, trying to get a grip on her hair, which he finds too short to hold, so rips the wimple off and slaps her across the face. Again and again, cursing her with every slap.

She should shout, she knows. The colony would hear, but her voice has dried up. All she can manage are little moans every time he hits her. Now he has her arm twisted up behind her, has picked up his sickle and is pushing her off the track into the forest.

When a cry does break out, but not from her throat. A long simian cry, taken up in the treetops roundabout and carried on and on until the whole forest is ringing. The man is startled, stops and looks around. Then, panicking, pushes Ritu from him with all his strength and runs off. She tumbles down a steep slope to land on her back.

Oozing ground here. Sky above. She lies there dazed, thinking, Marsh. Get up. But can't. The mud a soft pillow under her head, holding her down. When she forces her head up it lifts with a sucking sound, but then her shoulders go under. Her hands are covered in slime. Reeds all around her, tall as trees. Treetops, forest, at the top of the bank, sky.

Dizzy. She could sink into the marsh, slowly turn skeleton. Become a jawbone, some teeth.

Help. Yourself. She shuts her eyes, hears the ooze ticking at her ear, smells a sharp beetle smell, uses that to concentrate. Are you sinking? No. Rest a while, then. She gathers her strength and slowly rolls over. Draws herself, reed by reed, back to firm ground. Root by root up the slope.

The women of the colony wash her, dress her in a sari, lay her on a string bed. Lakhi goes to call the nuns.

Nobody wants the Packard.

No-one in Drummondganj. Jed has put it on the market in the classifieds, but everyone has heard the story of the German woman. The driver's seat has been stripped and re-upholstered, but even Brij's father, who coveted the car from the time he first serviced it, is no longer sure he wants it standing in the yard. Not that he could afford the asking price.

Jed is putting his affairs in order. The civil surgeon has called with new painkillers. Jed knows he must use the few clear days left him.

'I know I'm mad,' he says to his old friend. 'Senile.' What hurts is that he knows, can say *senile*.

'Confess!' he explodes when Father Lobo comes to counsel preparation. 'What do I confess to? Murder? Mayhem? Masturbation?'

The youthful Mangalorean, a giant with a treble voice, webs his long fingers and giggles.

When he's gone Jed lies there rehearsing the scene, embroidering, hamming it up. Confess to what? Molestation? Mangling? Measles? The sins pile up. He's grinning, enjoying himself, the spiteful stagey mouthing.

Mangaloreaneity, malingering, malodorousness? The brain still kicking, he's pleased to see. Melodrama, mockery, monkishness.

Misogyny?

How he would love to be working on *The Drummondganj Book of the Dead*! 'Concerning Deathbed Confessions' II, ix (a) Kings, Queens, Rulers: [Subs.] Leaders: Murder, mayhem, misprision, malfeasance, mischief, maundering . . .

Nachiketa has been in hiding. Send for him, sulk when he comes. Meandering. Myristicivorousness.

Mendacity.

Madness. He goes to the parapet and pisses over it, onto the periwinkle. Micturition. Looks out along the Via Mortis. Can it be?

Can it be? He looks again. It is.

The bamboo is flowering. All along Canal Road the dark-green clumps are enveloped in a yellow mist. The wind stirs it, sends it creeping towards Everest.

Mustard gas.

Sandhu knows nothing about bombs.

But he knows a young engineering graduate, unemployed, who can help. They'll need money, but he knows an NGO employee with access to Norwegian development funds. The NGO advocates small dams, grass roots action, fair enough.

'Weren't you one of those arrested in the Lohri crackdown?' Sandhu asks one day.

Brij nods and looks away. The word *Lohri* is still painful.

'I watched your release. The others went off to celebrate; you went straight home. I liked that. It's what we're fighting for.'

A few days ago Sandhu could not have said what he was fighting for. Or could have said and said. Now it's focusing. He loves Brij for that, and for embodying his lost youth. He's made his own adjustments. The dam was built with Soviet aid, but then Moscow went off the rails. The centre shifts, history shows.

Brij needn't worry about the device. He needs to get a job at the dam driving one of those trucks that are still clearing away detonated rubble from the site.

'You have a licence?'

Brij's hands shape *of course*. He was driving at seven, drove his first truck at fourteen.

'You have any local references?'

'My mamaji lives there.'

'Good. Go on, then. You stay there. Give me your address and I'll be in touch with you.'

Brij reaches across to Sandhu's pocket for his fountain pen and writes down his New Mandia address on the blotter. They are sitting in the Sonam Travels office. Sandhu reads it back to him.

'Read it again,' Brij says, unscrewing the barrel of the pen. 'And again.'

Then he squeezes the ink out onto the pad until the address is an egg-shaped black blot.

Sandhu looks up with a reluctant smile. He'll need a new blotter.

B AISAKH, *April can be chill — two pairs of socks for Jed — but the cold comes at dawn and doesn't last. The trees aren't fooled. The coral is budding, covered in lipstick tubes, the lychee grove is loud with bees. The brainfever bird is not yet in full throat. In his moody silences he steps gravely from twig to twig, the pretender in exile. Sudden dust storms blast Cecelia's roses, wrap Everest in sackcloth. Perpetua's water wars have resumed: she paces the line under Mrs Puri's terrace, brandishing the wrench in one twisted hand and a rosary in the other. Or crouches with the goongi at the mains tap, listening for the water hammer.*

B rij feels he can trust Sandhu. But he feels the old panic: his life is slipping out of his control. He envies those who act single-mindedly, resolutely. Himself, he'd like to talk about it. He can't approach Raju; his brother would think he'd gone mad. And maybe he has. His father would inform the police. His mother would look long and admiringly at him and have him locked up.

Jed, then. But Yama Raja would mock, and mockery of all things Brij can't take just now.

He hasn't been back to Everest since January. Has looked away from it in his head, especially during the month he spent with his uncle's family in New Mandia. It's still a blind spot; when he tries, certain images blur, and he's come in a morbid way to cherish that ghosting.

But there is a figure that hovers, alive, at the edge of his vision, who has never gone away, and today he recognizes her. Ritu. Talk to her.

He doesn't take the shortcut. Too much pain that way. He goes round to the front gate, which he latches softly behind him before making straight for the iron stair. Jed he'll have to endure if he is to meet her. He steps lightly. With a bit of luck Yama will be dozing.

He isn't.

'Nachiketa! Back from the dead!' Jed was never tactful, dressing up unconcern with wit. 'How are things down there?'

'Not bad.'

'My subjects behaving? No sedition in the ranks?'

'No.'

'Good. All well on ancestral ground? I assume that's where you've been. I refuse to believe that my neighbours at Everest would be home and not call on me.'

'I've been away.'

'Excellent. It shows in your cheeks. You've never looked better.' Spoken with the eyes shut fast.

Brij looks down at him. Does this man never tire of clever talk?

'Dam filling up nicely?'

'I'm going to blow it up.'

'Fine. You have every right. Have you flown any kites lately?'

'No.'

'Have you noticed the bamboo is flowering? Creeping up on me like mustard gas. You wouldn't like to take some dictation?' Jed opens his eyes wide. 'The *Book*?'

Brij sighs. How does it matter?

'All right.'

But then Ritu comes in off the roof, where she's been dipping sheets. Sunblind, she doesn't see him at first. Then her eyes pick him out, meet his.

Him. A man. Men. He doesn't know about the attack in the forest, yet reads all three in her look. But also, in the gaps, *You!* For which he's grateful and nods yes, smiling. The trace of a smile drifts back. He'd almost forgotten its beauty, this face which the other displaced. That one a fox, this one a bird.

Where to start? So many taboo subjects. Neither strangers nor friends, denied the barter of both. The silence is growing opaque when Jed says to the ceiling, 'Nachiketa is going to blow up the Mandia dam. He'll want a cup of tea.'

It rescues her inert hands. She takes the kettle to the door, shakes out the chips of kettlestone. Fetches down the tea caddy.

'What is it to be?' Jed demands. 'Orange pekoe or tisane of periwinkle?'

'Pekoe,' she answers. The voice soft, subdued. Tsering substituted for three days up here till she recovered. The forest walks are at an end, for now. So are the numeracy classes. Serve God on the roof.

'Some breeze, Nachiketa. I'm hot.'

Brij turns on the fan. The simple act, alongside her tea-making, draws them together, he feels. Recalling a past when he made free with every object in this room, when they did things together.

'And put on some music. Whatever's there.'

There's a record already on the felt mat. Brij winds up the gramophone and a quavery tenor shreds the yielding air. Powdered glass on kite string.

Lady of Spain, I adore you.
Right from the time I first saw you . . .

'There's no fresh milk,' Ritu announces. 'Shall I mix up some powder?'

'Make it up, make it up.'

Jed's impatient mind is already drifting up through altitudes of dogwood and musk rose. His eyes roam the iron corrugations, the lids growing heavy. The painkiller Ritu administered after changing the sheets is going to work. It takes longer now, on top of the other drugs. By the time the tea is drawn he's unreachable. She sets his cup down on the bedside table and covers it with the saucer.

My heart has been aching for you.
Lady of Spain, I love you.

Ritu hands Brij his without looking, has not made herself a cup. Smooths her veil down, making to go.

'You're not having any?'

She shakes her head. Then sees that a spoken answer would have carried fewer implications.

He puts his cup down untouched.

'All right,' she relents, and takes Jed's cup.

The song, foreign to both, comes to an end.

Silence, which Brij does not know how to break. The ghost of Inge fills the room.

Ritu sips her tea. Let him speak first.

He does. 'Are you well?'

'Much better.' But he wouldn't know.

'You were ill?'

'Yes.'

'You have a new guest, my mother was telling me.' When she doesn't connect he adds, 'The little girl.'

'Oh, Masha.' Lightly, with a faint smile. Ritu doesn't think of her as a guest. 'She's been with us a while.'

'Where is she from?'

'Who knows? That side.' She waves along the hills. 'All that trouble over there. She came with a note pinned to her frock.'

'How is she doing?'

'Well. She's learnt her alphabet, Hindi and English.'

'Are you her teacher?'

'Everybody teaches her.'

Brij smiles and tries to picture the lessons. 'You'll keep her?'

'Of course.'

Brij stares at his cup. Utter conviction in that response. This woman he abandoned for the other – if you can give up what is not yours. Such a woman he could keep safe. Could have kept. At such moments he knows only the urge to protect, to hold with his arms. But Inge is there between them. He failed Inge. He is about to fail his family. But would not fail this woman whom he loved. Loves, he realizes now, though he cannot expect to be believed. Doesn't deserve to be. What does he deserve?

And you? a voice is speaking in Ritu's head. How are you? Where have you been? Look, I'm not surprised you fell in love with her. It doesn't matter any more. But what is this nonsense about the dam? Jed's rubbish, surely? Stay here. Come and see us. The girl needs—

Needs what?

'I'll take the cup.' She's standing up.

He hands it to her and stands up, too. Dismissal in that tone. His mind is racing for something to say, some hold on the moment, on this room, some word that will check the slide.

'Ritu.'

It's all he can manage. She has turned away, is busy rinsing cups, taunting herself. You didn't mean to stand up. Pride. And all your talk of charity! The china clinking dully in her hands.

He waits for her to finish, still doesn't know what he's going to say. *Come with me. A dam is nothing*.

She's drying her hands carefully on a tea towel. Examining the label which says plainly, MADE IN INDIA 100% BAUM-WOLLE. *Say you need me and I will leave this place*.

'Ritu.' His tongue stiffens. 'Can I give something towards the girl's . . .' What is he saying? It's not what he meant at all. 'Will you take some money for her?'

Norwegian funds, for development.

'There's no need. The order is not poor.'

They're walking down the iron stair together, Ritu leading. Her dove-grey habit descending, step by step, so frail, so tangible, before him. The space between them constant, and yet widening so rapidly he fears he's going mad. He could lay a hand on her shoulder, but the habit is reproof.

Come back. There's more. His tongue is wood.

Mrs Puri watching from behind her pot of basil. Perpetua treading the line with her wrench. The goongi staring up at him with spaniel eyes. From the back of Everest a shout, then a girl comes running.

They reach the bottom of the stair.

'Well, bye bye. This is the girl?'

'Yes. All the best. Masha will reach you to the gate. Masha, this is Brij.'

Ritu turns and goes to her room, where she can be alone. Custody of the heart.

Masha holds Brij's finger with a fearsome grip and tugs him, laughing, all the way to the Everest gate.

Summer

*N*ow the brainfever bird is in full cry. His call climbs and climbs, then snaps off like a muezzin's microphone.

Last night's storm has spread a carpet in the lychee grove. Late blossom mixed in with stillborn fruit. The tiny fruit shaped like male genitalia. The carpet has a pattern, random yet assigned: dust on creamy blossom on green fruit on a ground of dead brown leaves. Small bees hover in formation over the carpet, imposing still another pattern, one that lifts and ripples, till it's hard to say where the true level of the ground lies.

The fountain is dry; ditch plants draw in. But new leaf fans appear hourly on the flamboyant, filling in blank spaces of sky.

It would show the world that the cause is not lost simply because the Soviet state is being dismantled. There are still workers in the world, and chains.

For the rest of April the Soviet bookshop is often closed as he goes about the logistics. The NGO supplies a wide-bore water pump, money, papers: a tubewell to be sunk for development. Sandhu buys batches of RDX in spot purchases, which Baingan coolie is pleased to negotiate through his sons, the scooter rickshaw drivers. The engineer finds employment. Brij trucks.

He's back in Mandia. Driving for a contractor grown rich in the shadow of the dam. There's no other shade to be had. The sun scorches the back of his neck, of his knotty hands. Dust coats his hair, his thick lenses, his city shirt; his city shoes are wearing down on rock and rubble. His first wage is not payable until July; the contractor keeps back a month's earnings.

'May Day would make bigger news,' Sandhu repeats, up to scout around, to report on progress.

Brij doesn't care. He listens stonily when someone talks; he drives by rote. His eyes take in the road, but he's looking at the dust, not through it.

Sandhu has picked up a survey map and a glossy brochure put out by the dam publicists. The brochure shows the dam, in surprising detail, with levels and spillways, an artist's view for the layman.

'We're laymen,' Sandhu jokes, looking down on the real thing from a park high on the hill in New Mandia. The blue lake swelling behind it.

Brij, in a Sunday T-shirt, dabs stolidly at his forehead with a handkerchief and doesn't smile. He no longer needs to please people.

Down in Drummondganj, sweat plagues the engineer, too. He works in a rented shed with a small table fan playing on him, but must turn it off when he plugs in the soldering iron. Then, just when the solder is beaded, a drop of sweat will fall beside it and the hiss and spurt of steam will jolt his nerves.

He leans back to rest his neck and stares at the rags of cobweb hanging from a roof beam.

If the drop fell between two wires in the circuitry . . .

He screws up his eyes. His jaw aches. He has been grinding his teeth in his sleep.

The water pump sits on the ground beside him like a giant boot. He is trying not to think about the foot.

JETH. *May Day burns. At one time, when the forest was intact and there were groves and orchards besides, the townspeople counted it the first day of summer and switched on their fans. Today the fans blow hot air; only a desert cooler will do. In Brij's house a cooler pump breaks down. Going to replace it, his father remembers that the spare one went to Everest last year. He curses and goes out onto the terrace, where his wife's pickle jars are still hot from the last of the day's sun. Carrot sticks crowd the top like dead goldfish. He leans on the balustrade where the Bhatts' one plant, a cactus, has withered in its tin.*

A dust haze hangs over the city; there's a green kite twitching in the sky. The mountains look their age, grey, exhausted. As night falls streamers of flame appear on them: the villagers are burning

off undergrowth. All along the range are patches where the fires

have got out of hand. There the orange glows like lava, whole trees

flaring up in seconds. The forest will smoulder for days.

'OK,' Sandhu announces, turning up one morning. 'We're ready.'

May Day didn't work out; there were delays, worries. Now he thinks he has it under control. He spreads out the map on the park bench.

'Where's the landfill?'

Brij turns the map round to face him and points to a gully. 'I think.'

He has the ground plan in his head from weeks of clearing at the dam, but he's not comfortable with maps.

'Good,' Sandhu says. It's off the main road, where he thought it was. 'Now listen. Tomorrow afternoon your truck will break down at the dam. Small problem with the tipper. You report it, but you repair it on the spot. Load up, take the load to the landfill. At the turn-off your truck breaks down again. You get out, fiddle with it so the other drivers see. Tell them you're OK, no problem. When they're gone you drive two kilometres down the road to the spring at the horseshoe bend. You know it? There's a pool there, with a sump. We'll be waiting for you. The labour will transfer the pump, cover it up. We'll pick them up on the way. You drive back to the dam just before the gates close. Then it's up to you.'

Masha under the pipal: a new red leaf.

Ritu is writing in her sketchbook, looking out of the glory-hole window. Masha has come to a halt under the tree where Inge worked, is standing there looking up at the new leaves. The girl has been swanning around Everest under one of Miss Sampson's hats. This one is red, with a long white feather in the band.

Ritu shuts the book. It's become a daily record and she knows Cecelia would confiscate it: diaries are against the rule. But for some time she has felt obliged to keep one. It began with Masha's coming, when she was struggling to communicate with her, trying to see the world with the eyes of a child, of her own childhood spent looking closely at nature. But she limits herself, must pick out one thing a day. Daily she reviews the minutiae of Everest and compels herself to pick out one.

Masha's hat is today's entry. It means she cannot record the tumbling of the green bee-eaters as they scallop the hot afternoon air, or the mauve ripples in the camel hoof buds that Neha's knife was slicing on the chopping board just now. Some days she will sit there swollen with detail, hardly able to breathe. The glut of sensation oppresses her, will not go away until she has detached one image from the mass.

The satellite dish a moon lily. Yesterday.

Extravagance some days: *Her smile would ripen green mangoes.*

The day Miss Sampson died: *Death, the tolling of a tongue-less bell.*

She has begun along the way to judge. *C. will haggle over the fare to heaven.*

J. climbed Everest, can't climb down.

But mostly she returns to one subject. *She's a mystery: a seashell on a mountain.*

Nape furry, upper lip tomentose.

And it's as she sits today looking over the month's entries that the idea ferns into her head.

But can't be written down today.

She needs a mother, not mothering.

B rij cuts sharp, backing his truck off the road. Sandhu's public carrier is waiting with the huge pump: he had no idea it would be so big. It's not going to bring the dam down, but it'll rattle the turbines. Brij has to dump half his rubble before he can take on the bomb. He sees a cut under the culvert where the spring water has eroded the bank. A precision drop would seal it and make the bridge safe.

For future generations, he smiles into the rear-view mirror. Going to your death and dabbling at minor surgery. He backs all the way to the edge, throws the handbrake, leans on the tip lever, toggles it. Shaking out gravel like salt.

Sealed. In three weeks he's mastered that. Look, Father, not useless. And maybe not going to my death, if I can jump from the truck in time.

The tipper bed drops back into place. Brij pulls out, drops another load on the road shoulder, then backs up against the tailgate of the other truck. The labourers, who've been watching from the roadside, go to work. Plainsmen Sandhu picked up from three widely separated villages.

It takes six men an hour. The pump is hooded over with a tarpaulin and the roadside gravel is shovelled back on board. Around and over it, Sandhu directs to secure the machine. No better way, the labourers agree, not even chains.

The engineer, unemployed once more, climbs into the

truck cabin and explains the detonator mechanism to Brij one more time. He has written it down, too, on the inside of a cigarette packet. They climb out, smoke a last cigarette together, two from the pack. Sandhu, who doesn't smoke, has the labourers top-dress the bomb with more gravel.

Then he comes round. 'OK, boss.'

Brij looks evenly at him. 'OK, comrade.'

They shake hands. For the first time in months Brij is grinning. The pain is gone.

'But single women *can* adopt.'

Ritu has seen the new legislation discussed, and denounced, in the *Tablet*.

'Yes, but Christians can't,' Cecelia replies, 'not in this country.'

Ritu is baffled. 'Why not?'

'In India only Hindus can adopt a stray child.'

Ritu frowns. 'But that's not right!' Her voice breaking.

'Maybe,' Cecelia agrees. 'But that's the way it is.' She'd like to nip this whole thing in the bud. If Ritu goes, Neha will follow, she's sure of that. The sketchbook is on her desk; it was what brought the whole business up. The bit about herself in heaven rankles, but she's trying to be fair, to keep that out of it.

'Where would you go?' She's being reasonable.

'I could take her home.'

'Really?'

Ritu knows she couldn't. Her father would not allow it. She'll have to go to Delhi, get a job at a hospital, or a nursing home.

'I'll get a job.'

Cecelia's lips tighten. 'You know what they'll say.'

Ritu lowers her eyelids. That has never been a worry. Now it decides her.

Cecelia sees her mistake too late. She was going to use the sketchbook to bargain with; now it's simply a book, soon to revert to its owner.

'A child needs a father,' she tosses out. Into the gap widening between them.

'Who does she have here?'

They're both aware of that. And both have seen the orphans at church. Twenty girls, eight boys, fed and clothed; scrubbed but never shining. Eyes glazed over with a crippling knowledge. Labelled, merging into one dull mass, fading before they open.

And this one blazes like a poppy.

Phillips looks again at the truck.

Coming down the service slope, one of the yellow tippers. There are twelve trucks working with the dozers: they carry earth up the steep slope to a landfill off the main road and come back down for more. The steep road serves a dam access six floors down from the top. It's here, outside Phillips' gate that the levelling is in progress. Below the access the road switches back and continues down to the foot of the dam, overhanging the first spillway. At any one time there are two trucks coming down or going up the slope, so what is it about this one that puzzles Phillips?

And then he sees it. The truck is coming down, so it should be empty.

It isn't.

Brij sees Phillips at the bottom of the slope, standing at the access gate. He knows him at once by his massive head and oddly short legs. He's never addressed the dwarfish man, though he's heard his name often enough. Everyone uses it; even those without reason to. It sounds modern, like the radio, the TV; Phillips is general property. Among the engineers with the hard hats it's Phillips this and Phillips that; even the drivers like calling out to Phillips as they go by. Phillips stands at his post staring up at the truck.

Brij brakes. He's been in a state of heightened awareness ever since he set the clock. Now he's tingling all over. He has two minutes to deliver the load.

He throws the handbrake and jumps out.

'Phillips!' he shouts and signals, come quick.

The man looks puzzled, starts moving on his short legs.

'Phillips!' Brij beckons urgently.

Phillips breaks into a run. Up the slope, just as the handbrake begins to give. Brij jumps back into the cab and grabs the wheel. The truck begins to roll down the slope. Phillips is drawing level with the truck, slowing down again.

'*Run*, Phillips!' Brij shouts, turning his head to the window without taking his eyes off the road. 'It's a bomb!'

Phillips runs.

Brij has stopped looking at his watch, is operating now by instinct. The truck gathers speed on the slope, roaring as it goes.

The plan was to ram the gate in the wire fence and direct the truck at the access door, a wide bay in the concrete hull of the dam. Leap from the moving truck, race back down to the lower service road, and jump into the spillway. Keep his head above water, then float downstream into the old river. It's why he's wearing a life jacket.

Now he's lost time. Things are starting to go wrong. The nose of a loaded truck appears at the bottom of the slope and

279

Brij sounds his horn. The truck backs off. Brij leans on the horn all the way down.

He doesn't need to accelerate on the level, but does. The gate is half open. The truck rams the other half as it bursts through the security fence, veers away from the access door. Brij must hang on to the wheel just when he should be letting go. He rights the wheel, points the truck at the entry bay and steps on the pedal once more to make sure. The truck leaps forward, covering the ground sooner than Brij expected. Now he jumps, falls, rolls over.

He's run out of time, he knows. His instinct is to take cover. But there's no cover. The only cover is the dam, where the truck has just crashed. He gets up and runs at the security guard, knocking him down at the door. And then he's inside the concrete shell.

It's dark inside. The neon light like moonlight. And oddly quiet. Just the hum of machinery, of giant turbines in the hall below. A companionway leading down.

He's on the iron stair when the bomb goes off.

Tonight Everest is a kiln.

The bedsheets burn, the twins cry out in their sleep. Ritu turns her pillow over repeatedly, looking for a cool surface for her cheek, till finally she swings her feet over the edge of the bed and sits up. She goes barefoot to the mesh door and lets herself out into the night. Against the rules, but the rules are fading fast now. She walks on the dry grass in the rosiny light of a shrouded moon. Thunder rolling on the horizon, distant lightning, someone else's storm. Her feet find the drive, begin to pace its length. She feels the pebbles underfoot, sharp and smooth, walks haunted by a nameless dread and longing. Something is wrong.

She turns and hurries back to her room, to the other bed. Leans over the bed and switches on the light.

Masha's bed is empty.

The bottom sheet smoothed flat, her slippers gone.

Ritu looks about wildly, her blood pounding. The thunder must have woken her, but where has she gone? The child fears thunder above all things. Ritu looks under the beds, in the bathroom, out of the door she just used. Hears a sudden sharp tapping of raindrops on large leaves, rain out of a clear sky. Is she out there?

More likely indoors, after taking a wrong turn into the hall.

She slips through the door that is always open, pauses at the foot of the staircase, where the clock used to stand. Stares into the enormous shadows of the hall, black wings folded on grey. The floor reflecting light from the landing windows, lapping around the legs of the long black pier of the telephone table. Not there. Cecelia's door stands open, beside it Perpetua's. Go quietly, try the chapel first. She crosses to it, genuflects, walks down the aisle, inspecting the pews, the altar. Not there. Try the parlour. She moves by instinct among the parlour furniture, instinct helped by memory, helped also by lightning that continues to flicker over the hills. Not here.

Turns, making for the dining room, when she sees her.

On the staircase, coming down. Holding the devil's arm.

Against the landing windows, a low sheeted figure in silhouette. Moving steadily by no light she can see, so steadily it's clear she's asleep. Wake her and she could fall, where Miss Sampson fell. Let her come.

Ritu goes softly to the foot of the stair and places herself there, waiting. Step by step Masha comes down. Looking for something that eludes her, the way the past eludes one in the harsh light of day but is there the moment the eyes are shut. Her eyes are open; she sees Ritu and doesn't see. Steps off the last step and buries her dreaming forehead in Ritu's stomach. They stand there, locked in sleep and sleeplessness. She has her plastic bag in one hand. She went up to the twins, to comfort and be comforted.

Presently Ritu leads her back to their room, puts her to bed. Then goes out and walks again on the grass, now wet with those few drops of rain. When she comes back in Masha is motionless on her bed, the top sheet bunched up under her chin.

She is breathing strangely, half choking. There's a band of sweat on her forehead at the cusp where the deeply arched eyebrows almost meet.

Ritu wipes the sweat away with the back of her hand. Then she undoes the small fingers and releases the sheet. Pulls it away, uncovers the sweating body. It's too hot for covering. She could lift the child up and hold her to her heart, push back the night terrors she remembers so well, and those she can only guess at in Masha's hidden past; hold and soothe and keep her from harm, put her own body in the way. Stroke that vulnerable skin, till a gentle current flows out of one and feeds the other. Because that is all one can hope to do. But that would wake her, and it's sleep she needs.

She takes the plastic bag and looks in it for the first time. Among the bangles and toys is a bloodied rag, the blood no longer fresh.

She turns off the light and returns to bed, and lies on her side staring at the pool of moonlight on the floor.

A sunbird's nest, with eggs.

Thapa angles the branch he's just cut off to catch the last of the sun. Three eggs, speckled grey. He stands penitent, brooding over how his blade always falls in the wrong place. Then hangs the nest back up in spite of his belief that disturbed eggs don't hatch. That done he returns to his room to dress for the wedding.

There's another nest suspended at his door, a weaver bird's funnel, hanging there since January to ward off ghosts, one in particular. It's done its job so far: Inge has not returned to haunt him. There are two ways to kill a ghost: you burn it or you drown it. Or else you ward it off with baya nests. Other nests are best left alone: the sunbird's nest is a bad augury on this day. Coming, too, at the end of his preparations. Why didn't he let the bougainvillea be? Primping like an old woman. He's swept the entire compound, trimmed the creepers, weeded the gravel paths, colour-washed the brick borders in alternate red and white. The place is as spruce as a cantonment.

True, the guests don't come till after dark, but it's not every day that a batman gets to send off his officer.

The wedding tents and awnings have been pitched on the open ground to the city side of Everest. Cecelia has watched the patterned canvas go up without a murmur; Major Bakshi went up to see Jed and Jed gave his assent. Behind a harlequin screen of red and blue and green diamonds the cooks are at work, sweating into vats of chhole and chicken dopiaza. A hill boy with his index finger bandaged has chopped eight kilos of onions single-handed. Bakshi has contracted out the occasion at ninety rupees a plate, with the crockery and cutlery and tents and chairs and carpeting and generator thrown in. He's bargained hard: the bride is in no position to pay, and he's taking on her family besides. He's made her back down on the bizarre notion that the tents should face away from Everest, so as to be visible from her terrace.

Mrs Bakshi wears less jewellery than she did the first time round, as Mrs Puri. Only one piece, a teardrop of diamonds clustered around a sapphire at her forehead, is new; the others – necklaces, bracelets, nosering – she wore fifteen years ago, when the navy band played and she was young and slim. Her sari too is new, peacock blue with Benares gold work. All through the reception she will glower at Perpetua, who has chosen an especially rumpled habit for this evening.

Thapa is in full dress, his shorts pressed, his kukri handle facings Brassoed, the scabbard Cherry Blossomed. The old Gurkha johnny hat dusted off and angled over his head. He escorts guests from the gate, marching up the gravel in front of them on boots that glitter like cat's eyes. He has drunk nothing.

Major Bakshi, in a wool-blend suit, has been sweating and drinking all evening. At the reception he sits with a rum whose level Thapa has kept constant; his paisley raw-silk tie is plastered to the glass. Officer and man are locked in a duel of misty origin; only the new Mrs Bakshi can begin to unravel the dialogue of their eyes. Every time a guest arrives Bakshi rises, accepts their felicitations, presents his wife with a wave of the arm that has the rum sloshing in its glass. Mrs Bakshi does not rise; the child the major has grown to hate is wedged between her thighs as she sits enthroned on red velvet and gilded wood. Only when the nuns arrive does Bakshi, out of habit, put away his glass. In deference to Perpetua he has dinner served at once, but eats nothing himself.

'There were three killed,' a guest is saying, a colonel from the local Sikh regiment.

'I heard six.'

'No, three. And fourteen injured.'

'And the dam?'

'Small crack. But they're letting out the water in case it develops. All the gates are open.'

'That'll take weeks.'

'It wasn't full. Not even half.'

'Have they found out who was behind it?'

'The usual theories. Akashkhand. Pakistan. But he was from here, local man. One funny thing. He was wearing a life jacket.'

'What, in case the dam burst?'

Muffled military laughter.

Ritu has heard enough. The nuns leave before the sweet dish, taking Masha with them. She has eaten a plateful of pulao with great civility. Thapa comes to attention as they go. He has positioned himself at the entrance to the tent, beside a guy rope, facing outward like a temple guardian.

Inside the tent the talk turns to shikar. The major tells his wild boar story, the colonel caps it with a leopard. Bakshi is not pleased: this is his day. He searches his mind for a fitting reply, but he's shot no tiger, no rhino, no elephant. His eye falls on Thapa, a shadow beyond the gauze of the chief marquee. Should he? He swallows down the rum in his glass and calls the man in. Thapa takes the empty glass and marches off to the drinks table.

'Smart man,' Bakshi says by way of introduction. 'He was with me in Jessore, in Chham, in Kutch, all over. Totally faithful, honest, reliable. Strong, my God! But . . .' Bakshi leans forward and lowers his voice, 'don't ever mention buffalo sacrifice to him.'

Thapa returns with a full glass, clicks his heels, and goes out to his post.

'Buffalo sacrifice?' the colonel says, with a conspiratorial twinkle. He's lowered his voice, too. A few of the guests edge closer. Thapa hears the voices lowered. They're using English but he can pick up certain words: regiment, kukri, a place name, a festival. He strains to hear, and as he does a flush comes over him, and deepens.

'We were posted in Ranikhet,' Bakshi says, 'and it was Dashera. Ten days of drinking, dancing, and gambling. With the johnnies the last four days are crucial and the big climax comes on the eighth night at midnight. That year our man had been selected for the eighth-night sacrifice because he was known to be good with his kukri. Lightning Thapa, they called him. One flash – and there was the goat's head on the ground. And he was handsome, too. Bit short, but well built. Anyway he was selected.

'For two weeks the chosen man goes into isolation: no drinking, no women, no meat, nothing. Rice, curds, water. Special exercises, prayers, rituals, baths. After all, the honour of the regiment depends on him. It has to be done with one stroke, clean.

'That night he came out from his puja smiling, confident. I remember there was already a bit of cheering as he walked up. The priest put the tilak on his forehead and handed him the kukri. The buffalo tied up and waiting. Our man takes up his position, closes his eyes, says a prayer. I remember the kukri going up.

'And then I don't know what happened. Some people said the buffalo moved, some said he lost his concentration. But the kukri came down at the wrong place. Or at the wrong angle. Or something.' Bakshi drains his glass. 'But after that he was known in the regiment as Two-Stroke Thapa.'

'Two-Stroke Thapa!' the colonel repeats, more in sorrow than in amusement.

He has spoken softly, but Thapa has heard the humiliating words. Their poison is burning in his chest. The cry that started there is shredding in his throat, twisting his mouth before it spills into the night.

Bakshi looks up sharply and sees his batman's shadow turn. He knows he's done wrong. Even as he spoke the last words he knew he was crossing a line, watched himself do it with red incredulous eyes. Now he hears the cry and flinches.

Thapa is rigid, the naked kukri in his hand. One thrust and he can cancel the shame of that night. Bakshi sees the man spring and shuts his eyes. Thapa lunges with such force that his voice box lifts.

There's a sudden slackening in the tent cloth at the entrance. Thapa has severed the guy rope where he stood on duty. He leaps again and severs the rope on the other side of the entrance. He runs from rope to rope around the marquee, slicing the air. Pole after pole jerks free from its mooring and tilts sharply inward, until the last rope is cut and the whole tottering structure collapses.

Screams, gruff shouts, arms poking up, sheeted ghost heads. A rented chandelier glowing under the jaconet.

Thapa stands there a while getting his breath back, then makes for his room. He cannot begin to think of what he will do when he gets there. He marches through the portico and around the corner, the kukri still in his hand.

And then he sees her.

At the garage door, against the old car. A white wraith, rising, her eyes fixed on him.

He stops, stands there breathing hard. So everyone, everything, has failed him on this night. Even the weaver bird's nest. Ghost after ghost returning to haunt him. This one, when she sees him stop, comes floating towards him.

He's never fought a ghost before. Let her come. He'll cut her into a hundred pieces.

The goongi hears Thapa's step.

She was moping by the car when she heard his terrible cry. Sat very still on the fender listening to the short rasps that followed it as Thapa ran around the tent slashing at the ropes. She's never heard a cry like that, not even in her tortured dreams. Now he appears, breathing hard. She sees him stop dead, the kukri in his hand.

The jolt of fear that floods her whole body brings her to her feet, the roots of her hair prickling, her eyes straining on their stems. She should be cowering, but she's frozen on her feet. And now unstuck, floating towards him. Borne on a cold current that's tossing her brain like a cork, as a white light cuts and cuts into the dark and she falls in a heap at his feet.

Thapa drops the kukri.

It's not Inge, it's the goongi. Having one of her fits. He stands over her, his breath still forced. What to do? He's seen the sisters jam a teaspoon between the woman's teeth to stop her biting her tongue. What to use? He drops to his hams, hears the teeth chatter. There's no other way: he shoves his fingers in there, feels the teeth clamp down.

Then picks her up with the free arm and carries her to the front door. Rings the bell repeatedly as her teeth sink in.

Mid-morning. Ritu stands on the roof looking out across the low hills.

She has steeled herself to look at the forest without

288

flinching. It's where she could have ended, among those trees. But didn't. This morning her eyes are not on the forest or the hills. She's staring at a point in the sky where a year ago there was a red kite which she helped fly.

She heard the guests talking about the dam last night. Picked up the bit about the bomber. This morning his name was in the paper.

A crow lands on the balustrade with a chicken bone in its beak. The caterers simply emptied their rubbish on the ground before leaving. After the tent fiasco. This morning the men came for the tent.

Brijeshwar. She'd never considered the whole name.

His face returns, his touch. She's forgotten the kiss, filed it away, remembers only his hands grasping hers on the kite reel. His wiry hair. Here on this roof. His saying, 'The world is full of dangerous people.' Her saying something about charity. She winces. Charity!

The crow's eyes glitter craftily as it regards her from its perch, the bone still held crosswise in its beak.

She goes over their last meeting. His confusion, her stubborn silence. Charity.

She makes a sudden movement and the crow takes fright, hopping away along the parapet. She follows its direction and walks to the back of the roof. The crow launches itself into the air as she passes and flaps back to perch where she was standing. It just wanted its corner back.

Now she's looking down on the walled garden. The fountain that never got going. A creeper has sprung up at her workroom window, its tendrils looking for a neck to throttle. The eucalyptus offers its smooth silver throat.

Go now, book a ticket. Be her guardian if you can't adopt. Jed shows no sign of dying, for all that the bamboos are flowering.

She continues her circuit of the roof. The dentures are still there by the pedestal, and the chair, though he doesn't come out now. The bottle of rubbery B-forte capsules. A new cake of soap with toothmarks in it. The other day, while she was bathing him, he took the soap from her and bit off a piece. Held it in his mouth, trying it – green cheese – then spat it out. Bitter food.

A haze has blotted out the mountains; the Himalayas could be a rumour. The dish looks out across a grey valley.

She picks her way back to Jed's room, across the maze of pipes that deliver the promise of water to the four corners of Everest. Past the bathtubs, the washing line. She finds she is carrying the bottle of capsules, the soap and the dentures. Let the chair stay.

K2. No, Everest. No, Kangchenjunga. It's black rock. Footprints flowering in dry snow. Daphne, no, Fay. In a hat with cherries. In the Packard. Rolling, rolling. Brake hard for jungle fowl crossing. What country is this? The camera, quick, where's the camera! It tastes like kibbled wheat. If we're going let's go. Nachiketa, take the keys, there's a good chap.

Now this old ram of Tollygunge
He had two horns of brass

Photographic evidence, and six toes up there to prove it. Tea. The Emperor of Tea, teaspoon his sceptre, cosy his crown. Yes. Tea, tea, tea, tea, tea. Where is she? Beer will do, the warmer the better. Ratskeller with Grete. With Inge in the ice cave. No, Kitty. Looked like that Gujjar woman.

Cheese. Any kind. This is soap. Mustard shirts and ice water.

Mind the seed tray. MIND THE SEED TRAY!

Idiot. IDIOT!

She takes the bridge between finger and thumb for the last time. Calms him.

Bakshi is gone, with his bride.

Up to the resort on the mountain, leaving the children with relatives. He said nothing to Thapa about the marquee. The sour smell of rotting food still rises from the midden left behind by the caterers, but the ants from the anthill are at work, and every morning the doves and mynahs go pecking in the grass for grains of rice.

Masha has tied a blue duster around her head and produced tin gold earrings from her polythene bag; for the past week she has been a bride. It's the one game the goongi refuses to play with her. 'Widding going,' Masha announces undeterred, and marches off to where the marquee stood. The red and gold throne might still be there. *It is!* She sits in the air, her eyes cast demurely down, glaring from time to time at Perpetua.

Perpetua's stopped skirmishing on that front. At the moment there's nobody behind the pot of basil. But let the honeymoon end.

Cecelia sits at her desk writing a letter to Mother in Delhi. The fan slackens suddenly, though it's not yet eleven, and the heat pounces. She shuts her eyes, sits back and sighs.

Under the silk-cotton tree Thapa is sweeping up a cloud of fallen silk.

'Strike! Strike! Strike! General Strike!'

'Do your shopping today,' the loudspeaker announces. 'Tomorrow the market will be closed!'

The announcer is in a scooter rickshaw, bumping slowly down Canal Road. He sits in the back seat, his speaker pointed at the driver's head. The volume is turned up high but the sound is muffled, a fog of noise, so people must still strain to make him out.

The Latvian leans over from his bed to soothe his distraught mynah. He's abandoned his hammock, which catches the afternoon sun.

'We request the public to stay home tomorrow as a mark of respect to the victims of last year's firing!'

A banner wrapped around the scooter rickshaw repeats the message in red letters.

Upstairs with the twins Tsering hears the loudspeaker and shuts her eyes as if the sound has pierced her there. A Tibetan, she speaks better Hindi than her Indian sisters from the coastal states, but her expression suggests that all language is noise. The twins halt their rocking and appear to focus for a moment on the outside world. The loudspeaker passes, the wave crests, clearing Everest. The twins register the Doppler shift, and resume their metronomic bleating.

'What was he saying, Thapa?' Cecelia calls from the verandah.

Thapa comes over, a bandage round his hand.

'A strike tomorrow, Sister. Buy your vegetables today.'

Perpetua, listening from the pantry, reaches for her shopping bag with fingers that have twisted back on themselves like coat hooks. Neha, who likes an outing, too, speeds up her sorting of the dhal. Ordinarily she will go into a trance, her fingertip working by instinct as it flicks aside the tiny sticks and stones before the mounting pink dune.

Masha, who ran to the IN gate as soon as she heard the loudspeaker, and followed it along the wall, has climbed the OUT gate and is leaning over the spikes, staring after the scooter.

'*Stupid!*' Ritu thinks out loud and holds her head. 'Why didn't I *connect*?'

She stands beside the open suitcase in her room, staring over the lid at the wall. She booked the train tickets a week ago, but she should have remembered when she wrote the date on the form: 14 June.

Well, history will repeat itself. She sees the police trucks, the looting. The crowd around the scooter rickshaw, rocking it. With Masha and herself in it. She shakes her head violently.

No. They're going, but they'll go the back way. She'll go to the station this evening and arrange for Baingan coolie to send one of his sons to Everest. Double fare, of course. But they're going.

She returns to packing the suitcase.

The book of ferns.
The book of mushrooms.
A botanical pharmacopia.
A small pair of sandals.
The Drummondganj Book of the Dead.

'Take it,' Jed indicates.

Or he could be waving her aside. From his thoughts. She takes a turn about the room, holding the loose sheets of his manuscript. Her manuscript. His moon lily. The death mask grins lopsidedly at her. Dust on the gramophone lid; the record rack covered with a dust cloth. Kettle, fish, car keys, tea caddy, tooth mug. She could place her finger on anything in this room, blindfold.

She sits down on the chair.

Jed's massive head on the pillow. All beak, in profile. Black rock, breathing gently. He's died once in this room already, on this bed. The civil surgeon certified it.

And here he is, blinking. Turning his head to look. At her. Without a trace of recognition.

'You,' his lips form. 'You.'

She leans towards him. His eyes are blank.

'Hot.'

She takes a face cloth, dips it in water and spreads it across his forehead. The feet begin to rock.

'Cold.'

She covers them with a sheet.

He shuts his eyes, dismissing her. Sleep returning, or what passes for sleep with Immanuel Jed.

In the afternoon, when the sun has come around to the city side, the banister on the iron stair could blister flesh. She goes down the twisting stair without support, treading squarely on the fish-plates so that her feet make a new and unrecognizable sound.

Baingan's son brings his scooter rickshaw early.

He parks in the portico and rings the bell, as if his engine were not loud enough to wake all Everest. There's a barricade outside the station, he announces, but the demonstrators won't bother with Canal Road. And it looks as if they could get wet, he says, taking his eyes off the sky above the lychee grove. The morning light has disappeared under black clouds.

'Better to wait at the station, anyway,' Cecelia advises. 'Go now.'

She's been sitting with Ritu in the parlour. The order will help, she repeats, as they rise. And the courts will move faster in Delhi.

'You have the tickets?'

Ritu has them, but checks again to satisfy her. She hasn't slept. Last night she heard the ripe fall of a papaya, heard Thapa's whistle and clank. This morning she heard Mrs Bakshi's rooster.

Neha carries the suitcase to the scooter. She's fussing with the lunch packs when the storm breaks.

Hail! Masha is delighted. White stones falling, skittering about on the gravel. She ducks out after a big one, and puts it in her mouth before Tsering can stop her. Tsering, who's just come down from Jed's room and got her feet wet. Her toes are smooth, pale gold, like ginger rhizomes.

Then they're in the scooter and Baingan's son is buttoning down the flaps. It's dark inside, with photos of painted actresses for company. Masha stares at them, awed, and takes Ritu's hand. The nuns wave, the goongi crows, Thapa salutes. The scooter moves off, hailstones smacking down on the roof.

At the gate they catch smoke from burning tyres. 'There's a barricade just beyond the gaol,' Baingan's son shouts, 'but we're going the other way.' He turns down Canal Road. During the night Ritu lay imagining this last ride down Jed's Via Mortis, saw the cemeteries, the flowering bamboo flash past, lit by the early morning sun. Now the flaps are down and she's riding blinkered under a deafening barrage of hail. She sees Baingan's son glance at the canvas roof in the rear-view mirror. Gives Masha's hand a squeeze. The squeeze comes back. Masha looks up at her, adventure shining in her eyes.

At the Parsee cemetery they turn right. Ritu catches a glimpse of the wrought-iron gate. This was the gate that always intrigued her on her morning walks. She always thought they used vultures. Oldcomers, come carrying their fire. She thinks of the Latvian, come with his chopsticks. He will die in his sleep and find a corner in the pauper section at Everest, a foreigner no longer. What a tangled world! Every atom making new.

The scooter rickshaw slows down. 'There's a barricade outside the station,' Baingan's son says, peering through the windscreen. The hail has changed to rain. 'My God! They're burning a jeep.'

He does a U-turn and draws up next to a side gate. Jumps out and is wet in seconds as he unfastens the flap. 'This is the goods entrance,' he says. 'You can get to the train from here.' He smiles his father's smile as Ritu pays him, twice the fare, when they're spotted.

'Get ready to run,' Ritu says to Masha, taking her arm. They dash through the gate and along the goods platform. Baingan's son runs with them, lugging the suitcase. Drops it as his windscreen shatters.

By the carriage is a trolley with hot tea. Masha has a sip from Ritu's glass. They climb aboard.

The train pulls out. The maze of tracks slides underneath the carriage with a luscious grinding, scissors on silk. They have a window seat. 'See the turntable?' Ritu points, and explains how one works. Have you been on a train before? she wonders as Masha gapes. Suddenly the enormity of her decision, of this journey, makes her gasp. But it's too late to go back. She's always risked the world, but now she's taken on a passenger. 'See the giraffe?' A swivel-necked column for watering steam engines. Then the outer signal cabin, the signal man leaning out of his upstairs window with a green flag.

They come to a level crossing, where the traffic is drawn up, waiting patiently. Bullock carts, bicycles, scooters. Ritu looks again. Sitting astride a motorcycle, with his head tilted in thought, is Bunny.

Rice fields now, filling up with rain. The scent of wet earth, no sweetness like it. How the whole chest heaves at the scent, how close one comes to being the scent.

In the distance, the mountains, a blue wall, retreating. She is leaving them behind. Checks in her bag for the tickets, spies the scallop shell he gave her. Takes it out, looks up again at the mountains. The dam is up there somewhere. Where? She is clutching the shell so hard the frilled edge bites into her palm, parting skin. For a moment the whole range splits open, light pouring through a crack in the wall. Her eyes fill with sudden tears and she draws Masha to her. With one arm, so the child must lean over awkwardly. What's the *matter*? Masha's look says. Ritu can't speak; her heart is breaking. She shakes her head swiftly, a small movement. Her eyes say, My love, and then, my dear love.

The track curves round towards the forest. As the engine slips into the trees, she sees them: a row of women walking in single file towards the city. Along a dust track, balancing headloads of firewood, each one intent on her load, as if she were balancing her whole life.

AFTERWORD

I have followed Kalidasa's ancient division of the seasons in his *Ritusamhara* (The Garland of Seasons) but the story of blighted love owes less to classical Sanskrit poetry than to the old *baramasih* (twelvemonth) tradition of folksong, where the lamenting voice is always that of a woman.

More than one young man has met his death in the troubles in our hills, but Brij is not modelled on any of them.

The adoption laws depicted here reflect those set out in our constitution, but they are now under review.

The discovery of a book of German poems by one Leo Kohs, wartime internee, in the rag-and-bone market of our home town changed the direction of my story, but I owe a greater debt to the many beloved dead who lie in the Dehra Dun cemetery.

The British Association for Cemeteries in South Asia and its journal, *Chowkidar*, have regularly enlarged my knowledge of Indian graveyards, but the germ of this book lies in the grave of my mother:

Dorothy Violet Sealy
née Clement
1924–1987

RIP